PRAISE FOR T
LISA VER(

Random Acts of Kindness

"4½ stars! Top Pick! Higgins' latest wonderful, page-turning novel further confirms her status as a master storyteller. Her narrative beautifully chronicles the relationships and adventures of former friends with a heady mix of belly-deep laughter, tears and empathy." —*RT Book Reviews*

"Women readers won't wish to miss one mile of this rich, thoughtful, and sagacious novel. Men smart enough to want to know what women really think would be wise to dip a toe in Pine Lake." —*Library Journal*

"Fans of chick lit will enjoy this humorous and uplifting homage to good friendships and a variety of Americana." —*Booklist*

Friendship Makes the Heart Grow Fonder

"This novel reveals the excitement of European travel while honestly reflecting on the pain and confusion that accompany the grieving process...[This] story of self-discovery is both heartwarming and thought-provoking." —*RT Book Reviews*

"Compelling...Readers who lose themselves in this wonderful book will be rewarded with the discovery of the value of true friendship.   —*Kirkus Reviews*

"Higgins does a nice job of balancing the characters' voices, and with each woman at a different stage in her life, diverse readers will find something to connect to. A natural for group discussions."   —*Booklist*

"Do not miss this rich celebration of friendship—its power to heal, to fulfill, and to put life's adventures into perspective. This book is as comforting as a cup of tea with your best friend."
    —Susan Wiggs, *New York Times* bestselling author
of *Return to Willow Lake*

One Good Friend Deserves Another

"Engaging...Higgins scores with a richly told story of what every girl wants, and the friends who'd sacrifice everything to help her get it."   —*Publishers Weekly*

"4½ stars! Higgins doesn't use flowery verse; she presents hard realities, dysfunction, and, best of all, possibilities and hope. Her research shines through with brilliant factual narrative in a novel that you won't soon forget."
    —*RT Book Reviews*

"Characters that could have been stock (the rich girl, the Trekkie programmer) have a depth that is strengthened by relationships with family, boyfriends, the past, and, most important, friends."   —*Booklist*

"Reminiscent of the *Sex and the City* TV series...easy and fun, chock-full of humor and entertainment...relays the necessity of taking risks and the power of friendship to pick you up when you fall."   —*Norfolk Daily News* (NE)

The Proper Care and Maintenance of Friendship

"A life-affirming novel...A happy reminder that life is all about taking risks."   —*Publishers Weekly*

"Quirky, original, and startlingly refreshing, this is a novel about friends. It's a novel about risks. And it's a novel about dreams, what we thought they were and what we discover them to be...Great novel. Great reading."

—TheReviewBroads.com

"A lovely novel with moments of deeply moving insight into what it means to be a mother, a wife, and a friend. Read it and share it with your own friends—you'll be glad you did!"

—Nancy Thayer, *New York Times* bestselling author of *The Hot Flash Club* and *Beachcombers*

SENSELESS ACTS *of* BEAUTY

ALSO BY LISA VERGE HIGGINS

The Proper Care and Maintenance of Friendship
One Good Friend Deserves Another
Friendship Makes the Heart Grow Fonder
Random Acts of Kindness

SENSELESS ACTS
of BEAUTY

Lisa Verge Higgins

GRAND CENTRAL
PUBLISHING

NEW YORK   BOSTON

Grand Central Publishing
Hachette Book Group
1290 Avenue of the Americas
New York, NY 10104

www.HachetteBookGroup.com

Printed in the United States of America

RRD-C

First Edition: March 2015
10 9 8 7 6 5 4 3 2 1

Grand Central Publishing is a division of Hachette Book Group, Inc.
The Grand Central Publishing name and logo is a trademark of Hachette Book Group, Inc.

The Hachette Speakers Bureau provides a wide range of authors for speaking events. To find out more, go to www.hachettespeakersbureau.com or call (866) 376-6591.

The publisher is not responsible for websites (or their content) that are not owned by the publisher.

Library of Congress Cataloging-in-Publication Data

Higgins, Lisa Verge.
  Senseless acts of beauty / Lisa Verge Higgins. — First edition.
      pages ; cm
  Summary: "A new novel of women's friendship from the author of Random Acts of Kindness that will appeal to fans of Kristin Hannah, Luanne Rice, and Karen White"— Provided by publisher.
  ISBN 978-1-4555-7287-8 (softcover) — ISBN 978-1-4555-7288-5 (ebook) 1. Female friendship—Fiction. 2. Chick lit. I. Title.
  PS3558.I3576S46 2015
  813'.54—dc23
                                                    2014048816

SENSELESS ACTS *of* BEAUTY

Chapter One

M aybe Tess would have noticed the police cruiser earlier, if she hadn't been shaking so badly.

Slouched in her car on the shoulder of the highway, Tess glimpsed the black-and-white rush by again, this time on the opposite side of the road. She imagined the officer eyeballing her through the driver's side window. She squeezed her eyes shut and wished away yet another ghost of her past, like the ones she'd been seeing ever since she'd left Bismarck—mirages of teenage runaways trudging on the side of the road, ghosts that had turned out to be nothing more than mile-marker signs, or a grocery bag snagged on a guardrail, or a yellow *No Hunting* placard nailed on a tree just beyond the shoulder.

But that police cruiser had been no ghost. Old instinct kicked in. She roused herself from the driver's seat, shoved open the door with a boot, and unfolded herself onto the road.

A wave of dizziness forced her to slap a hand on the doorframe. She blinked in the rain splatter that painted the roads slick. She breathed and tried to keep the sight of the Adirondack pines upright where they belonged. She told herself she felt dizzy because she'd driven eighteen-hundred miles in four days in a car overdue for a tune-up. She told herself it was the gas fumes filling her brain. She told herself she felt nauseous because she'd fueled herself with nothing but Red Bull, beef jerky, and pink Sno Balls.

Anything was a better excuse for this nausea than the truth—that she'd morphed into a quivering mess the minute she saw the green exit sign that said *Pine Lake*.

She stumbled to the front of the car, slid her fingers under the hood, and released the latch. She raised the hood only moments before she heard the gravel pop of another car pulling up behind her own.

As footsteps approached, she muttered, "Morning, Officer."

"Car trouble, ma'am?"

"It's nothing serious." Tess fixed her gaze on the workings of the engine, not the gray blur in the corner of her eye. "It's just overheated."

"If you drove all the way from North Dakota, I bet it is."

Tess nodded and hoped he didn't see her twitch. That license plate was sure to get a lot of attention in upstate New York.

He said, "That's a long ride."

"Yes it is, but I've done longer."

Tess didn't offer up any more information. She checked the perfectly good hoses and bent down to see the fluid levels. Back in Bismarck she drove an eighteen-wheeler for a living, so she'd been taught a lot about how to avoid jackknifing, but not a heck of a lot about the workings of a combustion engine. Companies didn't want drivers to represent their companies covered with grease from crawling under their rigs. Still, she'd hung around with enough mechanics so she could fake it pretty good when she had to.

She had to fake it now because she knew from experience that officers of the law became suspicious of strangers who parked for no rational reason on the side of a quiet country highway…unless the car was disabled.

As the officer leaned forward to look under the hood, she dared to glance up from under her bangs to give him a look-over. She was still twenty-odd miles from her hometown, but it would be just her luck to stumble upon some officer who'd once slapped her in handcuffs. But this officer was dressed in regulation gray with a thick, black belt and a silly white hat. State police, not local law enforcement. A young officer, by the fresh color in his cheeks. Too young to remember anything about Tess Hendrick.

She'd better suck it up. If she could ever muster the courage to cross the town line, she was bound to be recognized, sooner or later.

The officer straightened up and said, "If this car's disabled, you should set up flares or cones in intervals."

"I have them in the trunk," she said, "but I don't expect to be here much longer."

"I think you may need a tow. These foreign cars—"

"I'll know in a minute," she interrupted. "I'm just checking how hot the engine is before turning it over."

The engine wasn't hot at all, making a liar of her. The macadam was sending off more heat around them, rain-drenched though it was, and the air had that too familiar July storm chill that made goose bumps rise on her bare arms.

The cop eyeballed her. Tess pulled out the dipstick to check on the oil level, her heart stuttering as thunder rolled in the distance. She wondered what he made of the feather tattoo that covered her shoulder, the cheese puff–stained skinny jeans, and the lines of Latin tattooed on the inside of her left bicep.

He said, "I've been doing my circuit, ma'am, and I noticed you've been parked on the shoulder here for a while."

"Yes." *Damn it.* "I didn't want to burn myself on the engine so I waited until it cooled."

"Well, this may look like a little country road to someone who's driven halfway across the U.S., but it's a county highway. Parking on the shoulders is prohibited, and dangerous."

"Better to overheat on the side of the road than to stall in the middle of it. For safety's sake, right, Officer?"

She met his eye the same time she mentally told herself *stop*. She couldn't afford to tweak authority, her favorite sport when she lived around here. As if to prove her folly, the officer took a step back to glance through the car windows into the chaotic interior, no doubt searching for visible evidence—bags of weed, glassine envelopes, empty beer bottles, shotgun shells, cigarettes bought tax-free at the reservation in bulk for resale, something to give him an excuse to ask for her license and registration, to search the vehicle for incriminating evidence.

She wondered what he'd make of the gas mask in the backseat.

Think. Think like the adult you are, not the mouthy runaway you once were. Tess watched a drop of oil run off the end of the dipstick, trying to staunch the nerves that had abandoned her. What the hell was wrong with her? She'd thought she'd put all this behind her fifteen years ago. She thought she'd stuffed all those early, ugly memories in a box in some dusty corner of her mind, never to be referenced again. She hadn't realized how tightly she packed them away until she glimpsed that sign. One glance was like a box cutter, and the memories burst open.

Enough.

She shoved the dipstick back in the oil tank. "The engine is cool enough now," she said, knocking the prop loose. "I'd be grateful if you'd wait while I turn it over, just to make sure."

She closed the hood and then walked a steady line around him. His nostrils flared like he was trying to determine if she were stoned or had been drinking. She probably looked like she had been, after all these days in the car, unwashed, holding her head at an angle because she'd pulled a muscle in the back of her neck, her lips chewed bloody with worry. She could hear the cop thinking, deciding whether he'd take the next official step, but she just kept striding until she pulled open the door and dropped into the driver's seat.

She jangled her keys. "May I?"

He gave her an unconvincing nod and then slapped his hands on the rolled-down window as if to stop her from bolting. She shoved the key into the ignition. The car turned over and purred as she knew it would. She watched the dashboard as the red warning lights blinked temporarily, then, one by one, winked out.

She took a deep breath. "Sounds like everything's back to normal."

"Yeah."

"Sorry for the trouble, Officer. Next time I'll remember to put out flares."

"Where are you heading?"

"Boston," she lied.

"That's another two hundred miles."

"I'll make it before dark."

"Forget Boston."

"Sorry?"

"Get some sleep." He pushed away and squinted toward the wall of clouds gathering over the far blue peaks. "This storm is spitting now, but it isn't over. It's going to get worse before it gets better. It's dangerous to drive in this kind of weather when you're exhausted."

She wanted to blurt out that she'd driven a sixty-thousand–pound vehicle over slick roads during a High Plains snowstorm on less than the federally regulated amount of sleep. She could certainly handle a little mountain thunderstorm in a Volvo.

But the truth was that Boston wasn't an option. She

didn't *have* any more options. All troubles always came home to roost, and that's how Tess knew, bone deep, that the foolish, headstrong runaway she was looking for could be nowhere else but in Pine Lake.

"Plenty of hotels off the highway," the officer said, slapping the roof of the car. "I'll follow for a while, just in case that car fails on you. You take the next exit to Pine Lake, you understand?"

Her heart, her breath, and her stomach all crowded up to her throat.

"Yes, Officer. I will."

〜

Man, it was cold for July.

Inside the cabin, Sadie pressed into the corner as the wind sucked warmth through the uneven boards. She shrugged deeper into her soaked hoodie and blew into the fibers, trying to heat her stiff fingers. If she'd known it was going to rain like this today, she would never have set out to walk the miles to the grocery store. But the last of the peanut butter was gone so she had no choice but to risk the curious gaze of the storekeeper as she rang up Sadie's collection of granola bars, apple juice, Pop Rocks, skinny tampons, and a single roll of toilet paper.

No *way* was she using leaves.

Now she glimpsed a line of beaded blood on her arm and realized she'd scratched herself on something—a tree branch or a stuck-out nail—while she was rushing back to the cabin

7

in the rain. The Pop Rocks rattled in her backpack. They were rattling because *she* was rattling, the bones of her knees knocking together. She couldn't just keep sitting here and hope the rain would end. None of the camping books had warned her about how sudden the rain could come in the Adirondacks but they all warned about hypothermia. She was supposed to put on dry clothes and seek shelter.

Groaning, she shoved the backpack off her lap. She gripped the windowsill to help stand up, straightening out her cramping legs. Through the trees she saw the lake, gray and churning in the downpour. She saw the sweep of the back lawn, the empty picnic benches, and, finally, when she squinted, the wide porch of the main lodge of Camp Kwenback.

Inside that fancy log cabin, folks were clutching mugs of hot chocolate with three inches of marshmallows melting on top, sprawled on a couch just in front of that big fire. That's what she'd be doing, anyway, if she were inside. When she first scouted the place a week ago, she'd glimpsed the fireplace, the couches, and the redheaded woman offering coffee to a guest. There was even a bookshelf full of books in there, probably novels about smart girls who solved mysteries without being forced to haul their fourteen-year-old butts into the wild.

There was more truth in those novels, she thought, than in the wilderness guides she'd filched from the library. Those books had you believing that the Adirondacks were everyone's free grocery store, full of blueberry and wild blackberry bushes that were always ripe. Now, if she were eighteen years old, she could walk right up to Camp Kwenback and ask for a room. When you're eighteen, you're an adult, supposedly you can do anything. Well, she knew an eighteen-year-old boy whose momma still washed his clothes. Sadie had been washing her own clothes since she was ten. Being an adult at eighteen was just another stupid rule set up by the A-thor-it-ees. Like no flip-flops in school or ten points off if you don't write your name on an assignment.

You just going to shiver and whine about it, Sadie Tischler? It's not like she had a choice. If she banged on Camp Kwenback's back door right now, looking like some scraggly homeless person, the owner would call the police for sure. Sooner or later, she'd knock on that door. When she did, she wanted to be strong, confident, and *sure*.

Her stomach growled. She slapped a hand over it, focusing back on what was important right now. *Shelter, food, sleep.*

Sadie squinted across the back lawn toward a dim gray shape on the other side that she knew was a shed. Inside that shed was a big metallic machine that gave off heat when it was running. Around it there was a space just big enough for her to curl up and get some sleep uninterrupted by roving raccoons or biting flies or rain. That's where she'd dry off, have something to eat, take a nap. If she could just get to the shed without being caught.

Sadie assessed the distance between here and there, looking for places where she could hide so she wouldn't be seen from those glowing windows. The safest route was to skirt the woods the long way around, but the idea of all that walking made her head feel woozy. Better to be casual about it. The folks inside that camp were probably happy around the hot fire, not staring out at the lake looking for girls who should know better than wander in the rain. She would just walk across the back lawn like she owned the place. She had a lot of practice pretending she belonged wherever she happened to be.

It was a plan.

Once outside the tumbledown cabin, the rain hit her like someone had opened a fire hydrant. She flattened against the wall to try to use the eaves as protection, but all it did was snag her hoodie on splinters. Spitting rain out of her mouth, she pushed away and counted seconds as she headed into the open.

Each second was the next thing on the list. First, when she reached the shed, she would peel off her wet clothes and hang them on the corners of the furnace thingie. Second, she would paw through her backpack and put on anything dry. Third, she would press herself against the metal to get toasty until she felt herself thaw. Fourth, she would drink two juice bags. Fifth, she would eat the little blueberry pie she'd bought, the one that couldn't be stored for long anyhow. There was no one around to care anymore if she ate dessert before dinner.

She waited to hear the squeal of the sliding door, footsteps on the porch floorboards, a shout out to stop. It was weird to be out in the open after a week and a half of hiding. She kept marching with the rain pounding her face, while the fog crept up from the lake like some bad black and white movie, her mind working up excuses just in case she were caught.

When she reached the shed, she hurled herself in and shut the door. Her breathing sounded loud inside. The place had a tangy smell, a basement smell, copper and oil and dampness. Already it was warmer. Dropping her backpack, she sank to her knees next to the rumbling machine and flattened her cheek against the metal.

The rules screamed in her head—*shelter, food, then sleep*—but the hum of the machinery worked on her like a lullaby.

ॐ

The kid looked like a nestling bird dumped out of a tree in a storm.

Riley Cross knocked off the hood of her slicker and then reached for the bulb chain. When the light flooded the shed, she smiled right away so that the girl wouldn't be scared. Blinking, the girl had crouched into a defensive posture, backing up until she was practically behind the generator.

Riley said, "One heck of a storm, huh?"

Water dripped off the girl and joined the growing puddle at her feet. The rubber toe of one sneaker had separated from the canvas. The girl's eyes, an unusual pale green, were bug-wide.

"It's hard to know when a rain like this is coming," Riley continued, glancing out the small, high window. "Sometimes you can smell it in the air. It's ozone; it smells sweet, electric.

Or if you look to the west, sometimes you'll see a blue glow atop the mountains, which is the first of the lightning."

The girl didn't move as a wet shoulder slipped out of the neckline of her sagging hoodie.

"You can tell if you watch the birds, too." Riley swiped at her wet coat, shaking her dripping hands dry. "They get real quiet. Still, I've lived here pretty much all my life and even I can't always predict when a storm like this is going to come. But you're not from around here, are you?"

Riley would know if she were. Pine Lake wasn't a big town, and it seemed like half of it consisted of her own relatives. The rest she'd gone to school with. And she knew this girl wasn't with the growing number of tourists renting the little cape houses or camping in the Adirondack woods beyond the borders of Camp Kwenback. She'd glimpsed the girl several times, at a distance, walking alone in the woods, her curly, puffed, and coppery ponytail bobbing.

The girl still didn't answer. She tensed up, bracing her legs like a Carolina wren sensing the approach of a rival. The girl really could use a change of clothes, along with a solid meal. Maybe more than one. Riley remembered the sandwich that had gone missing from Mrs. Clancy's lunch tray on the picnic table last week. And the chip wrappers she'd found discarded in the corner of one of the old cabins. It was probably a good thing that the girl was wary of strangers, but Riley wasn't sure it was just wariness in that gaze.

"Listen, I've got a fire going inside." Riley gestured in the direction of the main lodge. "And I'm about to make myself some hot chocolate. Why don't you come on into the lodge and join me? You can use my phone if you want to call someone."

The girl didn't move. If anything, she shrank back deeper behind the generator. Wet as she was, Riley didn't want her to press back too far and get tangled up in the wires. There was a good chance squirrels and chipmunks had made lunch out of the rubber insulation, exposing the live insides.

"Ok, then, come on in whenever you're ready." Riley pushed open the shed door and then pulled her hood over her head. "The sliding back doors are always unlocked. I'll have some hot chocolate waiting for you, just in case."

Riley walked out, letting the door bang shut behind her. She strode across the squishy lawn with the rain pouring over her bill-cap. This wasn't Camp Kwenback's first runaway. She'd figured the girl would be inside within five minutes, maybe ten.

It took forty.

Riley had all but given up when she heard the squeal of the sliding door. The girl slipped in and hesitated on the all-weather rug, shivering. When she was crouched back against the generator, Riley had estimated the kid to be about twelve years old, but the girl unfolded to a good five foot two, all stick-thin legs, awkward proportions, easily on the far side of a skinny thirteen.

"Go ahead and kick off those sneakers." Riley gestured to a grilled cheese sandwich and a cup of hot chocolate sitting on the raised bricks of the hearth. "That's been waiting for you. Glad you decided to join me."

Riley took the soaking hoodie out of the girl's hands and saw goose bumps riddling her thin arms. All the girl wore underneath the jacket was a ribbed tank and a pair of jean shorts. Riley held out a hand for the backpack, but the girl just held the strap until her knuckles went white.

Riley dropped her hand and hung the hoodie on a nearby hat tree. "I'm Riley. What should I call you?"

"Sadie."

The girl spoke the name in a firm voice and then watched Riley's face. Riley sensed that a great deal of thought had gone into the decision whether or not to tell her.

"Pleasure to meet you, Sadie." Riley wondered whether the name was real. "First time in Pine Lake?"

"Yeah."

The girl followed her to the fireplace, looking all around her. Riley took it all in, too, trying to see it through Sadie's eyes, the soaring pine rafters with their glossy sheen and dark pine knots, the rustic hearth made with local stone, the six-foot taxidermy bear that flanked the fireplace on one side, and the wide, sweeping antlers of a moose mounted above. But Riley's eye inevitably caught on the duct tape holding the antlers together, the floor that needed refurbishing, the game table held stable by a rubber-banded deck of cards under the leg, and the glass-topped coffee table with the nicked edges. The 1970s no doubt wanted those faded plaid couches back, if she could ever afford to buy new ones.

At least she'd lit a fire. A nice fire always drew attention away from the failing zoo vibe and made the room cozy, timeless.

Riley slid a hip on the raised hearth and gestured for Sadie to sit on the other side of the tray of food. Sadie sat, dropped the backpack between her feet, and then seized the cup of hot chocolate. After drinking deep, she palmed the grilled cheese and took an enormous bite. The girl's eyes drifted closed like she'd never tasted anything so good.

"So," Riley began, as Sadie swallowed half the sandwich, "is there anyone I can call for you? The phone lines aren't down yet, but I wouldn't count on that for long."

Sadie shook her head and buried her face in the hot chocolate again. Riley wished she'd at least topped it with a layer of marshmallows. The girl needed some real meat on her bones. Riley considered making another sandwich in the kitchen, but she had a strange feeling that, if she left the room, there was a good chance Sadie would wolf down the last of the sandwich, shrug into Riley's own slicker, and then disappear back into the rain. After all, the girl had stolen a lot of things in the past couple of weeks.

Ah, yes. One theft had to be addressed. "Hey, Sadie, you wouldn't happen to have my Leica in that backpack, would you?"

Sadie froze with the mug between her hands.

"My binoculars," she explained, shrugging. "I have several pairs, some old ones that I really should give away. I don't mind if you borrowed a pair at all, especially if it were for bird watching. But the Leica are my particular favorite, and I've really been missing them these past few days."

Placing the mug down, Sadie tugged on the zipper of her backpack. "I was going to give them back."

"I know."

"I borrowed them," Sadie said, as she pulled out the binoculars, "because I heard something screaming in the middle of the night."

"A screech owl, I bet. Scary call, I know." Riley took the binoculars, cold and damp, hoping the rain hadn't gotten into the optics. "Did you find him? By the big oak? By the marshy area?"

"He's somewhere near that beaver dam."

"He's beautiful, isn't he?"

Sadie shrugged and gave her a look like she was wondering if Riley were dealing with a full deck.

Riley was used to that.

"Well, that owl is almost as beautiful as the crane you folded for me." Riley gestured toward the reception desk, upon which lay a bowl full of her mysterious visitor's origami. "I put that crane in with his brothers and sisters."

"I didn't want you to think it was stolen."

"I know apology origami when I see it."

"It wasn't—" Sadie stopped herself. She lifted the mug, then lowered it once she realized it was empty. She took a deep breath, her shoulders rising and falling. "Thanks," she finally said, "for letting me...borrow your binoculars. Can I ask you," she continued, as her gaze drifted to Riley's hair. "Is that color real?"

Riley ran her fingers through her frizzed hair. After last fall's drastic cut, it was taking its time growing back, and it had reached that awkward stage where it wasn't quite long enough to pull into a ponytail but just long enough to make her look like she'd stuck her finger in an electric socket. "One hundred percent real. Can't control it much in this weather. I guess we've got that in common."

Sadie didn't smile. In the silence, the fire crackled, something in the wood popping and shooting sparks up the chimney. Riley wished she could read the strange, fierce expressions flitting across this young girl's face. There was only one way to get the truth out of her, and that was to ask.

"Sadie," Riley put the binoculars aside, "I've stumbled upon a lot of critters in the generator shed during the years I've lived here. Raccoons, possums. Once I found a nest of barn owls. But a teenage girl? That's a new one. Is there anything you want to talk about?"

The look Sadie gave her was one that Riley sometimes saw in the sparrows that gathered by the feeding table on the back lawn when she came out with a new bag of food. It was a steady, assessing look, a look that spoke of hesitancy, of burgeoning trust, but also fear at the approach of such a large predator. The birds crouched with their heads cocked, their gazes steady, while the little muscles under their feathers grew tight.

Sadie reached down and unzipped her backpack. She pulled out a white hand towel. Seeing it, Riley had a moment of embarrassment for not being a good hostess. She realized that the girl could probably use a nice, fluffy hotel towel to dry her skin and hair, instead of being forced to dig for some well-worn towel in her soaking backpack. Riley was about to get up and fetch a fresh towel when she caught sight of the Kwenback logo at the edge of Sadie's towel.

"Wow. Are you planning a future in cat burglary?" Riley reached over to tug the fringed end of the towel. "I don't remember which origami crane went with that."

"I didn't borrow this."

"Oh?"

"I've had this towel my whole life."

Sadie spoke into the threads of the fading logo. Riley looked at Sadie's face more closely, trying to see in it the features of any one of the sixty or seventy families who used to come to Camp Kwenback on a regular basis, when this resort had teemed from June to October, when the back lawn was the center for fierce badminton competitions, when the lake was full of canoes and rowboats, and every swing was going full tilt from six in the morning when her grandparents served coffee on the back lawn, to midnight when they launched fireworks off the dock.

Riley had worked as the camp events director for six straight summers, herding the young ones for sack races and Red Rover, challenging the teenagers to shuffleboard competitions, playing bingo and Monte Carlo in the main lodge during the rainy days. Generations of families had spent summer weeks in the cabins that spread through the woods down to the lake. Riley could name every one of them, right down to the great-grandchildren, and some still sent Christmas cards. But she reasoned that Sadie was too young to remember any of that. It had been nearly fifteen years since Camp Kwenback had anything that looked remotely like a full house.

Sadie's shoulders rose and fell. A little line deepened between her young brows, and color darkened in her cheeks.

Riley leaned forward. "Sadie?"

"My birth mother," Sadie blurted, lifting the towel. "My birth mother wrapped me in this when I was born."

The term *birth mother* skittered across Riley's thoughts like a chip of flint sent flying over a lake, skipping in steps, spreading ripples in its wake, ripples that swelled as the implications became clear.

"I was just wondering," Sadie said, "what you were doing fifteen years ago, on August twenty-second?"

Chapter Two

Sadie had made a ritual of it. Standing in front of the bathroom mirror to brush her teeth, she'd find herself instead pulling her upper lip and noticing the two larger front teeth, the way the smaller ones on either side slipped slightly behind them. Or she twisted her head so that she could see the three freckles on the edge of her jaw. Or she pulled the little curls of her brass-red hair and watched them bounce back, noting the strands that were more gold than red, others more brown. Pressing close to the mirror to see her gray-green eyes and the streaks of rusty brown that splayed out from the center pupil, wondering as her breath fogged up the glass when she would come close to someone else's face and see in their eyes the same starburst pattern.

Riley's eyes were brown. Soft brown, melted chocolate chip brown. Sadie hadn't expected that. But after forty minutes of thinking about it, she realized that Riley's brown eyes didn't mean Riley couldn't be her mother. Sadie's seventh-grade science teacher had shown the class diagrams of Mendel's peas, and once Sadie realized what they meant, she'd made a beeline to the library to pour over eye color and hair color inheritance diagrams for people. So she knew brown eyes were dominant. But she also knew that if her father had green eyes and one of Riley's parents had light-colored eyes, then Sadie had a fifty percent chance of having green eyes with a brown-eyed mother.

She'd worked it out a couple of times already, drawing diagrams in the dusting of dirt on the floor of the shed.

"Sadie."

Sadie's chest felt tight, like something was swelling up underneath her ribs. She'd been watching Riley since arriving in town by train more than a week ago. She'd followed her from a safe distance as Riley wandered the woods every morning, pausing for long instances to peer through her binoculars. Sadie liked Riley's rolling laughter as she chatted with her guests on the back porch on sunny afternoons. Sadie liked that Riley spent most of her days barefoot. Now she stared at Riley's face, taking it all in—the freckles that covered her skin, the curve of the lobe of her ears, the bow shape of her upper lip, the gleam of her two front teeth as she opened her mouth on a breath.

"Sadie," Riley repeated, "I'm so, so sorry."

Sadie grappled with that while the pressure under her ribs stretched so tight that she couldn't suck in a breath. She grappled with that while the fire baked her right shoulder. Sorry for what? Sorry for not recognizing her own child right away? Sorry for giving her up for adoption? Sorry for not having stepped in after everything went wrong? Sorry for having wasted fourteen years they could have spent together under the rafters of this lodge, drinking the hot chocolate now curdling in her stomach?

Or sorry because it wasn't Riley, nearly fifteen years ago on August 22, who'd pushed her into the world?

And all at once, the pressure under her ribs collapsed like a balloon popping, and she tightened her grip around her knees so she wouldn't tumble off the hearth onto the hardwood floor.

Riley said, "You've been hanging around the camp all this time, working up the courage to ask me that, haven't you?"

"I've been wasting my time."

"How frustrated you must feel."

Sadie mouthed the word *frustrated*. Frustration didn't seem to say what she was feeling right now. For as long as she could remember, she'd been fed pretty much the same story told to every adoptee she'd come to know: That her birth mother had been a young woman, a brave woman, making a difficult choice when she was unable to take care of her own child. Her birth mother was someone like Riley, pretty in a country air, no makeup, soft in the middle kind of way.

Well, she should have known that script was a sketchy fairy tale meant to stop a boatload of ugly questions. She thought she'd prepared herself for all possibilities. But now she realized that, over the past two weeks, she'd opened herself up to dreaming again.

Sadie felt a tug and realized that Riley was pulling on the towel that Sadie had pressed between her knees. She loosened her grip enough for Riley to slide the worn terrycloth into her hands.

Riley fingered the fading logo. "I imagine you've done a lot of work to figure out where this towel came from."

"Search engines are your friend."

Sadie reached for the mug to hide her face behind it. She tipped the cup high, but there was nothing left at the bottom but thick, oversweet syrup. Her friend Izzy had been right. She'd been an idiot to think that when she skipped out of school, stashed her textbooks, and headed to the train station, that her birth mother would just be there, waiting, at the end of it.

"The camp has had the same logo since nineteen twenty-two." Riley passed the pad of her finger over the dark green threads of the three pine trees, two small ones nestled against a taller middle one. "My grandfather paid a lawyer to have it trademarked a long time ago."

Sadie knew that much was true. She'd saved up grocery money to pay for an online logo search two years ago, and up popped Camp Kwenback in Pine Lake, deep in the Adirondack Mountains.

Riley asked, "You said your birth mother wrapped you in this?"

Sadie tightened her grip around her knees. She supposed she'd opened the door to questions once she asked if Riley was her birth mother. She couldn't exactly shut it tight now. But there were risks in telling too much, so she weighed the truth carefully.

"My parents kept that towel in a box with my other baby

stuff." Sadie remembered the little porcelain shoe from the Ohio hospital, painted with the date and time of her birth, along with a first-year calendar full of her mother's silly comments about emerging teeth and when she first rolled over. "My parents saved all the stuff from the hospital, including that, which was underneath it all."

"Wow." Riley made a choking little laugh. "All my parents saved in my baby box was the knit hat that the hospital gave me. That's the hazard of being the sixth kid. But this...this is kind of nice, isn't it?" Riley brushed her hand over the towel. "To have something that you know your birth mother gave to you?"

Sadie shrugged. "It's just a clue."

"So I take it that your adoption was a closed one?"

"Of course." Why else would she be sitting here, making such a fool of herself in front of a stranger?

"You haven't seen your birth certificate."

"You've got to hit the magical age of eighteen before the wizards will unseal it."

"And your parents?"

Sadie's jaw tightened. "They told me everything they knew, which wasn't a lot."

"Well"—she raised the towel—"you're quite the resourceful one."

You don't know the half of it. Sadie let go of her knees and dropped her feet flat to the floor. "So," she said, "even though you're not who I *thought* you were, maybe you can still help me out."

Riley didn't answer right away, absorbed in smoothing

the towel while a wrinkle deepened above her brows. Adults thought they were so slick in hiding their feelings, but Sadie could read people. When Sadie had gone to the train station to buy a ticket, she'd taken one look at the faces of the three tellers and knew immediately which one wouldn't blink an eye about selling an unattended kid a train ticket for some-place five hours away. When she loaded up at the local grocery store, she knew which cashier wouldn't ask pesky questions about why she was buying so many groceries and how she got the money to do so.

So right now, looking at Riley, Sadie could tell the woman was hesitant about the idea of helping her.

Well, she didn't come all the way to the middle of nowhere for nothing.

"Fifteen years ago," Sadie ventured, "a woman must have visited this camp. I'd bet she was pregnant with me." She gazed up at the rafters again, knowing that once, a long time ago, her mother had stood under them, too. "Someone who maybe even gave birth here, in one of the rooms—"

"I was in college fifteen years ago, Sadie, but I can tell you that the only story of a woman giving birth in this lodge dates back to Prohibition."

"If you were in college, how would you know it didn't happen?"

"Pine Lake is a small town." Riley lifted a brow. "Some-thing like that would have made the rounds for sure. How long have you been looking for your birth mother?"

"A couple of months, maybe."

Sadie plucked at her wet socks and considered how

much more to say. When she was in grammar school, she didn't think twice about the fact that somewhere in the big, wide world was the mother who'd given birth to her. She was more concerned about whether Santa would ignore her parent's no video game rule and leave her a Nintendo DS under the tree for Christmas. All she really understood was that she was special because she was adopted. She'd been *chosen*, her mom used to tell her.

Only recently had she come to understand that she'd been *given away*.

"A couple of months, huh?" Riley said. "Aren't you a little young to be taking on such a difficult search?"

Sadie sighed. If she were just three inches taller, or ten pounds heavier, people wouldn't give her so much sass. But she'd always been small and skinny no matter how much she ate. "I'll be fifteen in six weeks. Isn't there a way to check when a towel went missing?"

"Actually, no."

"But you keep track, right?"

"A towel is a towel, Sadie. There's no individual identifier. Here at Camp Kwenback, we just figure out how many have gone missing by the end of the season, and then we order a bunch from a company in Rochester that does the embroidery."

Rochester. Sadie frowned. She didn't realize there could be another place that this towel might have come from.

"Every year," Riley continued, "we lose some in the wash, we throw the stained ones out, and many a guest has left with a towel or two in their luggage, either unintentionally or as souvenirs." She waved a hand around the room. "Maybe if my grandparents had searched luggage routinely all those years ago, we could have saved enough in the budget to buy new couches."

Suddenly Sadie imagined the crowds of people who'd used those towels—lodgers, Riley's family, friends, employees—and others, too, maybe a whole factory in Rochester. She had assumed that the towel meant something. Now she wondered if the towel was just a piece of cloth that a nurse had grabbed out of a lost-and-found box.

A shadow fell over her and Sadie realized that Riley had stood up.

Riley asked, "Is there someone I could call?"

"Nope."

"A friend, family?"

Sadie tightened her jaw so she wouldn't say too much. She probably should just make up a story about her parents camping in the woods. She could tell Riley she'd head back once the rain stopped. Then she could hike into the woods until Riley couldn't see her anymore, then circle around and set up camp in the farthest cabin. She needed to sleep but most of all she needed to think.

But the words wouldn't come. She felt odd, light-headed, sort of nauseous, like she'd drunk the hot chocolate and eaten the grilled cheese too fast. And it was weird having Riley standing right in front of her, smelling like vanilla and sugar.

Riley said, "The rain is likely to continue for a while. I've got a bunch of empty rooms upstairs. I've always found that everything looks better after a hot bath and a good night's sleep. You want to stay for the night?"

Sadie began to tremble. It felt like months, not weeks, since she lay her head down in her own room and fell asleep to the rumble of cars passing on the street outside. She could imagine the inn's bed, a real one, not the rain-slick, moldy, plastic-covered mattresses in the last cabin. A bed with a soft pillow under her head instead of her lumpy backpack. Clean sheets in a warm room with no blackflies or mosquitos.

But there was danger in falling asleep. She might wake up to find the police waiting for her.

"The room is free for weather refugees," Riley said, winking. "Besides, I suspect you could use the sleep. Believe it or not, I know exactly how you feel right now."

Sadie turned her face away. She'd heard words like that all her life, from social workers, teachers, and the principal at her school. She never understood why people said such things when they couldn't possibly know.

"Three years ago," Riley continued, "I asked someone a question very similar to yours, except I was too scared to do it in person."

Sadie looked up, confused.

"Yes." Riley pulled a little smile. "I was adopted, too."

Chapter Three

Tess took two steps inside Camp Kwenback, then stumbled to a stop like she'd tripped through time. Sunset flooded through the sliding back doors to gleam on the wooden floor. She glanced at the hearth, glowing with a dying fire. She saw that old toothless bear—*Bob*—perched upright, its once-patchy belly now completely devoid of hair. She arched her neck to let her gaze roam over the high ceiling, the dark pine knots arranged in the same constellation she remembered so well, memorized after long hours lying on those plaid couches.

She breathed in a long, deep breath, closed her eyes, and sent up thanks that her one and only Pine Lake sanctuary still existed.

Then she heard footsteps and her throat closed up. She imagined that they belonged to old Mary Cross bustling across the room and Bud shuffling behind her, sporting his usual red plaid LL Bean shirt—summer or winter—smiling behind his Coke-bottle glasses as he greeted her.

But when she opened her eyes what Tess saw instead was a woman her own age striding across the room from the kitchen, drying her hands on a dishtowel.

"Riley Cross." Tess felt a low, swooping sense of relief to see a familiar face—a rare, friendly one. "I should have known you'd end up here."

Riley's hair was shorter, curlier, wilder than the last time she'd seen her, but otherwise she was the same pink-cheeked, outdoorsy woman who'd been in most of Tess's classes at Pine Lake High. Riley could have waltzed into any greasy spoon trucker stop and Tess would have recognized her. But as Riley's steps faltered and the curiosity in her eyes intensified, Tess realized she herself might not be so easy to pin. Her boyish cut was Swedish blond now, not gothic black, and she sported a heck of a lot more tattoos. Tess figured she'd also put on a hell of a lot more life miles, and those probably showed in her face.

"Theresa?" Riley lifted her hand to her mouth. "Theresa Hendrick?"

"Tess," she corrected. She'd dumped the name Theresa the day she ran away from Pine Lake. "Everyone calls me Tess now."

"Oh. My. God." Riley slapped the dishtowel over her shoulder and, in one step, enveloped her in a hug. Tess stiffened at the shock of human contact. She spent most of her days alone in an eighteen-wheeler. For self-preservation's sake, she avoided human contact in the trucker's man camps. This might be as close as she'd been to another human being since she'd walked out on her husband two years ago.

Riley pulled back, gripping her by the shoulders. "I can't believe Theresa—*Tess*—is standing in front of me after all these years."

"Imagine. I survived."

"You look good, you look fit."

"Comes with being gainfully employed."

Well, she *had* been gainfully employed until five days ago. That's when she told her boss—who knew Tess had no family—that she had to take time off for family. She'd left his trailer to the sound of shouted curses.

Riley tapped Tess's left bicep. "That's a new one. I like it. Looks like a pheasant's wing."

Tess glanced at her tatted arm, a sleeve of overlapping feathers in black, burnt sienna, and rose, a tattoo chosen when what she most wanted to do was fly away.

"Pheasants are lovely," Riley ventured. "They're game birds."

"Then they're always an easy target."

"Unfortunately, yes."

"I chose well then." Tess nodded to the great room beyond Riley's shoulder. "I see you've won the Cross family lottery."

"Yup, I'm sole proprietor now."

"I love that you've kept up that late seventies vibe."

"I prefer 'shabby chic.'" Riley turned around and eyeballed everything. "If I wait a couple of years, I can upgrade to 'vintage.'"

"One more rub for luck and Bob's intestines are going to spill all over the hearth."

"Think of the Halloween possibilities."

"And Bud and Mary?"

Riley paused a moment, and the face she turned to Tess was full of apology. "Two years ago. It happened pretty quickly. They died within three weeks of each other."

So long ago and yet not so long ago. Tess tightened her grip on the strap of her overnight rucksack, trying to ignore the sharp, stabbing sensation in the middle of her chest. Of course Bud and Mary were gone. They'd sheltered her here three separate times, and they'd been in their seventies then. She'd always meant to send flowers, a note, to call and say thank you. Like all good intentions, they had a way of passing her by.

"Good people, your grandparents." Tess cleared her throat. "They always said they'd leave the place to you."

Riley raised her brows. "Did they really?"

"I heard them talking about it once when I slept in that back room by the kitchen. They spent a long time debating whether it would be the right move."

"Well, that would be news to my siblings and cousins. My grandparent's decision came as a shock to the whole family. Every one of them had been salivating, expecting a piece of the camp pie. That is until—" The bell over the front door jangled, and Riley's face paled. "Oh, Mom. There you are."

At the realization that Riley's mother, Mrs. Margaret "Don't Call Me Meg" Cross, was walking through the front door, a rush of heat flushed through Tess until even her fingers and toes prickled. She'd known that sooner or later she'd have to face one or another purse-wielding scion of old

Pine Lake. She'd just hoped it would be later, when somehow, miraculously, she'd be more prepared.

Now she turned to face the authority figure who'd been the only sour face at Camp Kwenback during Tess's visits. Everything about Mrs. Cross was sharp: the creases in her capris, the part of her blond hair, the click of her heels, and her opinions. When Bud and Mary first took Tess in as a runaway during the height of the summer season, Margaret Cross had a lot of strong opinions about Tess's petty rebellions, minor infractions, and juvenile delinquency. Margaret Cross didn't like teenage girls who left their mothers—even if it was only for a few weeks at a time—even if that mother was an unrepentant alcoholic.

Tess stifled the urge to toss her head so her bangs fell across eyes, but she just couldn't stop the resurgence of the old attitude.

"Hey, Meg," Tess said. "How ya doing?"

Mrs. Cross raised her head from her phone. And there it was—the shocked, horrified expression Tess had expected to slam up against over and over in Pine Lake, now that she'd mustered the guts to come back.

"Theresa Hendrick." Mrs. Cross blinked, struggling to bring her features under control. "What a surprise."

"Yes, it's been a long time. How are the Daughters of Old Pine Lake, Meg? Is that venerable association still strong?"

"Of course. We have a charity golf event coming up."

"I'll be sure to remind my mother to put it on her calendar."

Tess watched consternation twitch across Margaret

Cross's features at the idea of inviting the infamous Mrs. Hendrick of Cannery Row to one of the DOPL's events.

"I just arrived to ask Riley," Tess said, turning back to the registration desk, "if there's any chance one of the cabins is available for rent."

"Ha!" Riley rounded the reservation desk. "Only if you want to sleep with raccoons."

"I've slept with worse."

"I haven't rented out the cabins in a decade. Now they're only good for nesting sparrows."

"It's better than the back of my cab, I bet. I just need a place to lie low for a while. You know, from the FBI."

Tess winked at Riley, who dropped her face to hide her smile. Tess just couldn't help herself. Really, it was like riding a bicycle.

"Forget the cabins." Riley pecked at the keyboard of her computer. "We have plenty of rooms available here in the main lodge."

"Good. For safety's sake, I'll keep the weapons, the drugs, and the body in my trunk. Is it a smoking room?"

"Alas, no."

"I guess I'll just have to smoke on the porch." Tess glanced over her shoulder. "Maybe you'll join me, Meg. I've got some serious Jamaican ganja."

"The Jamaican blend is too harsh for me," Mrs. Cross said. "I prefer Mango Kush."

Tess blinked.

Riley sighed. "Really, Mom?"

"Really what? You're both adults now; I can make those

jokes." Mrs. Cross didn't bat a lash. "Now, Riley, while you're renting rooms don't forget you have the whole Milton family coming in next week."

"In *three* weeks, and it's all here in the computer."

"What about Mrs. Clancy?"

"She just arrived this morning. She's napping in her room right now, all worn out from the drive."

"And don't forget the Jeffreys, too—"

"They canceled. Mrs. Jeffrey had to have emergency gall-bladder surgery."

"Mmm. I'll send a card." Mrs. Cross granted Tess a curious smile. "So, Theresa, I assume you've come back to Pine Lake to visit your mother?"

"Of course."

The lie felt numb as it slipped across her tongue. It'd be a cold day in hell before she ever spoke to her mother again.

"Mom," Riley said, "why don't you get yourself a cup of coffee in the kitchen? I'll join you once I take care of our guest."

"You're getting so bossy in your old age, Riley." Margaret extended a hand to Tess and leaned in, giving her a perfect hospitality voice. "Pleasure to see you again, Theresa."

I doubt it. "Send my regards to the other Daughters, would you?"

"Indeed I will."

Mrs. Cross's heels clicked across the pine wood floors as she headed toward the kitchen, thumbs flying across her phone.

Once her mother was out of earshot, Riley said, "She

wasn't kidding about the Mango Kush." Riley swirled the mouse in little circles on the desk. "A good friend of hers has a card for medicinal marijuana. The closest dispensary is in New Jersey so Mom takes her down to buy it. Mom thinks she's an expert now."

"I'm more concerned that your mother is now alerting every shopkeeper, waitress, and cop in Pine Lake that Three-Tat-Terry is back in town."

"You must have known your return was likely to cause a splash."

"Somehow," Tess said, "I'd hoped Camp Kwenback could keep this secret, like it did once or twice before."

Tess couldn't quite meet Riley's eyes. The first time Tess chose to run away from home, Riley had been spending the summer here, too. Since they were of an age, they'd spent a lot of time together, roaming the woods, canoeing, climbing the big net between the oaks. But come school time, Tess had grown wary that Riley would whisper to her girlfriends all the gossip Tess had shared about the dysfunctional Hendrick family.

But Riley had never said a word. Which is why Tess had made a beeline here today, seeking a safe place to hide from the rest of Pine Lake.

"So, Tess," Riley said, lit by the blue glow of the screen, "how many days are you planning to stay?"

"Three, four. It depends."

"I can give you the friends-and-family rate."

"Sounds dangerous. Don't you have, like, twenty-seven cousins?"

"Only if you include the second cousins." Riley checked a ledger on her desk. "I used that rate for a bunch of Pine Lake girls who came here last August for a mini-reunion."

Mini-reunion. Tess swallowed the urge to laugh. Mini-reunions must be what people do when they have happy memories of childhood.

"It was an impromptu thing," Riley continued. "Jenna Hogan and Nicole Eriksen drove Claire Petrenko clear across the country to meet a bunch of us here. Claire had been diagnosed with breast cancer, did you know that?"

Tess shook her head. She'd liked Claire Petrenko once, before Claire started to make Tess feel like her star charity case.

"Claire's doing great now. She finished chemo. She's involved in some clinical trial out in Oregon. The reason I mentioned it," Riley ventured, "is that your name came up quite a few times over the weekend."

"I'd have been disappointed if it didn't."

"Jenna, Nicole, and Claire went looking for you in Kansas or Oklahoma or someplace like that."

"Oh?"

"Yeah, they drove, like, six hundred miles out of their way to stop by your house, but you weren't there anymore."

Tess's ribs tightened. That's Claire Petrenko. That woman never could give up a lost cause. She wondered what Claire had thought when she came upon the burned-out farmhouse that used to be Tess's home.

"I guess I was back in North Dakota by then." Tess rubbed the spot under her eye socket where the headaches always started. She'd spent the night in some anonymous hotel by the side of the road as the cop had recommended, but a restless night's sleep on a lumpy mattress wasn't helping her deal with this memory lane overload. "If you've got a room, Riley, I really need to crash."

"I've given you the corner room. Right near the fire escape. Just in case the FBI comes knocking." Riley gave her a wink as she placed the key on the counter. "Just as a reminder, we still serve continental breakfast here in the main lodge between six and ten a.m., though you can always brew a pot of coffee in the kitchen if you sleep in. The rooms are straight up the stairs, the last door on the left. But you know all this already."

"Yeah, I do."

"Good. Now I'd better go talk to my mother." Riley slipped out from behind the registration desk. "It's never a good thing to keep General Cross waiting."

Riley made her way to the kitchen. Tess grabbed the key, and then her gaze fell upon a teak bowl just behind the reception counter.

A bowl overflowing with origami cranes.

Once Tess had been cruising in her eighteen-wheeler on Interstate 94, her thumb on the splitter, her forefinger on the high/low, working the shifting of gears like she was part of the machine, feeling like she was flying—until ahead a car spun out on a slick of oil. She slammed on the brakes, forgetting for that crucial split second that she was driving without a trailer, thousands of pounds lighter than if she were hauling. Only the strap of her seat belt kept her from careening around the cabin as the rig screamed and bounced and missed by a hair a harsh roll on the grassy berm.

Now, staring at the origami, Tess braced herself for the cold wash of terror. She blinked and blinked and blinked but she couldn't make the evidence disappear before her eyes.

She'd found her runaway daughter.

Chapter Four

S o," Riley said, screwing up her courage as she strode through the swinging doors to face her mother, "have you set a date for Olivia's baby shower? I told her she could have it here in the lodge if she wanted."

"Your sister decided to host it at the Adirondack Inn instead." Her mother dismissed the subject with a wave of her hand. "What's with Theresa Hendrick?"

Riley crossed to the sink where the day's dishes awaited washing, pretending that the news about her sister's decision didn't pinch. "I don't know what you mean."

"Don't be obtuse, Riley. That thrice-arrested classmate of yours just waltzed through the doors of Camp Kwenback. No one has laid eyes on her since she skipped town over a dozen years ago."

"Do you blame her for leaving Pine Lake?"

"That's not the point."

Riley shoved the faucet on, feeling a kick of loyalty. The whole town loved to gossip about the dysfunctional

Hendricks—the husband who ran off with his daughter's own English teacher, abandoning his twelve-year-old daughter as well as an alcoholic wife. While Tess was at Camp Kwenback, it had taken weeks for Riley to gain Theresa's confidence enough for Theresa to lower the walls she'd erected and let some of the truth slip through. Riley respected those confidences, just as she respected those boundaries.

Riley had a few of her own.

"So," her mother persisted, tilting her head so her blunt-cut hair swung against her shoulders, "Theresa must have said something about why she's here?"

"She told you that she's here to visit her mother."

"After leaving that poor woman to fend for herself all those years ago? No, I don't believe that for a minute—"

"Then I can only assume she's here for vacation." Riley picked up a sponge and ran it around the inside of a mug. "A little R and R."

"If Theresa Hendrick was looking for rest and relaxation, I can't imagine she'd seek it in Pine Lake." Her mother set her coffee aside and pulled out a drawer to grab a dish-towel. "Officer Rodriguez was so furious when she left that I wouldn't be surprised to discover there was still a warrant or two out for her arrest."

"Really, Mom?"

"Maybe that's why she cut her hair short and dyed it blond. Maybe she really doesn't want to be recognized."

"Better alert the FBI."

"Did you see the muscles in those arms?" Her mother

wiped a mug dry with efficient, absent swipes. "You don't get that kind of definition daintily perspiring in a gym."

"I think she looks fabulous." Nicked and scratched and battered a bit, but still in one piece. Eyes like Sadie's, in an odd way. Like they couldn't shake last night's horror movie out of their minds. "And frankly, Mom, it's none of our business what she's doing here."

"All right, then." Her mother pulled a cabinet door open and clanked the dry cups inside. "If gossiping about the notorious Theresa Hendrick is off the table, then let's talk about other business."

A prickle of dread spidered down her spine. Riley told herself it wasn't possible that her mother knew she was harboring a runaway who was now sleeping in Room 6.

"You'll remember that I warned you," her mother said, "that the Pine Lake Credit Union would pass on your loan application."

Ah. So General Cross had heard the news. Riley could only assume that her mother had heard it while she lunched with the mayor's wife, or enjoyed a round of golf with the bank manager, or while gossiping at a planning meeting for the next charity event for the Daughters of Pine Lake.

"I remember the warning." Riley slipped a grilling pan on the dish rack. "But Ernie is the manager of the credit union—not you. Good proposals can change minds."

"Good business *ideas* change minds." Her mother wandered to the industrial range to nest a frying pan with the others in the lower drawer. "Ernie knows Camp Kwenback. He's a businessman who's not going to be swayed by nostalgia. I was just trying to save you some professional embarrassment. But as usual, Riley Cross plows forward." She straightened up from the range and then tapped a manicured fingernail against a new cabinet knob. "Red knobs? Really?"

Riley ignored her. These lacquered knobs had been in the sale bin at Ray's General Store, and Riley thought they'd be an inexpensive way to freshen up the place. Unfortunately, once she'd installed them, they just seemed to point out how scratched the maple cabinets were, how dull the countertops, how blackened the grout in the backsplash.

"So," Riley said, "did Ernie's wife give you any particular reason as to why they rejected my proposal?"

"Just the usual."

"That Ernie is still as miserly as Grandpa always insisted he was?"

"Your grandfather also let guests stay free for a summer week if he liked them. Your grandfather spent most of his last ten years entertaining a hefty proportion of his guests gratis, every week from June to September."

Riley ran a sponge along the edge of a butter knife. "If you die with your bank accounts empty, then you planned well."

"His quote, and the very reason you're in this fix." Her mother returned to the sink and picked up another dish. "If he'd left the camp to any of the rest of his twenty-six heirs, we'd have had this place sold to the highest bidder and the proceeds generating interest in tax-deferred college savings accounts for the grandkids."

Riley realized she was holding the sponge so tightly she

was squeezing all the soap out of it. "Are we really going to do this again?"

"I just don't understand why you continue to ignore common sense. You've seen the way this place has declined. Your grandparents resisted every step as we set up a website and tried to move into the twenty-first century. They just kept entertaining their old friends and letting the place fall to pieces."

"Because the credit union wouldn't give them a loan, either."

"Because your grandparents didn't understand that the camp needed a complete overhaul if it was going to survive." Her mother frowned at an origami bird sitting on the windowsill. "Have you at least called that last developer whose number I gave you?"

Riley felt around the bottom of the sink, seeking more silverware.

"I wonder about this every day, Riley. Why on earth would you leave a perfectly fabulous job in one of the swankiest hotels in New York City to come here and brush spiders out of the corners of log cabins with a broom?"

"Ordering five-hundred-count Egyptian cotton sheets for a fancy city hotel didn't fulfill my need to commune with nature."

"According to Declan," her mother said, waving toward the origami bird on the windowsill, "you did plenty of communing with nature running around with that odd bird-watching group in Central Park."

Riley's throat tightened at the sound of her husband's

name. "They were the Uptown Birders, Mother. Every year they added valuable information to a worldwide database about the migratory habits of many North American species."

Her mother didn't respond. Her mother didn't need to respond because her silence said that Riley should have spent those hours with Declan in their overpriced apartment rather than with a bunch of hipster retirees peering through binoculars. Her silence suggested that had Riley paid as much attention to her marriage as she had to summer bird breeding behavior then she wouldn't be here, separated, alone.

Riley plunged an arm into the hot, soapy water and pulled out the rubber stopper. She wished she could encapsulate why her marriage went wrong and be able to turn it around and toss it at her mother like a made-for-TV sound bite. Declan didn't beat her or cheat on her or abuse her, the only reasons her mother could ever imagine for why Riley would leave a man who oozed such rough charm with his Irish accent and longshoreman's shoulders. Why would she abandon a fashionable apartment on the Upper West Side and a middle-management job at the Aston Hotel that paid her a healthy salary? For the first couple of months after she'd left him, her mother had been sympathetic, patiently awaiting some clarification. A hundred times Riley had been tempted to launch into the explanation, but then she'd look into her mother's eyes and wonder why her mother couldn't just accept Riley's need to raise high, thick walls around that subject.

Just this once.

Then her mother did what Riley dreaded the most. General Cross released a long, weary sigh, murmuring, "Oh, Riley," and at the sound of that tone of voice, Riley's back tightened like a boat rope straining in a storm. General Cross was about to launch the second phase of her attack. The first phase was always a good strafing with emotional napalm; the second a calmer and more reasoned approach that left her and her siblings feeling like they were trying to punch shadows.

Her mother balled the wet dishtowel in her hands, closing her eyes as if summoning the strength of angels. "Why do we always argue like this?"

"Because you don't trust me to make good decisions?"

"You were like this from the moment you were born. A stubborn little redhead always shooting off in the wrong direction. And with five siblings older than you, it was easier at the time for me to give you your head. That was my weakness for loving you so much."

Riley braced her hands on the edge of the sink and watched the water swirl down the drain. She knew her mother loved her—had *chosen* her by adoption—thus making her special, different from her mother's five naturally born children, filling out the family to the six kids her mother had always wanted.

But when her mother spoke like this, it gave Riley flashbacks to grammar and middle school. In those days her mother would stand over her as she tried to get Riley to organize her backpack, as her mom quizzed her on what homework was due, as her mother called herself Riley's secretary in an attempt to make up for whatever common sense and organizational skills Riley just hadn't been born with.

More and more Riley felt like a cowbird that had been deposited in the nest of a family of phoebes. Big and ungainly as an egg, needing more care as a hatchling, and, in adulthood, gobbling up the family business that all the other nestlings had expected to share.

"Honestly," her mother said on a sigh, "had I known what Bud and Mary had in mind, I'd have talked them out of it. They probably thought they were giving you a great gift, but the truth is that they left you an albatross. But with this latest debacle with the credit union, I'm beginning to understand." Her mother gazed out the window over the back lawn, wrinkling her tiny nose as if she smelled the mildew of old dreams. "As I've stood helpless and watched you ignore good advice, spending what I suspect is your life savings to fix the roof on this building and renovate the bedrooms, all done—yes, I know—as a labor of love, I suddenly realized that for Bud and Mary, you were the perfect choice."

Riley followed her mother's gaze to the back lawn but what she saw in her mind's eye was her grandparents setting the picnic tables end-to-end, friends coming off the porch to join them, using their wineglasses to anchor the tablecloths as a summer breeze fluttered off the lake. She saw her grandmother in a simple cotton dress bringing bowls of fresh corn and heaping green salads while Grandpa turned barbecue ribs on the grill, laughing while drinking root beer. Then they'd all sit, Grandma with her long, salt-and-pepper hair piled up off her neck and Grandpa with his rubber marsh boots, their guests digging in with abandon, and conversation flowing as the fireflies started to blink and the kids leaped off the bench to chase them around the green, green lawn.

And then the scene morphed before her eyes to one weekend last summer, when her high school friends had returned home for a mini-reunion. Riley had offered up the camp because she had the room to house them all, if not in the finest of conditions, and she wanted to throw one last party before she sold it to a developer a cousin had recommended. It was a lovely weekend, with Sydney cooking in this kitchen, Lu and Nicole setting the table, Claire slicing tomatoes, and Jenna tossing the salad. Jin kept up an endless monologue while Maya looked on in bemusement. They'd eaten out on the lawn just as her grandparents had, laughing and crying and talking until the wee hours of the morning. That weekend she realized what her grandparents had *really* wanted.

No sooner had the last of her friends departed before she'd cratered the development deal, hired renovators, gotten in contact with old customers, and started working on the business plan that she'd spent the last six months presenting to banks.

But there was this thing about decisions, Riley had come to know. You think the hardest part is making one— taking the wavering temperature of your heart, weighing the pros and cons, choosing an option—but you'd be wrong. Making the decision was only the first tentative step. Once made, there was no knowing where that decision would lead you.

"Listen to me." Her mother leaned in, pinning Riley's flitting attention. "Are you going to delay and delay until you're so behind on taxes that the town—or the state—slaps a lien on this place? You know what happens when the government gets involved in any land situation around here. It'll be just like Camp Abenaki—"

"Mother." Riley threw up a hand, trying to ward off the words.

"—the whole place swallowed up by the land trust, every building torn down to the dirt, and every last dollar from the sale swallowed up by back taxes."

Riley turned her back on her mother, like she wished she could turn away from the image in her mind, of Joe and Geri Stenton—the longtime owners of Camp Abenaki—standing stunned, watching the bulldozers knock down their eighty-year-old home.

"Closing your eyes won't make that truth go away, Riley." Her mother leaned back against the sink, stretching in an effort to make her meet her gaze. "You have to evaluate, like any good businesswoman, all of your options. And you have to do it while there's still some value in the old place."

"Let me guess." Riley turned, tugged the dishtowel out of her mother's hands, and dried her own hands on it. "You have the business card of one of those options."

Her mother pushed away from the counter to zip open her purse. Riley heard a card hit the butcher-block table. "I met him at the nineteenth hole during the firefighter's charity game last week. He said he'd still use Camp Kwenback as a resort. A different kind of a resort, but still a gathering place. He might even let you manage it."

Riley knew what the developers wanted to do. They wanted to chop down the wild woods that encroached on the back lawn, pull out the old slide as a safety hazard, rip up the obstacle course her grandfather had built through the forest, pull down the tree house by the beaver dam. They wanted to clear-cut twelve of the fourteen acres to build a golf course.

She couldn't explain to those developers any more than she could explain to the banks and credit unions what it meant to grow up running wild through the woods, playing manhunt amid the trees, making stick figures with acorns and milkweed, and watching birds teach their young to fly.

She couldn't explain to the developers that reviving Camp Kwenback was her Plan Z, and if it failed, she was out of luck, ideas, and a future.

"Riley, my darling daughter, there's no way to revive this broken-down place." Her mother's manicured finger tapped the business card. "Time has already passed it by."

Chapter Five

Y our turn, Mrs. Clancy."

Sadie dropped the dice into Mrs. Clancy's hands, then stretched back in the cushioned wicker chair to feel the sun on her face. She felt like a snake warming herself on a rock, her belly full of the half quart of orange juice, a banana, and two bagels she'd eaten after rolling out of her soft bed at eleven a.m.

Mrs. Clancy's bracelets rattled as she tossed the dice across the board. "Hah! I crapped out. How much did I lose?"

"You didn't lose anything yet. You've got a five and a two." Sadie glanced at the Parcheesi board, stained and warped, with two different colors of wooden elephants in a dead heat for the finish. "You can move both your pieces."

Mrs. Clancy raised her chin to peer at the board through her reading glasses. "Which one is mine, Sissy?"

"The blue ones are yours."

Sadie didn't bother to correct her name. This was the second time Mrs. Clancy had gotten it wrong since Sadie had finished breakfast in the kitchen and come outside, only to find her sitting on the porch perusing a local newspaper. Now she watched Mrs. Clancy pick up a green elephant and move it forward seven spaces, plus a few more. This was the third time they'd switched colors.

She gave Mrs. Clancy a look-over as the older woman reached for the dice out of turn. She was wearing only one earring. There was a stain that looked like ketchup on her Camp Kwenback T-shirt. Under the paisley scarf knotted carelessly at her nape, her wispy hair needed a good brushing. It looked soft and cotton ball white, just like Nana's.

Sadie felt a sudden ache in her chest, a hollow that no amount of breakfast could fill.

"Snake eyes!" Mrs. Clancy smiled at the dice on the table. "That's always lucky you know."

"Lucky?" Sadie pushed each of the blue pieces up a space. "It doesn't get me very far on the board."

Then the sliding doors squealed open and Riley edged out, laden with a tray.

"I made your favorite, Mrs. Clancy, Cape Cod chicken salad." Riley walked to the wicker seating area and nudged the Parcheesi board to make room. "I thought you might be ready for lunch."

"Just one more minute," Mrs. Clancy said. "I'm beating Susan in parmesan."

Riley gave Sadie a smile. "I hope you don't have money on the game, Sadie. Mrs. Clancy is a shark."

"Yeah, I've noticed."

Mrs. Clancy threw the dice again. "Hah!" With a sweep,

Mrs. Clancy gathered all the elephants to her side. "Better luck next time, kiddo."

"Maybe Sadie will play another game later, but right now I'm stealing her from you." Riley raised an eyebrow at her. "After that enormous late breakfast, I figured you and I could use a little trail walk."

"Sure, I'm game."

Sadie spoke the words lightly, but there was nothing calm about her nerves. Riley was looking at her like second period had just ended and it was time to hand over the test. *Here comes the grilling.* Sadie just wished she'd left her back-pack in a safer place than her upstairs room so she could make—if necessary—a quick escape.

Riley headed down the porch stairs, sweeping up a paint-brush and a small can of paint perched on the rail. "The markers on the red trail need freshening," she explained, as she headed full stride across the back lawn. "It's a bit more than a mile, there and back. Are you up for that?"

"Bring it on." Sadie put her head down and did her best to keep up with Riley's athletic pace, waiting until they were out of earshot of Mrs. Clancy before launching into a safe topic in the hope of avoiding a dangerous one. "So," she said, "is Mrs. Clancy a relative of yours?"

"No. Why do you ask?"

"You're feeding her. That's a little weird, in a hotel, isn't it? I mean, do you cook for all your guests?"

Not that there were many, Sadie noted. In all the time she'd been checking out the place, she'd seen no more than four.

"Mrs. Clancy is a special case," Riley said. "Her whole family used to visit Camp Kwenback every summer for the last two weeks in August. The Clancys have been guests for decades. Mrs. Clancy still has good memories of those summers so her family sends her here for a couple of weeks every year. But there was a time," she added, "when we used to feed breakfast and dinner to more than fifty guests and ten employees. We didn't bother with lunch because most folks would be canoeing on the lake or hiking through the woods or swimming at Bay Roberts. They'd go into town and get some of Josey's maple pecan pie or bag a lunch on their own."

Riley's description pretty much synced with what Sadie had supposed long before she'd come here. She'd spent late evenings waiting for her slow computer to upload all those pictures on the Camp Kwenback website: photos of folks eating on tables under the shelter of the boathouse, swinging on ropes in the woods, fishing in rowboats just off shore, and gathering in the main lodge by the fire.

Pictures that had convinced her that the woman who'd wrapped her in the Camp Kwenback towel had to be someone who really loved this place. How else did a towel from some Adirondack camp end up in an Ohio hospital?

Then Sadie thought of another subject she could bring up to avoid the grilling a little longer.

"So, Riley," Sadie said, as Riley paused before a tree, "do you have a library card?"

"A library card?" Riley ran her fingers over the traces of pale red paint remaining on the furrowed bark. "I guess all those potboilers and romance paperbacks in the lodge aren't to your taste?"

"Oh, I'll read *anything*." The longer and thicker the book, the better. "But I thought I might go to the reference desk of the Pine Lake library and look at the birth announcements in local newspapers or page through some old high school yearbooks."

"To look for your birth mother."

The instinct to make some sassy remark was strong but Sadie squished it down. She still needed something from Riley.

Two somethings, really: a library card and time.

Riley pulled at the top of a can of paint until the lid popped. "Don't you think that's a stretch, Sadie?"

"Did you forget you're talking to a girl who chased down a logo on a towel?"

"Yeah, but what do you expect to find?" Riley dipped the brush into the can and then painted one solid, thick line. "They don't exactly make birth announcements for babies placed for adoption. As for the yearbooks, you're assuming your birth mother was a local teenager. You're going to have to try to look past the hairstyles and bad clothing choices for any vague resemblance—"

"It's a start."

Riley dipped the paintbrush back in the can and did another coat. Sadie wondered if Riley remembered that you didn't need a library card to use the reference section. You *did* need a library card to use the computers though, and Sadie really had to find a way to update her online status before her friend Izzy got nervous and started asking questions about her to the wrong people.

"Listen." Sadie climbed on a log just off the path, throwing out her arms to keep balance. "I've been thinking about this for a long time. I figure that the person who had that towel—my birth mother—could be someone who came here every year for vacation. Someone who loved it, like Mrs. Clancy does. But I figure it's even more likely that it was someone local. Someone more like yourself." Her face warmed. What an ass she'd made out of herself last night, half blubbering with the hope that Riley would be *the one*. "The town Fourth of July parties used to be held at Camp Kwenback every year, right? And the Labor Day picnics?"

"Wow." Riley scraped the brush against the inside edge of the can. "I guess you saw the photos upstairs."

Sadie nodded. Old photos of Camp Kwenback lined the hallway on the upper floor. She'd fogged them up with her own breath this morning, looking for any teeny-tiny face that resembled hers. "My point is," Sadie said, hopping off the end of the log into a cushion of leaves, "that the library is a good place to continue my search. But...I just need a little time."

"Ah."

Sadie tried to read the meaning of Riley's "ah.'" She watched as Riley took care in settling the metal top back onto the paint can, tapping it in good with the butt end of the paintbrush.

"I'm not a charity case, you know." Sadie kicked around a few leaves. "I can pay."

Riley looked up sharply.

"I've been saving up." She squinted back down the path they'd come on, not in search of a glimpse of the lodge, but just to dodge that look. "I spent a long time planning this."

"So you did."

Riley picked up the can by the handle and headed back on the trail, falling into that athletic, loping stride again. Sadie had to walk double fast to keep up, which she did, just to stay beside her so she could glance at Riley from beneath her lashes and try to figure out what the woman was thinking.

"Here's the thing," Riley finally said, exhaling deeply. "Most people wait until they're eighteen to find their birth mother. Then they request a copy of the original birth certificate."

"Is that what you did?"

Riley stumbled a bit, but Sadie didn't notice any roots on the ground.

"I was a lot older when I started my search." Riley gazed in the far distance, though Sadie didn't see anything ahead but trees and more fuzzy trees. "When I was your age, I was terrified my birth mother would show up and steal me away from my family."

Sadie remembered that Izzy had said something like that once, before Izzy really understood what the "international" meant in international adoptions, and thus how far away her Chinese birth mother really lived.

"Life was good in my house," Riley continued. "I have five brothers and sisters. I was on the softball team in high school. I spent summers at this camp, playing with the come-aways—the visitors—and then I worked here as a teenager. I was terrified that a stranger would show up, call herself my mother, and disrupt all that."

"It didn't happen, did it?"

"No. But my feelings about my birth mother were so different from yours at the same age...I'm just worried that you've set out on this quest for the wrong reasons."

Here we go.

"The truth is, every teenager looks at herself in the mirror and wonders where she came from."

Sadie rolled her eyes.

"I saw my sisters do the same thing," Riley continued, "and they were brought up by their own biological parents—"

"They were just being idiots." Sadie caught herself. "No offense or anything."

"None taken." Riley's smile was a little sad. "Right now one of them, my sister Olivia, is acting like an incredible idiot."

"What I meant," Sadie rushed on, "is that they don't have any reason to ask those questions. But you and me, we've got a mystery in our past, so we have a reason to be curious."

"Oh, yeah, curiosity. I used to imagine that my father was a professional baseball player. Did you ever do that?"

"Mine was a professor." She dragged the toe of her sneaker in the needles to kick up a spray. "In my head I could see him, wearing a tweedy coat, round glasses, in a house full of books."

Riley said, "Once you find your natural parents, you know, you won't be able to imagine anymore."

"Imagining is for little kids."

"And then you'll get the answer to that other question, the harder one." Riley looked down at her. "You know the one."

Why was I given up?

Sadie nodded. The question didn't need to be spoken aloud. She heard it in her head all the time. The fact that Riley had the same question in her head made Sadie tremble a little, like she and Riley were the two tines of the tuning fork Mrs. Schein sometimes struck in music class.

But that didn't change her mind.

"Here's what I figure," Sadie said. "When I was ten years old, I really, *really*, wanted a puppy." Sadie remembered the pokey, unsteady mutt she'd wanted so badly, rust brown, licking her hand through the cage at the animal shelter. "But I knew that I couldn't take care of a dog. Not at that time, anyway, no matter how badly I wanted to."

Riley paused by another faintly marked tree. "A puppy is a lot of responsibility."

"Yeah, I heard that a lot." Sadie could still hear the puppy plaintively yipping as Izzy carried his brother away. Sadie's arms had felt so empty. "Later that night, while I was lying in bed trying to figure out a way I could keep that puppy, thinking about how much I wanted him . . . it just kind of hit me. Like when you play dodge ball, and you get hit right in the stomach and you can't breathe for a little while? My birth mother must have felt the same way I did when I had to leave the puppy behind."

The can of paint opened with a subtle pop. Sadie watched as Riley swirled the bristles of the brush inside, frowning. She straightened to sweep the color in a block over the old, faded paint. And then Riley stopped painting. She crossed her arms with the brush still in her hand, as the paint oozed to the end and dripped on the forest floor.

"If you find your birth mother," Riley said, "what are you going to do then?"

"What do you mean?"

"You know you can't just change one set of parents for another."

"Like, *duh.*"

"Your family may seem like the enemy now—"

"Oh, please."

As if her issues had to do with parents who refused to buy her a cell phone, or sign up for a social media account, or buy a hot pair of sneakers. As if Riley knew anything about what she was dealing with.

But, of course, Riley didn't. Sadie hadn't told her a thing. It dawned on Sadie that the best way to get Riley to do exactly what she wanted was to tell Riley some small part of the truth.

Sadie closed her eyes and took a long, deep breath.

"I couldn't exchange my parents," she said, "even if I wanted to."

"Oh?"

"I don't have parents anymore." She balled her hands into fists. "Both of them are dead."

Chapter Six

Tess lurked by the sliding glass doors of the main lodge, pressed against the wall in the shadow of the curtains, watching her natural daughter stride behind Riley as they both headed toward the lodge.

The last time Tess had laid eyes on Sadie, her daughter had been only three days old. Tess had been so loopy from pain medication that she'd somehow convinced herself if she just swaddled her daughter right, then the Camp Kwenback towel would protect her baby from all harm. But Sadie kept stretching her legs—plump with rolls—as Tess tried to bundle her. The baby girl inadvertently nudged away all the careful folding, making Tess laugh, making the whole process a wonderful game. Just when Tess thought she'd finally done it right, the nurse had swept in, startling Tess, startling Sadie. Sadie had let out a cry that released a slow, sliding weight in Tess's chest that she later recognized as her first milk dropping.

Help me, Tess had said to the nurse, who stood there implacable, holding out her arms.

Help me. Tess had fumbled to gather Sadie and all her twisted blankets close.

Help me.

"Hey, there you are."

Riley stepped through the sliding door, leaving it open for the shadow coming in behind her.

"You were starting to worry me, Tess." Riley toed off a sneaker. "How's the headache?"

Tess pressed her thumb against the throb pulsing behind her right eye socket, the medicine-muffled remnant of the migraine that had descended with a vengeance last night. Her palm obscured her vision—and her face—as Sadie stepped into the room.

"It could be better," Tess said, blinking. "I could use some industrial-strength joe."

"I've got some of that made already, as well as some cranberry muffins in the kitchen. Let me just take care of Sadie here. Sadie, don't bother taking off your sneakers, it'll only take me a minute to fetch the library card."

Riley set off toward the reception desk. Tess held her breath as she lowered her arm and faced her daughter. She tensed against a thunderclap of recognition, a lightning flash of womb-deep acknowledgment of shared blood and body and bone, expecting it, dreading it, and hoping to God that it wouldn't happen.

Then the reality of Sadie came at her in a rush: The sharp jaw, the narrow shoulders, the wide cheekbones just starting to emerge under the rounded face she recognized from the social media photos. Sadie's nostrils flared as if she sensed she was under perusal. She crouched to tighten the laces of her sneakers, the ridge of her spine visible under the ribbed tank top. Her hair was a bright red, the legacy of an aunt Tess had only seen in pictures in her childhood home—her mother's only sister, the one who'd died in her teens.

Sadie's ponytail dangled with bead charms.

Tess had rehearsed a little speech last night as she struggled to sleep, and now it stuttered out, her voice artificially high. "Sadie, is it? Is this another niece, Riley?"

"No, she's a guest," Riley said, from where she dug into some drawers across the room. "Sadie, this is my friend Tess. Tess, Sadie. Tess and I go way, way back to our high school days."

"Sadie." Tess spoke the word like it was foreign, like she hadn't rolled it over a thousand times in her mouth. "That's not a name you hear often."

"My parents met each other at a Sadie Hawkins dance."

Her daughter's voice was monotone and husky low, as if the girl was reciting something she'd memorized by rote.

"Are they around here right now?" Tess asked. "Your parents?"

"Nope."

Sadie's reply was hard on the *p* and offered up no other explanation. Tess didn't really need an explanation. She'd learned many months after it happened that Sadie's parents had died in a car accident, a wreck on the interstate six years ago involving an eighteen-wheeler like the ones Tess drove across North Dakota.

Then Sadie stood up, sweeping up the backpack poised by the door. The girl gave her a baleful look, and with a gut kick, Tess realized that the eyes Sadie turned upon her were pale green—green like alfalfa fields in the early spring when the shoots first rise out of the ground—and without stepping any closer, Tess knew there would be a rust ring around those pupils.

Those were her mother's eyes.

Just then the migraine shot a shiv through her skull, a cold, sharp pain that buried deep in her brain.

Sadie said, "Hey, are you all right?"

Tess squeezed the skin between her nose and brow, hoping Sadie didn't notice that it was the sight of Sadie's green eyes that had cut right to the soft unprotected pith of her, cracking the shell of numbness she'd spent fifteen years developing.

"Tess gets migraines," Riley explained as she approached and handed Sadie a card. "The library's only open for a few hours today, so you'd best head into town now. You can take one of the bikes in the barn."

"Okay...thanks."

And then Sadie was gone, her shadow slipping out the back door and into the sunshine as swiftly as if she'd gone up in smoke.

"Wow." Riley came close, folding her arms and peering at her in concern. "You really don't look so good."

Tess closed her eyes and fought to pull her shattered self together. "About that coffee...?"

"Right."

Tess stumbled after Riley, resisting the urge to glance out the sliding back doors, telling herself the worst was over because she'd made it through the initial contact and Sadie hadn't recognized her. She told herself that it was *good* that Sadie hadn't recognized her, even as she felt some lonely ghost of herself peel away to trail the young girl toward the barn.

She'd been lucky, she thought, as she pressed her thumb against her eye socket. She shouldn't risk another face-to-face. She had to get this wayward runaway back to her home before Sadie got herself in real trouble. And Tess had to do it without revealing herself, something she could do only if she played her cards right with Riley.

So she followed Riley into the kitchen, which looked exactly the same as it had all those years ago, right down to the long butcher-block table and the battered white cabinets. Tess turned and gripped the edge of the table. With a little push, she lifted her backside onto it.

"Ancient reflex," Tess said, catching Riley's over-the-shoulder grin. "I don't see any health inspectors around."

"No health inspectors. This is no longer a commercial kitchen." Riley poured the last of the coffee into an old mug emblazoned with the faded letters *CK*. "And keeping up to code is the least of my worries these days."

Tess took the mug in both hands. The coffee was thick and strong and well-cooked and lukewarm, just like it had come out of some brown-stained glass-bottomed industrial coffee carafe in any truck-stop diner. She gulped it down and concentrated on the weight of it sliding into her.

She stopped long enough to breathe. "Being in this kitchen again makes me think of your grandmother and her legendary gingersnaps."

"Nothing is as good as Nana's gingersnaps. I swear we ate half the dough whenever she made them."

"Have you made any cookies with that runaway of yours?"

Tess watched over the rim of her cup as Riley blinked. Riley opened her mouth and then shut it just as quickly. Her old friend had a face as transparent as glass. Riley should never play poker for money.

Tess said, "You seriously thought I wouldn't know?"

"Not unless you're psychic. You haven't left your room since you arrived yesterday afternoon."

"Runaways give off a vibe." Tess pressed the coffee mug against her thigh, grateful for the caffeine hit just starting to dull the pain in her head. "Skinny kid, dirty clothes, battered sneakers. No parents in the vicinity. A rucksack she grabbed when I eyeballed her. She answered my questions with one syllable. She kept ducking her head. Remind you of anybody?"

"About six of my nephews."

"I drive trucks. I come upon runaways all the time hitching on the road and in the parking lots of roadside diners. You start to sniff them out after a while. How did this girl wind up crashing in Camp Kwenback?"

Riley shrugged and leaned against the sink. "I caught her in the generator shed yesterday, when she was trying to find shelter from the rain. I lured her into my clutches with the offer of a warm fire and hot chocolate. If I had to guess by the bug bites on her legs and the clothes I found drying in the farthest cabin, I'd say she'd been hanging around town since the end of blackfly season."

Tess feigned surprise, though she knew it had been at least two weeks since Sadie had gone silent on social media. "She's not a local?"

"No."

"But you checked for alerts, right?" Tess took a sip of coffee, leaning back on her other hand. "Missing children websites, that kind of thing?"

Riley grabbed a dishtowel and did her best to rub a layer of skin off her hands, watching the process as if she had money on the outcome.

"Oooookay," Tess said, trying to keep her voice light, like this wasn't any real concern of hers. "I'm just thinking about her frantic parents."

"She told me that she doesn't have any."

"Oh, I'm sure no runaway has ever said that."

"She said they died in a car accident." Riley tossed the dishtowel aside, opened a cabinet, and grabbed a canister of coffee. "And yes, I believe her."

"Having no parents doesn't mean she doesn't have a guardian. She may have grandparents, aunts, even foster parents—"

"I've considered all that." Riley swiftly shoveled ground coffee into the filter.

"Have you considered checking those skinny arms for track marks?"

"Oh for goodness sake, Tess, she's not a junkie. She's here because she's looking for her birth mother."

Tess started. She grabbed the counter for stability and felt the grit of embedded flour under the edge. Tess hadn't expected Sadie to confess her real motives to Riley. That made Tess's situation in Pine Lake all the more difficult.

"She owns a Camp Kwenback towel," Riley explained, as she closed the coffeemaker and hit the On button. "She told me that she was wrapped in it when her adoptive parents picked her up from the hospital."

Tess pinched the bridge of her nose again, even though the migraine had ebbed, because the action would hide her face.

"I know it sounds crazy," Riley said, "but just think of what that kid had to do to trace the logo to this place."

Tess didn't have to think. She knew. Sadie must have found a service that did searches for trademarks and logos. Sadie had saved up money somehow, paid for the search. Sadie had posted something mysterious a couple of months ago about finding what she'd been looking for. Oh, she was a smart one, her daughter. Knowing herself and Sadie's bastard of a father, Tess wondered where the brains came from.

Tess willed the throbbing behind her eye to ease. "So you're a redhead, Riley," she said lightly. "Got any secrets to confess?"

"What?"

"With that hair, you could pass as her mother easily."

"No, no, no way, no how." Riley raised both her palms and leaned back against the counter. "I've never had any kids. And I have a soon-to-be-ex-husband to vouch for the fact that I never intend to have any."

That hung in the air for a moment, a confession of a different sort. Tess paused, debated whether to follow up on it, and then seeing how Riley looked away, Tess chose instead to stay on track.

"Okay, then," Tess said. "I have to assume your runaway came here because she knows you're an adoptee, too."

"No, I told you, there was a towel—"

"Easily filched."

"—and she didn't know I was adopted. She was surprised when I told her."

"It's a small town, Riley. She's had a couple of weeks to ask around, right? Heck, five minutes in one of the booths at Josey's and any stranger would know everyone's business, including yours."

"C'mon, Tess. Who's gossiping about me being adopted?"

"Fair enough. I'm just saying it's quite a coincidence." Tess raised her hand to gesture to the solid roof, the kitchen full of food. "Being an adoptee would make you sympathetic to her situation. It'd make you more willing to help, give her place to crash, whatever. All it would take is a sob story about dead parents and the theft of a single towel."

Riley blinked, nonplussed. "You're making it sound like Sadie's some kind of manipulator."

"On the street, kids learn how to hustle. Real fast." Tess, sensing Riley's hesitation, took the chance to press a little harder. "You know Sadie's last name. Right?"

"No."

"Do you know where she came from?"

"No."

"Do the authorities know she's here?"

Riley crossed her arms as the coffeepot began to gurgle behind her, looking around the room as if seeking spiderwebs in the ceiling corners. "The girl is just looking for her mother. She needs a couple of days to do some research. Once she realizes that her birth mother hasn't been hanging around for the past fourteen years, waiting for her to show up, I'm sure she'll go back to where she came from."

"Riley, did you ever go searching for your own birth mother?"

Riley turned so pale so fast that Tess felt a kick of guilt. She'd gone too far. Tess didn't have the right to ask that kind of question.

Tess raised a hand in apology. "Hey, look, I'm—"

"It's okay."

"No, really, it's none of my business and—"

"I did look for her." Riley rocked against the counter. "It didn't turn out well."

Riley stared at the kitchen floor, but Tess could tell Riley wasn't seeing the odd-size gray slate tiles.

"I'm sorry." Even as she spoke, Tess knew she had to use this unexpected vulnerability for Sadie's sake. "Did you and Sadie talk about that? About how a search for a birth mother could go wrong?"

Tess hoped the terror of the idea didn't skitter across her own face as violently as it now skittered across Riley's.

"We discussed it. A little." Riley swiveled against the

counter, flipped open a cabinet, and pulled down another mug. "So," she said, her voice firm, "you think I should just throw this girl out."

"Runaways mean trouble."

"I remember a time when everyone told me that *you* were trouble."

"Hell, I was trouble."

"Not while you were here eating gingersnaps."

That much was true. And she would have loved to have stayed here, instead of crawling back to the dirty house in Cannery Row where her mother promised to get better and then pretended she wasn't drinking cheap vodka for breakfast.

Sometimes loyalty was a bitch.

"I was trouble, yeah," Tess agreed, "but Bud and Mary knew my name, where I came from, and why I was here, and so did the cops. But you," she said, pointing a finger in her direction, "are currently harboring a minor—a stranger—a runaway. It could get you in loads of hot water."

"Getting in trouble might be a nice change from following the straight and narrow path and disappointing everybody, anyway. And I can't exactly envision a Pine Lake police officer breaking down the door to slap handcuffs on Sadie or me."

Tess had seen Officer Rodriguez break a door down in the Cannery. She'd seen him come busting through and then seize her by the coat, throw her against the wall, and slap a cold set of handcuffs across her wrists. She'd had a bruise on her cheek for weeks.

"Unfortunately, it could happen." Tess figured if you're always staying on the right side of the law, you don't learn these things. "Depending on what this Sadie's *real* story is, her guardians could send the cops here and charge you with endangering a minor, even kidnapping."

"For giving a kid hot chocolate, a library card, and the loan of a bike?"

"Sounds like aiding and abetting, or it would, in the hands of any two-bit lawyer."

"I just keep thinking," Riley said, "that maybe Sadie is running away from a bad home life. Maybe she needs sanctuary. Like you did."

"All the more reason to get this kid the help she needs right now, before she learns how to jump railway cars, beg for change, and hustle more soft-hearted Good Samaritans like you, Riley Cross."

Riley frowned at her. "I can't believe I'm hearing you say all this."

"I've learned a lot from my bad choices. The juvenile delinquent you remember from Pine Lake is long gone."

"So much so that Tess Hendrick advocates for handing a runaway over to the police?"

Tess felt the twitch in her jaw, the one thing she couldn't suppress. She remembered her own wayward travels: Cleveland in the summer, Chicago in the early fall, St. Louis in the winter, back north in the spring, every day the same— wake up, beg, buy food, smoke, hang out, dodge the cops, move on. And she thought, yes, *yes*, she'd do anything—quit her job, drive eighteen-hundred miles, even call the cops on her daughter—to prevent Sadie from going down that same road.

She'd do anything except tell Sadie the truth.

"Hey, if you can get your runaway to go home without calling the authorities, that'd be great," Tess said, forcing her stiff shoulder muscles to mimic a careless shrug. "But knowing what I do about the mind-set of a rebellious teenager, I don't think you'll have much luck with that."

Riley chewed on her lower lip. Tess knew she was wavering. So she nudged herself off the butcher-block table, strode across the kitchen, and took the phone receiver off the wall. It was tethered, so she stretched it to the end of its springy cord. "You want me to do it? If I make the call, then Sadie can't blame you."

Tess hesitated as she heard a hiss from nearby. She glanced at the kitchen door, now rocking gently on its hinges. Riley must have heard it, too, because she clattered her coffee cup on the counter and shot over to the window by the sink.

Riley said, "Damn it."

"What?"

"She heard you." Riley pushed past her. "She's running."

Chapter Seven

S adie just ran.

She flew into the pine woods. She kept her eyes on the ground, watching the needles she was kicking up, seeing her half-tied laces, the leaf that had gotten stuck between the rubber sole where it separated from the canvas. The word *police* rang in her ears.

The first time she saw the police she'd been sitting in Izzy's house in her penguin pajamas watching Japanese cartoons. Her mom and dad hadn't picked her up that morning like they'd said they were going to. She'd liked staying at Izzy's house, which was messy in a pillows-on-the-floor kind of way, but she'd spent a whole weekend there and Izzy's brother was annoying and Sadie really wanted to go home. When the doorbell rang, she'd leaped up to greet them—but her parents weren't there. Instead, two policemen blocked out the sunshine, talking to Izzy's mom, and then those two policemen looked at her.

She'd had a box of cereal in her hand, she remembered,

and then suddenly it wasn't in her hand and little oat pieces pinged and bounced and scattered all over the hall. Later— much later—she'd found a heart-shaped marshmallow in the pocket of her pajamas, sticky and covered with lint.

Now Sadie rounded a tree to catch her breath and squeeze the memory away. She'd made it to the marshy part of the lake near the beaver dam. She realized she should have taken the bike. She could have gotten away faster. That was the problem with panicking. You get that squishy feeling in the middle of your gut, like the floor just disappeared, and then your stomach is in your throat and the two bagels and orange juice with it.

Think.

She bent in two to ease the pain shooting between her ribs. Her backpack shifted, tugging her tank top. She told herself she had been lucky. If she hadn't decided to go back to the lodge before leaving for the library, to dump out the two survival books in her backpack and stash them in her room at Camp Kwenback, she would have never heard Riley and her friend talking about her in the kitchen.

That Tess-woman had been doing most of the talking. It was hard to believe that skinny, tatted-up, hard-faced woman was a friend of Riley's. She looked like she had a getaway motorcycle idling outside. Or a pack of lock picks in her back pocket. Sadie hadn't liked the way that woman skewered her with one look from under those silly bangs. So-cial workers gave her that kind of piercing look. Like they could, with one glance, see right through Sadie's head to all the lies she'd worked hard to keep hidden.

She leaned over even further. Her heart was battering the inside of her chest. One thing was for sure: No way, *no way* was she going to the police. She knew what would happen then. They'd put her in a room and talk to her—*talk, talk, talk*—and then send in social workers who knew how to get information out of you like they had psychic powers. You go in and they ask questions about your whole family, brothers, sisters, aunts, uncles, grandmothers, neighbors, and all that information comes right up to the front of your brain whether you want to tell them or not. And if you don't tell them what they want to know, then they've got to find another way to get rid of you, so the next thing you know, you're on your way to some group foster home. Then you're sleeping in the lower bunk while the kid on the top tells you he's got a dead gerbil in his pocket that he stabbed with a stolen knife.

A branch cracked. She straightened like a shot. Peering around the tree, she squinted through the woods to see a woman jogging in her direction. The sun hit the woman's hair, and that's when Sadie knew it was Riley.

"Sadie, I know you're out here."

Riley approached closer, close enough that Sadie could see she was sweeping the whole forest with her gaze. Sadie fumbled for the binoculars around her neck and scanned the woods behind Riley, looking for a herd of blue uniforms, seeing nothing but trees.

Riley said, "I just want to talk, okay? Just talk."

Talk, talk, talk.

Sadie dropped the binoculars to her chest and stepped

out from around the tree. "I'm not hanging around here if you plan to call the police."

Riley's whole face softened. "I'm so glad you're still here."

"For now." Sadie looked Riley straight in the face because grown-ups always thought you were telling the truth when you did. "All that stuff your friend was saying—she's wrong. There is no one who cares enough about me to show up, drag me away, and charge you with endangering or kidnapping or abetting or any of those other stupid things that Tess-woman said."

That woman was messing everything up. And Sadie was so close. Just a few more days and maybe Sadie would have found someone in the high school yearbooks whose face looked like hers. A few more days and maybe she would have found the one woman in the world who *would* give a damn.

"Try to understand." Riley wandered toward a fallen log and sat down. "Tess got a shock today when she saw you. You're like a ghost from her past. She was a runaway, too. She ended up right here in Camp Kwenback, sleeping in one of those outdoor cabins."

"You told me that you knew her from high school."

"Yes, that's true."

Sadie rolled her eyes. Little tiny town with itty bitty problems. "It's not 'running away' if you end up a few houses over."

"Those two trips were tests. Later she took off for good. That's why she looks like she eats nails for breakfast."

"Ex-runaway, ex-con, I don't really care who she is. She shouldn't be sticking her nose in this."

"That's true. But for some reason, people stick their noses in my business all the time." Riley squinted off in the distance. "And I can't seem to help myself—I always listen. Which is why one day I woke up and realized I was living in an apartment that someone else decorated, working a job that I hated, and married to a man I couldn't possibly make happy. Go figure."

Sadie's jaw hardened. She didn't need the sticky mess of someone else's problems. She had plenty of her own. "Well, I can take care of myself, as long as the police aren't interfering."

"Good for you. Me, I seem to give off a perfume of desperation. But I'm trying to change that."

"So are you going to call the cops on me or what?"

"No, I'm not."

Sadie's heart leaped. "What about your Tess-friend?"

"Tess will keep her mouth shut if I ask her to. She owes me."

"You're not worried about being arrested if you let me stay?"

"Not if you tell me the truth."

Sadie took a step back, hesitating. "I never lied to you."

"I believe you. But Tess made one good point back there. You never told me where you came from and who might be waiting for you back home."

Sadie stilled. Her ribs tightened. She cast about for some half-truth that would satisfy Riley's curiosity. Half-truths were always better, and a lot easier to remember, but her mind kept stumbling over what she couldn't reveal. No, she couldn't tell Riley *that*. She just…couldn't. But she'd risked so much already—stealing books from her hometown library, using Nana's ATM card, traveling five hours away from home, telling so many half-truths to this one, kind stranger.

"I think you owe me this, Sadie."

Sadie closed her eyes against the kick of guilt. Then she whispered what she knew she shouldn't.

"I lived with my grandmother." She crouched down and plucked at a pinecone with a fingernail. Stupid tears prickled at the backs of her eyes. She blinked fast to keep them there. She wasn't supposed to talk about this. She'd kept all this inside of her for so long, clamping her teeth together when she was tempted, and now she felt her throat close so tightly she could barely breathe.

Riley asked, "Is your grandmother missing you now?"

She curled her hand around the sticky pinecone. If she just hadn't been in such a hurry that day. She'd had an algebra test and she hadn't been able to think of anything else. She knew she had to eat a good breakfast that morning, but that meant making more dishes to wash, less time to do it in. So she didn't have time to comb Nana's hair, make sure she was dressed properly. She remembered thinking what difference did it make anyway? What was one day wearing slippers and a bathrobe? It wasn't like they were going to have visitors or anything, and she could always take care of Nana once she got back home.

Sadie whispered, "I forgot to bolt the door."

One stupid mistake. All her fault. One stupid mistake and the whole world turned upside-down again.

"Sadie?" Riley stood close beside her, watching her, all gentle brown eyes.

"The police found her before I did," Sadie said. "Nana was wandering in the middle of Skillman Avenue. All she was wearing was a bathrobe and one shoe."

Chapter Eight

I t felt odd to be approaching the Pine Lake police station in broad daylight. Without wearing handcuffs, that is.

Tess dropped into her strut like fifteen years hadn't passed since she'd rolled over these sidewalks. She knew the exact distance between trees boasting little wooden signs admonishing people to curb their dogs. She knew the angle of the summer light, the air that smelled like maple syrup, the temptation of freedom provided by the thin alleyway between the yarn shop and the station. With her hands in her back pockets, she braced herself to enter the booking room of the police station without Officer Rodriguez nudging her ahead of him, pushed beyond all levels of tolerance, his overdeveloped neck muscles twitching.

No, this time she was heading into the belly of the beast on her own. This time she was acting like a good citizen, an upstanding, taxpaying member of decent society. Though if she thought about it for more than a minute, she knew she was riding a thin moral line between getting a runaway back to her family and ratting out Riley, a woman to whose family she owed a great debt. Just the thought of it made her twitchy for nicotine.

She pushed through the revolving door nonetheless. Her nostrils flared as she entered the old room. It smelled of mold and humidity, tinged with testosterone with a top note of dirty socks. The place was locked into the mid-twentieth century, with the same linoleum floors, the same old oak information desk, the same Plexiglas shield with the circular cutout, and maybe even the same female cop behind it.

The cop didn't turn away from her computer screen as Tess approached.

"Can I help you?"

"Yeah, I was driving over on River Road just off I-90 a couple of days ago, and I saw this kid wandering on the side of the road." Tess pushed away the memory of Riley demanding Tess respect her wishes and not report Sadie to the police. Technically Tess wasn't reporting her at all. "She was a young girl, fourteen or so, skinny, alone in the rain with a backpack."

"Yeah?"

The policewoman jiggled her mouse and kept reading something on her monitor. Tess wondered what kind of hot crime wave was going on in Pine Lake that the report of a runaway elicited such a dull response. Was the town secretary skimming from the city budget? Had someone set up a meth lab in the woods? Back when she was raising hell, the toughest thing the cops did in any given year was to bust a bunch of pot-smoking kids spray-painting the inside walls of the old cannery.

"She was a runaway," Tess said. "I'm here to see if there are any alerts."

"We haven't gotten any reports lately." The woman stretched back to pull some flyers from a pile. "The NCMEC keeps an updated list of runaways you can search online state by state." She slid the flyers through the slot in the Plexiglas. "You can also try the Polly Klaas Foundation—"

"Done both of those." Tess ignored the flyers. "I've also checked the FBI list of missing persons. I'm here to see if you've got a better, more up-to-date database."

The policewoman lifted her head. Tess felt the woman's gaze pass over her butch-cut hair, her shoulder tat, and her black ribbed tank. Tess didn't recognize the cop, but Tess could see the officer's mind working, flipping through some mental Rolodex. Somewhere in the basement storage of this very building there was probably a nice fat file on Theresa Hendrick, the edges of the pages yellowing, the paper spotted black with mildew.

The policewoman picked up a phone. "Have a seat. I'll send someone out to write up a report."

Her butt remembered the wooden bench sitting like a pew against the front wall. She slipped right into place. She ran her hand over the finish, worn in places where many a soul had languished. She wondered if she ran her fingers just underneath the edge she would find layers of ossified gum stuck there in youthful protest. All she needed to make this picture complete was that hard-nosed cop, Officer Rodriguez, walking through the door.

Then the far door swung open and a cop rolled out.

Sweet Jesus, no.

Rodriguez still had the same musculature that got him mocked as "Rod the Bod" by the late-night cannery crowd. The years had filled him in so he looked less like an obsessive gym rat and more like a fitness acolyte who liked to play tag football on the weekends. Or like one of those militant, angry fathers who beat the spine out of their kids.

Instinct kicked in. She rolled up out of her seat and slipped her hands in her back pockets. What the hell was he doing in Podunk Pine Lake? He should have blown this small-town police station a long time ago. He should have climbed his way up the ladder to Albany, where he'd have something better to do than harass teenagers. Or he should be living off a city pension somewhere, fishing and hunting his way through his forties. He'd certainly put in his twenty years. She hadn't even considered he'd still be kicking around, an ugly reminder of everything she'd left Pine Lake to forget.

He stopped square in front of her and gave her a hard-eyed glare. "Well, if it isn't Theresa Hendrick."

"Rodriguez."

"I called Gloria a liar when she told me you were sitting out here. You just cost me twenty bucks."

It wouldn't be the first time she'd cost him money. He'd once thrown ten bucks on a shopkeeper's desk to pay for the tampons she'd stolen by stuffing them in her coat.

"You shouldn't be gambling, Rod." She tried to raise her gaze above his chest, but it got caught on the regalia. "A guy with that much brass should know gambling is illegal in Pine Lake."

Rodriguez shoved his hands under his biceps so they bulged even more. "Blond suits you."

"I'll take the compliment." She squinted at his salt-and-pepper head. "But I'm just not feeling the gray, Rod."

"Blond is better than that goth thing you once had going. You know how many times I wanted to take a scrub brush to your face?"

"A scrub brush? And I pinned you for a whips-and-handcuffs man."

"You always did pin me wrong." He gestured to the tat covering her left arm. "I see you're still committing ritual, socially sanctioned self-abuse."

"That's a lot of big words."

"Still the smart mouth."

"You're looking pretty smart, too." She nodded to his uniform, crisp and blue as always. "You've earned a few more patches for your sash, Girl Scout."

"That's Captain Girl Scout to you." A muscle flickered in his cheek. "So what the hell brought you back to Pine Lake?"

"I'm visiting friends."

"And I thought I'd put all of them in jail."

She tried to straighten up like the adult she was, but all she managed to do was swivel from one hip to the other, regressing from thirty-something to a teenager in one minute flat. She seemed to be having no effect on him, as usual. He glared down from his six-foot-three-or-so, sporting the cop stone face, his lips pressed in a slashing line like an Old Testament god.

Well, she didn't owe anyone an explanation for why she was back in Pine Lake, least of all this cop who'd all but driven her out with his harassment. She was tempted to ask him if he was still throwing hungry teenagers in jail for shoplifting at the Food Mart. She wanted to ask him if he still did nightly drive-bys to harass the good folks of the Cannery. She was tempted to ask him if he was still working that battered wife case, the one when he helped the father retain custody of his biological children.

But if she gave in to the powerful urge to turn on a heel and leave the station, she'd only trigger Rodriguez's cop intuition. The last thing she wanted him to do was dig into the archives and investigate.

She steeled herself for the inevitable mockery. "Believe it or not, Rodriguez, I've come to ask for your help."

He turned his head. "Come again?"

"I saw a kid on the side of the road a couple of days ago."

"Did you just ask for my *help?*"

"Don't be a prick."

"For a decade of your young wasted life, I tried to give you help." He rocked back on his heels. "And here you show up fifteen years later asking for it."

"It's not for me. I need to see the most recent list of missing children and runaways."

"Gloria said you mentioned something about a girl walking alone on a county road."

"A runaway."

"Or a local kid coming back from some pickup soccer game—"

"I know a runaway when I see one. You think I'd drag my ass into this police station because I've got nothing better to do?"

"Oh, I don't know. Maybe you came here to get fingerprinted again, just for old-time's sake. Or to check on outstanding warrants."

"You told me that you buried all of those."

"The juvenile delinquent I remember never believed anyone's word."

"Are you going to help me with this runaway? Or are you going to harass me for old-times' sake?"

"You could have looked up this stuff online yourself."

"Sorry, I left my tricked-up laptop back in my eighteen-wheeler, and, geez, I must have misplaced my library card."

"So it didn't work out so well for you then."

"What?"

"Running away."

Tess's jaw hardened. She wished she could excise that terrible year from her brain and stitch the edges back together so it didn't include the cold, the damp, the sick, the lonely realization that no one in the whole wide world gave a shit about Tess Hendrick, least of all herself.

Her jaw had turned to stone so she just looked at him from beneath the swoop of her bangs, looked at him with all their conflicted history rolling between them, and waited for him to make the next move. She could see his cop mind working overtime. She could see him wondering what game she was playing. But she wasn't playing a game—not this time—so she didn't have to school her face. She'd come here for one reason alone: To ferret out some kind of proof that Sadie was lying to Riley—that Sadie's relatives *did* care that Sadie was gone. By now Sadie's Nana or aunt must have sent out an APB for a missing child. Finding that proof was the only way Tess could think of to shake Riley's all too trusting nature and get Sadie back where she belonged.

He unknotted his arms and said, "Freddie Taylor's got an autistic boy who wanders off sometimes, but we always find him splashing around at Bay Roberts. We haven't gotten any other local notices of runaways or missing children." He walked toward the door to the inner station, talking all the way. "You'll want a statewide database. If that doesn't work, I can get you access to the Canadian records. If the kid was that close to the highway, she could have hitched, she could have come from anywhere, and you know that, right?"

"I've ridden a few circuits."

"How good a look did you get of her?"

Tess thought of Sadie's bright red hair, the dimple in the lobe of her left ear, the alfalfa green eyes.

"Good enough."

Rodriguez led her into the main room of the precinct. He wove through the desks, past a few officers in uniform and a few without. The room had the kind of hush that came when everyone had just stopped whispering. She forced herself not to dodge eye contact. She wasn't being dragged in in handcuffs now. She wasn't being put in a holding cell until the cops could rouse her mother out of a drunken stupor long enough to sign her out. And a quick scan of the room didn't register any recognizable cop faces, although that husky guy in the corner with the thinning hair could be Officer Casey.

Rodriguez led her all the way to the back office, the one with his name stenciled on it, Captain Jorge E. Rodriguez.

"All the years of working here," she said, as she entered the one-windowed office, "and now you're den mother."

"It's almost as shocking as finding you alive."

"I'd imagined you'd be in Albany or New York City, capturing the real bad guys, instead of here harassing the stoners."

"I did five years in Albany."

She snorted. "You make that sound like a prison sentence."

"I worked homicide."

He didn't elaborate. He leaned over his desk, flattened his palm on a pile of papers, and with the blue glow of the computer screen lighting his face, he tapped the keyboard one-fingered. A diploma from the police academy was the only thing hanging on the walls. On top of a file cabinet stood a picture of two young boys and a dog frolicking in autumn leaves. No pictures of a wife, she noted. Next to the picture was some sort of blocky plastic award whose brass placard she couldn't read.

"Come around here," he said, "and I'll show you what's what."

She rounded the desk and saw a screen full of computer files. He hesitated for a moment, his finger hovering on the mouse, before he finally clicked a window and a database popped up. It was set on the most recent missing child report, only a day old. The missing kid was a six-year-old Vietnamese boy from Riverdale.

"It's set up by descending date," he explained, "so this listing is the latest. Clearly he's not your runaway. Click here and then you can go and see the main list and choose only the reports for female minors. Be patient. I'm fighting with city hall to approve an upgrade to the wi-fi so it's going to take a while to load each listing."

She glanced around the small office. "You want me to do this right here?"

"You wanted access." He nudged a coffee cup that said *World's Best Dad*. "There's a coffee maker in the break room. It's pure industrial sludge, but you know what they say about beggars and choosers."

"So you're going to let an ex-delinquent rifle through all those files of yours."

"All my files are password protected."

"I don't want to tie up your computer." *Or have you watch what I'm doing.* "I could be hours at this."

"You've got one hour. I'm going to lunch with Gloria."

"All right then." An hour would do it. "You girls take your time."

"There's hot chocolate in the break room, too," he said as he paused at the door, patting the frame. "I remember how much you loved hot chocolate."

Heat rose to the roots of her hair. The first time she'd been dragged into the police station, barely fourteen, when she'd been caught smoking pot with her new friends at the Cannery, Rodriguez had separated her from the others. He'd taken her into the break room and offered her hot chocolate. It was instant, watery, and served in a Styrofoam cup. It was the best thing she'd tasted since her father had dumped her and her mother gave up parenting.

She sank deeper into the Rodriguez-size hollow in the seat, determined to get this done and then get as far away from Rodriguez as possible. In the search box she typed Sadie's full name.

She watched the little hourglass spin as the search commenced. Sadie had been gone from the Queens house for two weeks, according to Tess's best estimate. It was long past time for someone to notice the girl's absence. Tess knew Sadie's Nana hadn't died—she'd searched all the local funeral homes and the newspapers for obituaries, but that search had come up empty. Tess could only conclude that Sadie had conned her Nana somehow, given her some kind of elaborate story to explain why she wasn't around. Like she was going away on vacation with a friend or she got a scholarship to some upstate camp. Sadie probably had an accomplice or two. Maybe that Izzy girl who posted on her social media all the time.

Then the hourglass stopped, the screen refreshed, and Tess frowned.

No matches.

Tess leaned back, worried. She'd received no hits from the other databases when she'd searched, either. She wondered if the authorities had screwed up the name. Tischler was one of those names that people always misspelled. She would search again using just Sadie's first name; it was unusual enough that she shouldn't get too many hits. And if that didn't work, she'd search for age, gender, and county.

Tess sat back in the chair, willing there to be a hit. A few Sadies popped up, but none of them were her Sadie, and the hourglass still spun. It spun and spun and spun. It felt as if it were spinning her anger into a tighter ball just under her ribs. What kind of family didn't keep tabs on a fourteen-year-old girl? No matter what lies Sadie might have told to shake free of her guardians, wouldn't they have checked on the "friends" whom Sadie was spending the summer with? Wouldn't they have expected an occasional phone call? How much effort did it really take to track a teenager these days? Tess herself had managed it over the years just by connecting with Sadie through social media. To Sadie, Tess was Mindy, a quiet ninth-grader who lived in Minnesota with two dogs, someone who friended her because of the pictures of Sadie's cool origami. Mindy rarely posted, but she occasionally "liked" one of Sadie's pictures, and she sure did monitor that page. Mindy had pinned the exact moment that Sadie decided it was time to hunt down her biological mother. It was written right there, a plain text post, blinking.

I'm not waiting anymore, Izzy. I'm leaving today to find her. You won't hear from me for a while, not until I can get to a computer again.

The hourglass stopped. She scanned the list twice, sighing. None of these Sadies were her Sadie.

Tess tried a different set of search parameters. Her anger

at the Tischler family was becoming a burn under her sternum. She kept thinking about the bundles of photos she'd reviewed while under the care of the adoption agency all those years ago. Tess hadn't even wanted to look at them when she first stumbled into the hospital, half-starved and five months pregnant with a child she wasn't supposed to be carrying. But the adoption agency preferred open and semi-open adoptions, and the adoption counselor didn't want to hear when Tess insisted on a closed adoption, sealed, done, *forever*. The folks at the agency were feeding her and clothing her and giving her a place to stay that wasn't behind a garbage dump under the dubious shelter of a fire escape with one or another boyfriend of the moment. The counselors kept telling her that she'd feel differently after the baby was born. They urged her to make an adoption plan. So they left laminated photo albums from potential adoptive parents on her bedside table. They left DVDs by the television. Bored and constantly under curfew, she'd page through those pictures of happy couples, pristine homes, sweeping lawns, educational wooden toys, TV-ready versions of families too perfect to exist.

Tess knew what these airbrushed, prepackaged lives were for. They were meant to give the birth mothers some sense that they were handing their precious babies over to Mary Poppins—and not Ted Bundy. They were meant to give the birth mothers some measure of comfort.

The screen refreshed. No hits again.

Damn it.

Tess pulled the chair closer to the desk. *Think think think.*

Someone in the Tischler family had to be looking for Sadie. She paged through their photos in her mind, trying to remember the relatives. She hadn't known the family was called Tischler when she first looked through their leather scrapbook. She discovered that only later, talking to another pregnant girl at the agency who was looking at some of the same profiles. This ever-weeping sixteen-year-old had opted for an open adoption. She recognized the portfolio Tess had been looking at, referring to it as the Tischler photo album. Then she wrinkled her nose and called them *weird*.

Tess had known them only as George and Rose, whose getting to know us letter talked about how long their family had lived on their apple orchard. The album was full of black-and-white pictures of pale-faced ancestors with their pants pulled up above their ribs, of women with wild, curly hair, laughing with their mouths open. There were pictures of parties held in the orchard, checkered tablecloths on old picnic tables, men with pipes, and generations of soft-bodied relatives laughing over pie with friends. Their opening letter was a chronicle of Tischler genealogy coming down to its very last twig.

But what seized Tess in a way she didn't understand were the pictures of the family's dried apple doll collection. And the shots they took every winter of the snowmen they dressed in sequins and feathers. She couldn't stop looking at their quirky autumn display of hipster scarecrows in thrift-store tuxedos.

Such strange, senseless acts of whimsy.

"No luck?"

Tess startled. She glanced up to see Rodriguez leaning in the doorway. She shot a glance at the clock and realized it had been over an hour since she'd sat down to search. She had an odd feeling that he'd been standing there for a while.

She closed the computer window. "No luck. Maybe she was just a kid walking in the rain."

"Or you're seeing ghosts."

"Whatever." She stood up and slipped around the desk. "It was big of you to help out, Rod, though I can't say it was a pleasure—"

"You're not even going to ask?"

Tess approached the door but he made no effort to move aside. She met his eye, and her stomach did a looping drop.

She hadn't come here to talk about this.

"Come on," he said. "Aren't you in the least bit curious?"

"Nope."

"I figured that's why you made up this flimsy excuse about a runaway." Rodriguez still had a gaze that could cut through bone. "Just so you could access my old files, see how things stood after all this time."

"I didn't touch your files."

"Not even the Hendrick file that I left sitting right on the desktop?"

She hadn't looked at the desktop. She didn't want to know anything. But now she remembered how he'd hesitated earlier, before he opened the window of the missing children database, as if he wanted her to see something on the screen.

Her ribs contracted. "It's a cold case, Rodriguez."

"Not necessarily—"

"The statute of limitations has already passed."

"So you've done your research."

"I'm gainfully employed and a tax-paying citizen. What is past—is over."

"I know you don't believe that."

Oh, but she did. She stepped right up to him. She looked into those hard eyes, into the face of the man who'd thrown her in cuffs and subjected her to dozens of scared-straight talks. She looked at the man she'd laughed at, even while he was fingerprinting her, and spoke her mind.

"Just leave it alone, Rodriguez. Let the muck stay on the bottom of the pond."

Chapter Nine

W hen Riley went searching for Tess, she found her friend perched on a stump outside the last of the cabins, her arms banded around her knees, rocking. Dappled light flowed over Tess's colorful tattoos. Riley thought she looked like a hummingbird, suspended but anxious with thrumming.

"Hey," Riley said as she came close, "you're up early."

"Old habit." Tess let go of her knees, then tucked a pack of cigarettes into the breast pocket of her denim button-down shirt. "When I'm working, the earlier I'm on the road, the quicker my route is done. I can't seem to shake the schedule, even on vacation."

"How's the migraine?"

"Better."

Riley reserved comment. She had a suspicion those migraines could be summoned at will. Her and Tess's friendship had always been an uncertain thing, born as they were in the same town but worlds apart. Riley didn't want this dispute over her resident runaway to drive a wedge between them.

"If you've got a minute," Riley said, "I'd like to show you something."

Tess snorted. "Last time I heard you say that, you showed me a box full of baby birds."

Riley remembered that spring when a clutch of fledgling starlings had been knocked out of their nest during a storm. "When I find them hopping around here now, I just put them back in their nests."

"Such a softie."

"It doesn't always work. Half the time their nests are in pieces on the ground."

"Still," Tess said, brushing off her jeans as she stood up from the stump, "it's always a good idea to return 'fledglings' to wherever they belong."

Tess looked at her from under the swoop of those bangs, and Riley suddenly remembered that hummingbirds were believed to be the reincarnated spirits of Aztec warriors.

"You and I are talking about different kinds of fledglings, I think." Riley gave her a sideways squint. "We seem to be talking across each other a lot lately."

"What we have here is an honest difference of opinion."

"Our little runaway isn't any trouble." Riley turned toward the path, gesturing for Tess to follow her. "You've noticed that, right?"

Tess fell into pace beside her. "I haven't seen her much."

"She's sitting in the kitchen right now polishing off blueberry pancakes while she reads *War and Peace*."

"Can't say I ever cracked that book."

"I'm just saying, I can't imagine many child grifters read Tolstoy."

"Riley, you've made your decision. You don't have to justify it to me."

"I'm not."

"Then why do you sound defensive?"

Riley blinked, nonplussed. "Maybe because you told me that I was crazy not to call the police?"

"Look." Tess raised her hands, and the way the light moved over her tatted shoulder gave Riley the impression of a bird ruffling its wings. "I see situations like yours and I think up worst case scenarios. That's what I do. But, hey, this is your business, Riley. I wish you and Sadie luck." Tess peered ahead. "Where exactly are we going?"

"To the barn. Trust me; you'll want to see this."

Riley led Tess across the sun-blazed lawn, past the table feeder and the pole with the house for martens, to the opposite side of the clearing. She felt a little off balance at Tess's swift dismissal of their dispute. Riley wasn't used to people ceding disagreements, accepting differences of opinion, and breezily changing the subject.

She'd better not get too used to this behavior. She was meeting her mother for lunch this afternoon.

At the barn she flung open both doors so light flooded through to the back wall. One side was cluttered with the usual machinery: a sturdy ride-on mower, an industrial snowblower, rakes and shovels and hoes and gardening equipment, tins of oil and bottles of blue windshield wiper fluid.

Fishing tackle and rods were lined up against the wall by the workbench, which had a clamp on the edge for making flies. In the corner leaned a fleet of rusted bikes she should really put out for bulk waste collection, but she kept thinking she could restore some of them. Scattered all about were old canoe paddles, boxes of shotgun shells, bear mace, and a new plastic kiddie pool, bought when Riley's nine nieces and nephews visited for a summer afternoon.

Riley breathed it all in for a minute, the mildew of the old wood, the faint scent of her grandfather's pipe tobacco, the aroma of oil and rust, the perfume of a half century of a well-lived life.

Tess's whistle pierced the hush. "He was a bit of a pack rat, old Bud, huh?"

"He'd say he was a 'collector of American art.'" Riley picked her way between the lawnmower and a pile of inflatable rafts to an area covered by a canvas painter's tarp. "Grandma wouldn't let him put any of these in the house, but that didn't stop him from buying them."

She lifted one end of the tarp and Tess took the other end. Dust billowed in a shaft of light flowing in from a high window. They rolled the canvas back until it collapsed into a heap on the floor.

Riley saw Tess take a sudden breath and then walk over the tarp to stride among the carved wooden bears, the five-foot-tall ones as well as the smaller foot-and-a-half baby bears that nestled up against the larger ones.

Tess flattened a palm over the surface of the largest sculpture. "I can't believe you still have the bears."

"Teddy's looking good for his age, don't you think?" Riley knocked on the shoulder of the one closest to her. "Winnie's over here."

Tess said, "Do you remember when—"

"Absolutely."

"—we dressed them in cheap beads and old hats and whatever we could find in Mary's old trunk in the attic—"

"It was raining that day, and we had to push them away from the corner of the barn where it was leaking—"

"—we held a wedding ceremony for Winnie and Teddy—"

"—and we stole one of Bud's shirts and tried to tape a pipe on Teddy's mouth but it kept falling—"

"—and we jumped every time it hit the ground." Tess made a little sound deep in her throat. "I thought your grandmother was going to kill us when she came in to see what we were up to."

"She was just furious that her clothes fit Winnie."

"Bud was standing right behind her, and he couldn't stop laughing."

Tess covered her mouth, and Riley realized that Tess was hiding a smile, maybe the first smile Riley had seen on her face since she'd arrived. She wished Tess would drop her hand. Just the way Tess's eyes crinkled made Riley think of young Theresa—not the brooding girl in her eighth grade class who liked to carve the wooden desks with her penknife, or the sullen runaway her grandparents had taken in the second time, but the imaginative younger playmate who'd been a lot more fun than Riley's cousins and most of the summer visitors.

When Tess dropped her hand, the smile had faded to a twitch. "I haven't thought of these bears in years. I see they've been breeding."

"Grandpa never stopped collecting. He found a chainsaw artist from Saratoga and bought a bunch from him. Others were gifts from some of his friends, his guests, or pieces he picked up at county fairs or roadside stands."

When she was little her grandfather used to tell her stories about them. He said they were originally local black bears who'd been frozen into place because of a woodland witch, and once a month, when the light of the full moon fell upon them from the window above, they twirled into life.

How many hours had Riley spent staring out one of the windows, watching the barn through the trees in the hope of seeing the doors open and the wooden bears sneak out to dance by the light of the moon?

Then Riley heard herself say, "I have to sell all of them."

The words dropped like lead in the silence. Riley felt Tess's sudden attention.

"I figure that I could get a good price if I sell them as a set. Maybe it'd pay for a plumbing upgrade or new roofs on the cabins."

"Things are that bad?"

Riley ran her finger down a furrow of fur on Teddy's belly, debating how much she should say about her shrinking bank account, the dearth of summer reservations, the struggle to get a business loan, and every other questionable decision she'd made since she'd packed a suitcase and walked out of her New York apartment. "If I could spruce up the place, fix those rusty swing sets, buy some new paddleboats, advertise some specials for the young families of my grandparent's former clients, I might be able to lure in more bookings, which would bring in more cash."

"I noticed the place looked a little...tattered."

"I prefer 'well-loved.'"

"You know I live out of a semi half the year, right? I've got no place to put these."

"I wasn't trying to sell them to you, Tess."

"Why did you show them to me then?"

Riley shrugged. "Because you know them, that's all."

Tess dipped her head so her bangs covered her eyes. Riley knew it was always the guests who loved Camp Kwenback the best. The folks who wrote long apology letters about how their teenager's schedule didn't allow them to reserve a week's vacation, but *how we loved those long, lazy summer days at the camp*. She never felt the same kind of nostalgia among her family. The folks who truly loved the place were like this former runaway, who still rubbed Bob's belly for luck when she didn't think anyone was watching.

Now Tess wandered amid the maze of the bears, the heels of her sandals scraping across the debris on the floor. "What about that old mini-golf area down by the entrance to the camp?"

"Other than that it's on my very, very long list to be repaired, what about it?"

"Your grandfather let my first grade class have our end of year party there."

"I remember those days. The clown with the rust-streaked face used to scare the crap out of me."

"That's a good reason to pull down all that rusty stuff." Tess ruffled her fingers through the short hair at the nape of her neck. "I thought...maybe you can replace all that with these bears."

Riley blinked at the sculptures, most of them mounted on solid poly-coated stumps. "How?"

"I could saw some holes in the bases for the balls to go through. It wouldn't take much effort."

Riley had a vision of Tess in a high school woodshop, bent over some machine spitting sparks that reflected in her safety goggles.

"I used to work for a contractor," Tess explained as she walked to the workbench, poking around the tools in search of something. "He was a friend of my father's. I ended up at my father's house after...after I'd had enough of the run-away circuit. His friend took me on his crew as a favor, and I picked up a lot of skills."

"I thought you just drove eighteen-wheelers."

"Being a Jill-of-all-trades has its advantages in a tough labor market. Ah." She lifted a silver box. "I knew Bud would keep a measuring tape here."

"It's an interesting idea," Riley said, as Tess strode back to the bears, "but the mini-golf has always just been another perk of staying at the camp. Even if I had it fixed up, it won't draw in more bookings."

"Make it public."

Riley blinked, surprised at the idea.

Tess asked, "Isn't the Putting Palace the nearest mini-golf around here?"

"Y-yes."

"That's ten long miles up the road. You could call your mini-golf the Bear's Den." Tess crouched by Winnie's base and pulled out the metal measuring tape. "I'd be happy to fix it up for you."

Riley stuttered, "Tess, I don't—"

"I'm not used to hanging around, Riley." The tape closed with a snap. "Gives me too much time to think. A project like this would give me something to do other than dodge grammar school teachers in downtown Pine Lake, as well as cops who should have retired years ago."

"So I take it that you still haven't visited your mother."

Tess's jaw tightened. She paced to a far bear as if she hadn't heard the question at all. Riley wondered if Tess was using this project as an excuse to give her more time to muster courage. She felt a twinge of sympathy for Tess—and admiration, too—for having the guts to come back at all.

"It'd be great to have you stay longer, Tess. Claire Petrenko is visiting soon and I know she'd love to see you. But though this is a great idea, I'm not sure I can afford the materials—"

"That's on me. As is the labor."

"I can't—"

"Consider it a gift." Tess avoided Riley's eye. "It'll be a bit of senseless whimsy in honor of Bud and Mary."

Riley opened her mouth but words failed her. Of all the

things she expected Tess to say when she saw these bears, this was certainly not one of them.

"I can't say no to free labor." Riley planted her hands on her hips. "Though I don't know how I'm going to run it."

"Hire your runaway."

"Sadie?" Riley laughed. "She won't be here that long."

With a slow tilt of her head, Tess gave Riley a one-eyed look.

Riley knew that look. She'd been getting that amused, knowing look ever since she was ten years old and proposed a new law at a city council meeting requiring every resident of Pine Lake to adopt a cat.

Riley said, "What?"

"I'm just saying." Tess raised her brows. "You seem so sure that Sadie won't be here long."

"Of course she won't. She'll do her research, and then . . . she'll go back to wherever she came from."

"I hope that's true." Tess stood up and took her time clipping the measuring tape on the waistband of her jeans. "But if I were the runaway eating blueberry pancakes in your kitchen, Riley, I'd be dreaming up some way to stay here forever."

ॐ

Going to lunch with her mother was bad enough. A thousand times worse was arriving for lunch only to discover that the person waiting in the far booth was her estranged husband.

Riley stood just inside the door of Josey's staring at the nape of her husband's neck. He sat in the booth with her mother. His elbow was extended like he was taking a sip of coffee. Black coffee, she knew. No sugar, no cream, and no nonsense.

Her mother caught her eye and then slipped out of the booth, placing a hand on Declan's shoulder before striding down the aisle.

Riley said, "Mom—"

"Just hush for once and listen."

"No. I can't believe you—"

"I've been thinking about this for a long time." Her mother placed both hands on Riley's shoulders. "I will have my say."

Her mother's grip was strong, riveting Riley to the black-and-white laminate floor. Riley went mute.

"When your father and I first started our family, I was so sure I could handle anything that came at me, Riley. I thought I could mold my children like you were all made out of clay. But by the time you became young adults"—she squeezed Riley's shoulders—"I wondered if I ever had *any* influence with any of you, ever. Sometime along the way, I just figured I'd stop wondering and just do whatever I think is best, whether it's right or wrong. Like I'm doing today. You can hate me for it later, but I'd hate myself more if I didn't try."

The pressure of her grip eased. Her mother stepped back. Then she was gone, the chimes over the front door ringing.

Riley closed her eyes, but it didn't help. Against the

inside of her lids she could still see the tapering point of Declan's hair on the nape of his neck.

She strode across the black-and-white tiles and tossed her purse on the far end of the red vinyl seat.

"Don't blame your mother," he said, settling his cup back on the saucer as she slid in. "Both of us thought this would be easier than me showing up at the camp."

"Mom always knows best, doesn't she?"

His cheek twitched. She stifled a pinch of guilt. She had no reason to feel guilty. Showing up in a public place with her mother was an underhanded, manipulative thing for him to do. For maybe the first time in their relationship, she was on the moral high ground.

"Hey, Riley, can I get you something?"

Riley glanced up at Josey's daughter, April, the twenty-something who ran the place now that her mother had decided to retire to Trinidad. "I'm fine, April. Short on waitresses?"

"I can't always depend on these college girls." She hefted the coffeepot. "What'll it be today?"

"Just coffee."

April filled the cup. "I've got a maple-pecan pie coming right out of the oven."

"Tempting," she said, "but I won't be staying long."

Declan didn't respond. He just raised a brow as he looked into his coffee and somehow that old politeness only made Riley feel worse. Declan had always been so well bred, so diplomatic, so kind in the face of what others thought of as her quirks—her hesitance in making even the smallest decisions, her shyness amid his boisterous friends, her obsession with birding. There was good reason for why she'd fallen for him straight out of college. It didn't help that right now he looked so good, even just wearing a faded Villanova T-shirt over a pair of khaki shorts. It was the easy athletic build, the barber-tamed black hair, the low brow, and the steady blue eyes that made women think of movie stars.

Everybody always told her she'd chosen well.

Riley looked away from those eyes. "Dec, I thought we agreed it was better if we did our talking long distance."

"If you'd pick up your phone whenever I called, I wouldn't have to hike up here and conspire with your mother."

"I get your messages. I've called the lawyers whenever they needed something. I've done everything you've asked."

"You don't call me back."

"There's nothing left to talk about."

"Isn't there?"

He gazed at her with those vivid blue eyes, and whatever moral superiority she had shriveled. Until the day she destroyed their marriage, their life had been ticking along nicely. She'd been pulling down a respectable income, he had a healthy 401(k) plan and had just received a raise at his architectural firm. Only when the keys to Camp Kwenback were dropped into her hands had she realized that their future had been imagined, drafted, and created by his dreams.

Declan leaned forward. "I keep waiting for the lawyer to call me and tell me that this is all over. But he still hasn't received your signed copies."

It'd be easier if she could claim those divorce papers were lost in the mail, but the tracking labels were right there on the envelope, sitting on the reservation desk at Camp Kwenback amid the rest of the mail she just couldn't open because it meant she had to make decisions. She had no rational explanation to give Declan, so she didn't bother making one up. She dropped her gaze to his hands instead. He'd always had lovely draftsman's hands, wide-knuckled, long-fingered, flecked with pencil lead, peppered with splinters on the days he visited worksites.

"Riley?"

Mechanically she picked up a spoon. "I've been busy."

"So your mother told me. Three banks have rejected your business plan."

Thanks, Mom. "There are a lot of banks in the world."

"I know the finances. The details were in the divorce papers. After all this time you can't have much more capital on hand—"

"It's my business, not yours."

"I want you to succeed at this, Riley. I really do."

She didn't bother to call him out on the lie. He'd just say he'd forgotten how doubtful he'd been after they'd received the news that Riley was the heir to the camp.

"I'm serious." His fingers flexed around the coffee mug. "I've been thinking about this. When your grandparents left you that camp, I guess you must have seen it as an opportunity to run your own business. I was ready for a different future, but I understand the urge."

She laid her spoon on the saucer and suppressed a sigh.

Ambition was Declan's specialty—it had never been hers. She just wished he could slip into her skin for one moment and see the world through her eyes. Then again, nobody seemed to be able to understand the world through her eyes.

"If you make this camp viable," he continued, "then you'll have checked that box. That's why I want you to succeed. Because after you've succeeded, maybe you'll be willing to move on to other things."

"I don't want children, Declan."

His eyelids twitched like he'd been hit by a blast of sand. He'd heard these words before. The first time she mustered the courage to tell him—a few weeks after their engagement—a smile had flitted across his lips, like surely she must be joking. But she hadn't been, and she'd braced herself for the condemnation she expected—that sense that she couldn't possibly be a *natural* woman if she didn't want to take the next logical step in life.

The truth was that she understood the sacrifices a woman made when she committed to a family. With three sisters, she'd seen up close the full-body, twenty-four-hour, never-ending immersion, the crazy three a.m. feedings, the emergency room visits, the moments when you thought you lost them, the fears that kept you up all through the night. Society questioned why a woman would choose to be childless, when considering the stress, level of commitment, and sacrifices involved in raising children, Riley always thought the real scrutiny should be about why a woman would choose to have babies at all.

But poor Declan. She must have seemed like a natural

mother, having been raised the youngest child in a big family, growing up among dozens of cousins, working as the children's activity coordinator at Camp Kwenback from the age of fourteen on, saving enough money from babysitting gigs to afford her own car at eighteen. She adored other people's children. She loved being a godmother, a favorite aunt. She'd known the truth about her feelings for a long time, but Declan had convinced her that her feelings would change. He didn't want children, either, at least not right away, he said. But that urge to have kids snuck up on everyone eventually, didn't it? She found herself thinking maybe he was right. Maybe someday she'd feel that womb pull of maternal instinct, that fecund hormonal rush that made people ooh and aah over newborn babies, that overwhelming need to breed.

Riley figured that if she hadn't felt that burning urge in bed beside this wonderful man, she likely never would.

He said, suddenly, "I just made partner."

"Oh?"

"Effective last month. No corner office yet, but...someday."

"Congratulations, Dec." She felt a rush of warmth. "I know how much you wanted this."

"It means a good step-up in pay."

"Don't worry, I won't amend the papers—"

"It means that you wouldn't have to work." He brushed imaginary crumbs off the red laminate table. "You could stay home. I could take care of you, until you...decide."

Riley looked at the face of the man she'd vowed to love

through sickness and health, till death do us part, and felt a twist of regret. Declan wasn't wrong. There was a part of her that still wanted to return to their lovely apartment with a sliver of a view of the East River, to settle into the easy routine of sharing coffee in the morning, walking to the subway together, coming home after picking up Thai food at the corner hole-in-the-wall, watching home improvement shows and talking about the dream house he wanted to build someday—yes, one part of her, deep inside, still wanted to burrow in someone else's nest, to have someone else to make all the hard decisions for her.

But she'd spent a lifetime doing what her family wanted her to do, and then what her husband wanted her to do, like a mute brown wren tumbling helplessly in the gale-force winds of other people's advice.

She reached across the table and took his hand, warm, just like she remembered. "My feelings are not going to change."

"You're not your birth mother, Riley."

Riley froze. The words had a taste like vinegar on her tongue. She tugged her hand away, but he just tightened his grip.

"You have a mother who loves you," he said. "She'll do anything to make you happy, even if it pisses you off—"

"Stop." She yanked her hand so hard that, when he released it, she slammed her elbow into the back of her seat. "I don't want to talk about this."

"You never do."

Of course she didn't. Who would want to talk about a

biological mother who'd given her away with all the care of putting a TV on the curb for recycling?

"I shouldn't have pushed so hard," he said, reaching across, trying to touch her as she dug out her wallet. "That was my mistake. But your birth mother is in the past, Riley, and you're letting her destroy your future—"

"This isn't about my birth mother." Not in the way he thought, anyway. "This is about us."

"Weren't we good together, Riley—"

"I can't do this."

Riley threw a couple of dollars next to the coffee. She slipped out of the booth and made a wide berth so Declan couldn't grab her arm. He called her name but her legs kept moving. She ignored the looks cast her way by the folks at the counter as she pushed out through the front door and into the sunshine.

She was fumbling in her purse to find her car key when he finally caught up to her in the side parking lot.

"Riley, stop."

"You shouldn't have come all the way up here."

"You're just scared."

"I'm not scared. I've never been scared."

"Then why haven't you signed those papers?"

She found her key in her purse and pressed the button to unlock the car door. The beep echoed in the parking lot. She slipped into her car, closed the door, and put it in gear. As she backed out of her parking spot, she came up beside him. She pressed the button to lower the window.

She wanted to yell at him to get a wife who wanted the

same things that he wanted—the satisfying career, the domestic life, the dinner parties with colleagues. She wanted to tell him to find a sane, smart woman who'd decorate his dream house with care and style and enjoyment, not with odd red-lacquered knobs, not with wallpaper covered in roosters. A man like Declan deserved someone who shared his ambitions, someone very different from herself.

She deserved something different, too, if she could just figure out whatever the heck that was.

"Declan," she said, her heart filling her throat, "I'll get to the papers. Don't ambush me like this again."

Chapter Ten

On the beach of Bay Roberts, young boys raced down the length of the dock to hurl themselves into the water, only to swim back to shore and do it again. A clique of teenage girls planted their blankets close to the lifeguard's chair, talking behind their hands and giggling and trying not to get caught looking up at him. Toddlers struggled to stay upright on the sand, clutching pink plastic shovels, followed by their mothers. White clouds like cotton candy floated across the sky.

Sadie lay on her stomach on a towel with her chin propped on her hands. Nearby, under an umbrella, three kids sat in front of their mother playing Old Maid. They hid their smiles behind oversize playing cards while their mother tapped her chin and screwed up her face as she eyed the backs of their cards. The mother reached out and pulled a card out of the middle boy's hand, looked at it, gaped, and then rolled back on the towel in mock horror. The boys squealed in high-pitched unison, bouncing and laughing.

A weak, shivery sensation started in her stomach. It was

like when she picked up that photo of her parents and held it real close to her face. In the picture her mom's and dad's smiles were fixed, but Mom's hair was all messed up like the wind was tossing it. When Sadie brought the photo real close, she could imagine that wind blowing. She could almost hear her mother laughing. Sometimes she swore she smelled a sweet scent, an apple and dirt scent, the kind that used to cling to Daddy's clothes.

Sadie sat up and swung her legs under her. It didn't do any good to think about Mom and Dad. It wouldn't do any good to think of Nana, either, alone in the hospital. If she spent too much time thinking about them, she'd end up brooding in a corner somewhere. She had to think about her future while she still had time to make it for herself. So she opened her composition notebook and flipped through the pages—eyeballing the scribbled notes, sketches of the Camp Kwenback logo, eye color inheritance diagrams—until she found the first empty page.

Bay Roberts, Wednesday—
Mother, blond, and three kids, two blonds and a brunette,
one of the blonds called Mikey. I can't see the color of their
eyes, but their hair is pin-straight and there's not a freckle on
them. Not likely.

She flicked the end of the pen, seeking other subjects.

Father with a young boy, curly hair like mine but not a
lot of it. The son is Asian, I think. He reminds me of

Izzy. There's a lifeguard, too, probably a local. He's six-teen or seventeen. Long, straight hair in a ponytail, skin like caramel. Oh, Izzy, you'd go crazy over him.

Sadie lifted her pen from the paper as a thought struck her. She really had to sign onto one of the public computers at the library. Izzy had promised not to say anything, but if Sadie didn't send her a message soon, her friend might get all scared and do something stupid.

"Writing poetry?"

A shadow fell over her. She looked up to find that Tess-woman, that interfering friend of Riley's who'd threatened to call the police. She was dressed in cutoff jeans and a tank top with her face half hidden behind a pair of sunglasses. Except for the baseball cap, Sadie thought Tess looked like the singer Pink on an angry day.

"Poetry sucks." Sadie closed her notebook. "The disguise isn't working, you know."

"Disguise?"

"Riley told me there were people in Pine Lake who wouldn't be happy to see you're back." Sadie pulled an imaginary cap. "A hat and a pair of glasses aren't going to hide those tats."

"Pine Lake hasn't seen these tats." Tess's flip-flops hit the ground and then Tess did, too, dropping down in the sand right next to Sadie like she'd been invited or something. "So have you found any likely suspects?"

"Suspects?"

"Riley told me you're looking for your biological mom."

Sadie stilled. A tingling swept up the back of her neck. Riley shouldn't have said anything. The fact that she did made Sadie want to curl in on herself, like the turtle she'd seen the kids playing with by the reeds. Instead she pressed her notebook against her chest and gave the woman her best back-off glare. But all Sadie could see in the shiny surface of the woman's sunglasses was her own distorted reflection.

"You're in Pine Lake, Sadie." Tess shrugged a shoulder. "It's tough to keep a secret here."

Sadie turned away and squinted over the water like it didn't matter, though she couldn't help wondering what else Riley had told this woman.

"I've been away from this town for fifteen years, but I've been recognized at least twice since I arrived." Tess wrapped her arms around her knees. "Now the whole town knows I'm here. I give it a day or two before folks start asking who the young redhead is who's hanging around Camp Kwenback."

"Riley's got my back."

"And I've got hers."

"What's your problem?" Sadie reached for her backpack. "I've got nothing to do with you."

"You're putting my friend in a difficult situation. And you're putting yourself in a worse one."

Sadie fumbled for the zipper. "You don't know anything about my situation."

"Have you thought about what you're going to do when you're done here?" Tess rocked herself back so the sun fell on her face. "There's still enough summer left to stay on the northern circuit, but big cities are better to hide in. Will you be hopping a train to Buffalo? Or will you be jumping the freight train that cuts through the southernmost part of town, the one that goes direct to Cleveland?"

Sadie twitched at the mention of that Ohio city, but she figured it was just coincidence that Tess mentioned it. No way did Tess know about her cousins in Ohio, because she hadn't even told Riley about them.

"I'd advise against Cleveland," Tess continued. "You can usually depend upon a train station for a safe public place to sleep, but not that one. Not while I was last there, anyway. I had to dodge a lot of junkies and some tough guys looking for lost young girls to pimp out. And the Dumpster-diving wasn't so good, either. You'd do better in Cincinnati—"

"I've got no reason to go to Cincinnati." Sadie shoved her notebook into her backpack and zipped it back up. "Or Cleveland or any of those places."

"Yeah, it's all the same, right? Whether you go to St. Louis in November or New Orleans in December. It's just the weather that's different. Every day you wake up, beg for change, hang out, and then, if you're lucky, score some happy-happy."

Sadie eyeballed her. "Oh, I get it now. This is the scared-straight talk, right?"

Oddly, Tess laughed. "Someone tried that on me once. Didn't work. So just consider this a little advice from one runaway to another."

"I don't go anywhere near drugs."

"Glad to hear that."

Tess's smile was thin and Sadie couldn't help but squint at her more closely. When she'd first seen Tess at Camp Kwenback, she'd pinned her as a hard-working woman. It showed in the ropiness of her arms, built like she used them all the time doing something real physical, like the guys always fixing the roads under the elevated train in Queens. The woman had a face that didn't like to smile, and Sadie thought she might work a little too hard to radiate hardassness. But a runaway? Being a runaway implied being young and a little clueless, and looking at this woman, Sadie just couldn't imagine that.

"You've got me all wrong." Sadie swept the backpack over her shoulder. "I'm no runaway. I'm here for a reason."

"Then you'll be going home soon, right? Because there's nothing out here that's worth leaving home for."

"Depends on the home, doesn't it?"

Tess turned her face away to look down the far end of the Bay. "You've got me there."

Sadie flexed her hand over the strap of her backpack, hesitating. She didn't want to leave the beach, but the library closed early on Wednesdays and there wasn't anything else she could do except wander around town. And it was nice on the lakeshore, warm and quiet. She'd come here to write descriptions of the folks on the beach, but she also had a couple chapters of *War and Peace* left to read. She didn't like the idea of this woman running her off.

Then Tess murmured, "I know why you like this place."

"Who wouldn't like this place?" Sadie squinted across the shore, to the bristly island in the middle, the one she could see so sharply with Riley's borrowed binoculars. "Cool water, soft sand." *Cute lifeguard.*

"This side of town is a hell of a lot nicer than Cannery Row, where I grew up." Tess let go of her knees and threw her hands back to support herself. "I imagine Disneyland would be like this, full of clean-scrubbed people."

Sadie had been to Disney World once. She remembered it because it was noisy, full of people and scary robotic creatures in the dark.

"I used to sit right here, too." Tess shifted her butt deeper in the sand like she was putting down roots or something. "I used to smoke cigarettes and watch everyone having a good time. I used to wonder why the hell I couldn't have been born into a nice, shiny, happy family."

A startling thought popped into Sadie's mind. "Are you adopted?"

"Nope."

"Then stop talking like you were."

"There were plenty of times I wished I had been."

She groaned aloud, not caring if it was rude, because what did this woman know about having a huge part of yourself kept secret forever?

"The first time I wished that," Tess said, "was when the cops arrested my mother. They called the house in the middle of the night, looking for an adult to come fetch her from the holding pen."

"Wow. TMI."

"Public knowledge." Tess shifted her weight onto one arm as she swept her hand across the expanse of the lakeshore. "Talk to any of the locals and they'd tell you the same story about Mrs. Hendrick."

"Should I break out the tiny violin?"

Tess's lips stretched into a grim smile. Then she motioned toward the mother and three kids, still playing the card game. "Do you think she's a possibility?"

Sadie squinted down the far end of the beach, like the question wasn't worth the bother.

"A woman like that," Tess persisted, "the kind who takes her kids to a sandy lakeside on a midweek afternoon...she's your ideal birth mother, isn't she?"

Sadie shot to her feet, not caring that she kicked some sand on Tess. Her spine straightened like someone had stuck a ruler up her back. "You can talk, talk, talk all you want, but you're not getting rid of me. Not before I find my birth mother."

Sadie realized how stupid she sounded, like a little girl looking for Mommy, but she couldn't help herself. This woman couldn't possibly understand. Even Izzy didn't understand. Sadie wasn't sure that even Riley understood, not completely, because Riley's adoptive parents were still alive.

Sadie's first vivid memory was of her mother. Sadie had been strapped into something, a toddler seat or a bouncy chair, she supposed. She had a stuffed rabbit in her hand. It had pink fur and Xs for eyes. She knew the memory was real and not something she'd thought up later because she still had this toy, Bunzy, back in her room at Nana's, now gray and worn and sour-smelling.

But in her memory Bunzy smelled like vanilla. In her

memory Bunzy was in her hand, and then Bunzy was gone. She must have cried out because, a little while later, her mother came into the room. Sadie didn't remember anything her mother said, just the tone of her voice, the way she made her forget about the rabbit. And then suddenly Bunzy was in her hand again. But when she looked up, her mother had disappeared.

"Sadie."

Sadie flinched. The Tess-woman's voice was soft and round. At first she couldn't believe the voice had come out of a hard mouth like that. But Tess was looking up at her from under the bill of her cap, and the sun at that angle cut through the lenses of the sunglasses, so Sadie could see that Tess was looking at her—searching her face—with the strangest, tightest, and oddest of expressions.

"We all want perfect parents," Tess said. "Hell, I did, too. But the truth is, your birth mother may not be one of them."

Sadie swallowed down her own sigh. She had had this conversation with the guidance counselor at her middle school, the social worker who followed up once a year after she'd been transferred into her nana's custody, and all the well-meaning adults who felt they knew what was best for her—to wait, always wait, until she was mature enough to handle the "possibility of failed expectations," and what they called "the inevitable emotional upheaval."

One set of parents dead and a grandmother in a nursing home. Uh-uh, don't talk to Sadie Tischler about emotional upheaval.

"I'd settle for a mother who just didn't disappear." Sadie wiggled her feet into her flip-flops and turned away.

"Sadie."

Over her shoulder she barked, "What?"

"Ask Riley."

"Ask Riley *what?*"

"Ask Riley what happened when she found her own birth mother."

Chapter Eleven

R iley's old friend from high school Claire Petrenko had a certain effect on people. Riley figured it had something to do with the fact that Claire had once been a Buddhist nun, because during the six-mile ride back from the Pine Lakes train station, Riley had opened up like a spigot, telling her everything that had been going on at Camp Kwenback.

"So let me get this straight." Claire sat in the passenger's seat of Riley's car. "You're telling me that Camp Kwenback is now housing a dementia patient, a teenage runaway, and ex-juvenile delinquent Theresa Hendrick?"

"Just another day in the life of Riley Cross."

"You poor thing."

"Trust me, I didn't plan for this." Riley turned the car onto the graveled road that led to the lodge. "It just happened. One moment it was just Mrs. Clancy and me, and the next—"

"The next you know, the universe is sending you lost souls."

"That's a Buddhist thing, right?"

"Sort of." Claire ran her fingers through her short hair, just growing back after the last round of chemo. "Last year, when Jenna showed up at my door, she said she wanted to help me after my mastectomy—but really, she was just running away from her divorce. She was broken, the poor woman, and in desperate need of support."

Riley tried to keep up with Claire's thought processes. "So you think Tess is running away from a divorce?"

"I haven't the faintest idea what Tess is running away from, though I know she was once married. I was actually talking about you." Claire hung her elbow out the window and gazed off toward the debris piled around the old mini-golf. "Every once in a while, whether you're ready or not, Karma sends you lost creatures. Since I was diagnosed with breast cancer, I've got a farm full of blind possums, three-legged goats, and one crippled raven, and darned if I know why." Claire gasped as she caught sight of Tess working amid the piles of wood. "In Buddha's name, she's gone blond."

"It suits her, don't you think?" Riley could just glimpse Tess walking between the trees. "The ink-black hair made her look like a vampire."

"Did you ask her?"

"Ask her what?"

"About the burned-out farmhouse in Kansas." Claire turned, the whites of her eyes bright. "When Jenna, Nicole, and I went looking for her last year, all we found was an abandoned wreck. It was practically still smoking."

"I mentioned it once." Riley turned into the parking area in front of the lodge and took the far spot. "She didn't answer, and it was like the walls came down hard. And, honestly, I haven't had more than a fifteen-minute conversation with her since, and it has all been about the renovation of the mini-golf."

"We'll have to do something about that, won't we?"

Riley stepped out of the car, then pulled Claire's suitcase out of the backseat. Claire came around and pushed the button for the handle. Claire hadn't opted for reconstructive surgery after her mastectomy so her T-shirt billowed over her chest. In pink letters it said *Chemo Ninja.*

"You're back!"

Riley glanced up to see Sadie's head pop up over the railing of the porch.

"Thanks for holding down the fort, Sadie." Riley squinted across the empty parking lot. "Any chance a busload of vacationers arrived to check in?"

"Um…no."

"A minivan full of hikers?"

"I didn't see—"

"How 'bout an SUV full of bicyclists?"

Sadie screwed up her face. "You said that the only one coming this week was your friend Claire."

Apparently not all fourteen-year-olds picked up on sarcasm. "Claire, this is Sadie," Riley said, as they bumped the luggage up to the shade of the porch. "Sadie, this is another good friend of mine from high school, Claire."

Claire thrust out her hand. "A pleasure to meet another redhead. The three of us should have some kind of secret handshake."

Sadie's face pinched in perplexity as her gaze grazed Claire's short hair. Riley realized that Claire's hair had come in dark, and it was too short yet to see the auburn highlights.

"So," Riley asked, "is Mrs. Clancy still awake?"

"She's dozing on the back porch. I made some of that Cape Cod chicken salad for her. She ate it right up." Sadie bounced on the balls of her toes. "Her hair needed a good brushing so I took care of it while she ate."

"I'm sure she loved that," Riley said as she pushed open the door to the lodge. "I'm going to get Claire settled and then—"

"Riley?"

Sadie stood on one foot, pulling on her fingers in agitation.

"Yes?"

Sadie said, "I've been thinking."

"Uh-huh?"

Sadie's gaze skittered to Claire, and then that gaze searched for a landing spot somewhere on the porch floorboards.

Claire caught the vibe. "Riley, I've been dying to give Bob's belly a good rub ever since I hopped on that train. You come fetch me when the room's ready."

As Claire's footsteps receded, Sadie slid her hip onto the porch railing. "So I was thinking," Sadie repeated, "I noticed that you've got those ledger things that you write in to track reservations and who is registered and what room they're in, right?"

"One for every year," she conceded, "though I've been

doing both ledgers and the computer registration since eighteen months ago because the new program is glitchy—"

"Do you save past years' ledgers? Like in a big box somewhere?"

Riley thought about the low-beamed attic over the guest rooms, the boxes and boxes of photo albums and memorabilia and stuff from her grandparent's bedroom she hadn't had the heart to throw away.

She knew where this was going. "You know you're looking for a needle in a haystack, right?"

"That's such a weird expression. I mean, if you're looking for a needle in a haystack, why can't you just use a magnet?"

"You know what I'm talking about." It pained her to think that Sadie's search would probably lead to one dead end after another. "In these ledgers, they'll all just be names to you. They won't mean anything—"

"You'd know them though. All those people who stayed here."

"Many of them, but not all."

"Maybe you'll see a name and remember something you'd forgotten. Maybe I can make a connection with the research I've been doing."

Riley hesitated. Sadie had been here a week now. She'd left just about every morning to bike to the library and returned each night sunburned from the beach. She'd also tagged along a couple of mornings when Riley went bird-watching, peering through the binoculars with the awe of a newbie. She'd been a great help around the lodge, playing cards with Mrs. Clancy in the evenings, keeping watch at the reservation desk when Riley had to pop into town. Riley had to admit that she liked the young girl's company. But with each passing day, Tess's concerns about legal complications weighed more heavily on her.

In for a penny, in for a pound. "Let me take care of Claire first," Riley said. "Then get ready to get dusty."

A half hour later Claire headed to the mini-golf to say hello to Tess, and Sadie bounced behind Riley as she led the way up the stairs to the second floor. In the ceiling halfway down the hallway hung a chain that connected to the pull-down stairs to the attic. She tugged on the porcelain grip and unfolded the stairs. Testing each creaking wooden riser, she made her way into the gloom.

The central air conditioning her grandparents had reluctantly added to the lodge twenty years ago didn't quite reach this space, so climbing the stairs was like walking into soup. The air smelled of pine resin and musty books. Decorations for various holidays were stacked up on one side, Fourth of July taking up a goodly amount of space. Riley had a moment's thought that there might be some decaying old fireworks in some of those boxes, until she remembered that it was her grandfather who took care of the fireworks, and he kept a separate storage space in the barn. These eaves were mostly Grandma's, and the boxes were packed so tight there wasn't enough space between them to slip the width of a pencil.

"Wow." Sadie ran her fingers across the boxes. "Your grandmother would have been epic at Tetris."

"She once told me that there were ledgers up here dating

to the turn of the twentieth century." Riley sought among the boxes for her grandmother's round Palmer-method handwriting. "She said they were part of the camp's history and refused to throw them away, so she shoved them farther back to make room for more. I keep meaning to go through them myself, but I can't seem to find the time." Riley paused and tapped a lower box. "That's my grandmother's writing. The ledgers in this box date back to the nineteen forties."

"We shouldn't go back more than fifteen years."

"Just so you know," Riley said, as she tugged one box out to eyeball the dates on the one behind it, "my grandmother wasn't the gossiping type. She wouldn't record if someone was pregnant. She just kept lists of names, the numbers of adults and kids, and what rooms or cabins they were in."

Sadie tapped a box close to her. "This one is marked photos."

"Oh, wow, I remember those. For a while I made photo albums for every summer." Riley shoved one box aside, still looking for the ledger box labeled with the right span of years. "What a lot of work that was. It's not like now, when you can go online and click and drag and make a photo album in an instant. We had to take pictures, get them developed, pin them in, label them by hand, and add cute scrapbooky things. It was a serious project. But everyone loved paging through them so much that, after I left, Grandma hired a teenager to be Camp Kwenback's official summer photographer."

"Photo albums are awesome." Sadie's voice went high with excitement. "This box covers the right dates."

Sadie hauled the box down and tugged the top open, flicking away dust-heavy strands of old spiderwebs. Inside were ten photo albums made of faux leather, the earliest over twenty years old.

Settling cross-legged on the floorboards, Sadie cracked one open. Riley caught sight of the first picture and stuttered, "Oh, lord."

Sadie's mouth dropped open. "That's you?"

"Yup, braces, skinny legs, bad hair, and all."

"Love the shorts."

"Hey, pleated fronts were all the rage back then." Riley reached over and flipped the page. "You want to see funky shorts? Get a load of those. Those are my grandparents holding court by the bonfire on opening day."

"Seriously?"

"They're wearing lederhosen," Riley explained. "This camp came down through my maternal grandmother's side. She was German through and through. She could cook pastry like nobody's business."

"She's round."

"And short. Grandpa sometimes called her 'dumpling.'"

"And your grandfather was so tall. Knobby knees!"

"Yeah, he was a bit of a giraffe. Apparently my grandmother's parents never liked him. He was *Episcopalian*, you know."

Sadie said, "You talk about them as if you're German, too. As if they were your own birth grandparents."

Riley didn't comment right away. She pulled a box off the pile and settled it in the alley between them, using the exertion as an excuse. The pine resin scent of this attic reminded her of when she used to climb here with her grandmother to haul down the holiday decorations, her grandmother batting at the dust with a dishtowel, muttering now and again in German. She remembered sprinkling the butcher-block table downstairs with flour as Grandma made dough. She remembered sleeping in a cot in the laundry room during the busy season, the scent of humid air and clean sheets, the *thwump-thwump* of the drier white noise to snooze by. Whenever Riley felt like an oversize cowbird in the nest of tiny Crosses, she would retreat to this camp where, for reasons unknown, she always felt like she belonged.

"They helped raise me," she said, debating how to sit comfortably in the narrow alleyway. "They were my grandparents. The only ones I ever knew."

"But you found your birth parents, right?"

Riley's sneaker caught on one of the uneven boards and she sat down clumsily, hitting the attic floor with a force that she knew would leave a bruise.

She should have known Sadie would ask her this question sooner or later.

"Eventually I did." Riley reached into the ledger box and pulled up one of the books. "Do you want to start on one of these?"

"Are they dead?"

Riley settled the book on her lap and wiped the dust off the cover. "No."

"Did you meet them?"

The spine of the ledger cracked as she pressed it open. Riley stared blindly at the pages in front of her, realizing she was tracing the old ink with a hand that had begun to tremble.

This shouldn't matter anymore.

"I'm on this website for adoptees," Sadie ventured into the growing silence. "We share stories. Most are adoptees who want to find their birth mother but we're too young to go through the process or we're having trouble opening the records. Some of the kids manage to break through the roadblocks, one way or another." Sadie shifted her seat. "But sometimes the mother doesn't want to be found. Sometimes she doesn't answer the phone or letters."

"Everyone's experience is different." Riley gave the ledger a little lift. "Why don't we just focus on yours?"

It had all gone very still in the room. No noises from downstairs. The air conditioning generator in the corner of the attic hadn't yet kicked on. All she could hear were the pops and creaks of an old wooden house and a rustling outside, of birds coming in and out of nests tucked in the nooks of the roof.

And Sadie, perched across from her like a curious little starling, canting forward, her clear green gaze bright.

Riley sighed and watched the movement of tiny dust motes through the light pouring through the small window. "My husband started the search."

"Husband?"

"Ex. Soon to be." Riley raised her left hand and wiggled her fingers, the pale swath across the ring finger evidence of the band she once wore. "He wanted to start a family. Before we did, he thought it would be smart to contact my biological parents and get all the medical history, like some kind of...prescreening."

When Declan had first badgered her about this, she'd put in a phone call to her old friend Nicole. They'd been on the softball team together in high school. With Nicole as the pitcher and Riley as the catcher, they'd made an unbeatable team that had won the regional finals for the first time in Pine Lake history. Nicole went on to graduate school in psychology and ultimately ended up working as a life coach. She'd seemed the right person to call for such a serious issue. Nicole had assured Riley that her feelings were absolutely valid. She should seek her biological parents only when *she* was ready.

If only Declan hadn't been so insistent. If only Riley hadn't been such a shy little wood thrush.

"Declan hired one of those firms," Riley said. "The ones you pay to unseal the adoption records or else find the biological parents some other way? I think he sensed that if he left the search to me, I wouldn't do it at all."

"Why not?"

"Sadie, if your adoptive parents were still alive, how do you think they'd react if you told them you were searching for your biological parents?"

Sadie's avid gaze faltered. She flipped over a page. Her jaw worked like she wanted to say something but thought better of it.

Riley said, "I love my parents, though they can be meddling and annoying. My mother tugged out my loose teeth, she took care of me when I had the flu, and she got me through

Algebra Two." Riley looked down at the ledger, swallowing hard. "She's blood and bone to me now. Outwardly they'd support me, of course, but in some part of my mother's heart, she'd always wonder if I were looking because she hadn't been good enough for me. I didn't want to hurt her that way."

That was my initial excuse, anyway.

"Izzy's like that." Sadie sucked in a little breath as if she wished she could suck the name back. "Izzy's a friend of mine. She was adopted, too. She says she doesn't want to know the woman who gave her up. She says she has a mother and a father and that's enough. But I think it's something more though." Sadie's knee beneath the photo album bobbed. "I think Izzy is afraid her biological mother wouldn't want to see her at all."

"And who wants to be rejected twice," Riley murmured, "by the one person who should love you most?"

This shouldn't matter anymore.

Riley ran her fingers down the ledger page, glancing at the names, *Tom & Lisa Sibelius Room 8, kids Caitlin, Molly, and Maeve in Room 1.* She remembered the whole family playing a fierce, noisy, fast-paced card game—Gnome Toss—in the main lodge every night.

"Back then closed adoptions were more the norm than they are today," Riley said, "so it was almost impossible to unseal the records. The people my husband hired had to find my birth mother through back channels." She shrugged, but the movement ached. "Eventually they succeeded."

The Diaz-Martins, Harry and Lexus, Room 4. Grandchildren, Ashley and Jennifer, 3 and 5, Room 6.

"I knew they'd found her because, well, I saw a picture of her online." Riley tugged her bright, chin-length curly red hair. "There's no hiding this, or the freckles, though hers were lighter, like they'd been bleached. From what I could tell from her Facebook page, she was married and lived in a big house outside Tucson. They gave me her address and phone number."

"Did you call?"

"Not at first. I went old-school and sent a letter." She'd agonized over every word before Declan finally took the paper from her, read it, and then stuffed it in the envelope. He'd hugged her afterward when all she wanted to do was to run back to the post office and yank the letter out of the mail slot. "I thought it might be easier that way, to give her some space to think about things."

"And?"

"We waited four weeks but never got a letter or a call."

Sadie asked, "You sent another?"

"Two." Riley's heart began a skittering little skip beat. "After that Declan insisted that I call."

Her fingers shook over the numbers.

Schroen residence, Peg speaking.

"I introduced myself." Riley's ribs tightened. "I actually wrote down the words I needed to say. I was that nervous."

Riley remembered the sudden hush on the end of the line. She remembered the sound of footsteps, a hurried rustle, and the click of a closing door.

Most of all she remembered the furious whisper.

How the fuck did you get this number? You're after money,

right? That's what this is all about? You'll never see a penny from me. And if I see you on my doorstep, I'm calling the police, do you hear me? Don't send me any more fucking letters. I'll just burn them. I don't have a daughter. I've never had a daughter.

You are not my daughter.

The words were like fangs full of venom, rendering her so numb that she hadn't been able to feel her fingers as the phone fell out of her hand, clattered to the hardwood floor, to the scream of the dial tone.

A sharp pain brought Riley back to the attic. She realized she was digging her fingernails into her biceps. She let her arms go and took a deep breath of the scent of pine resin, old books, and warm paper.

"She didn't want to talk to you." Sadie's eyes were round and disbelieving. "She didn't want to meet you."

Riley's throat closed to words. She considered which was worse: divulging the terrible truth or letting Sadie continue on in blissful ignorance. Some calmer, more rational part of herself—a consciousness hovering over her shoulder, separated from the memory of pain—realized that this was one of those moments a parent must encounter all the time. Do you tell the vulnerable child the harsh truth? Or do you instead make up some cotton-wrapped version of it so she's not made bloody by the sharp edges?

"Sadie," she heard herself say, "are you absolutely sure you need to find your birth mother?"

Sadie ducked her head so that Riley got a good look at the part in her hair and the springy curls around it that wouldn't be confined. Sadie riffled the corners of the black photo album pages as her leg continued to bob, bob, bob. A filmy spiderweb floated down from the rafters and drifted over her shoulder until she reached up and brushed it away.

"If everything were perfect," Sadie said, talking into the photo album, "I'd want to get to know my birth mother before I met her, and I'd want to do it on my own time. I'd want to know how old she was when she had me, where she lived, whether she's married now or single or has other kids or lives with her parents." Sadie tilted her head, like she was just stretching it, to one side and then the other. "I'd want to see a picture of her. I'd want to know what she does all day. Whether she likes to read. Whether she has a lot of friends or just a few." She breathed hard, her nostrils flaring. "That's kind of what I was doing in the woods, before you found me in the rainstorm."

When you thought I was your mother. Riley felt a pang in her heart that burrowed deeper than she thought possible.

Sadie continued, "I'd be pretty mad if my birth mother was an alcoholic or a drug addict or something. It would totally suck to have come all this way just to find out she didn't care about anything but her next fix. That she didn't want anything to do with me. Maybe didn't even remember me. Your birth mother is an idiot, by the way."

Riley tried to muster a smile, but she couldn't control the muscles of her face when all she could think about was the same emotional wallop that she'd experienced in her early thirties transferred to a fourteen-year-old who, Riley suspected, was as soft as an unborn bird inside that sturdy shell.

"But," Sadie said, closing the photo album, "my situation is different from yours. My parents are gone so I don't have to worry about how they feel. My nana is in a nursing home and hardly remembers her own name, never mind me." She rose to her knees to pull another photo album out of the ledger box. "I need to find my birth mother, because she's really all I've got left. And I have to do it soon, or else I'll be shuttling through foster homes for the next four years until I age out of the system."

Riley admired Sadie's conviction. It was so simple, so solid, and so very pure, and you couldn't argue with the logic. Riley wondered how different her own life would have been if she'd possessed only a fraction of Sadie's force of will, of Sadie's fierce determination, of Sadie's fearlessness.

And in any case, Riley figured there was no true harm in continuing the search like this, pawing around ledgers, looking at old photo albums. Such a search—without professional help—would likely never bear fruit. So she bent her head over the ledger, running her finger down the familiar names, turning page after page.

Then Riley sucked in a breath so fast that spit hit the back of her throat.

"I know," Sadie said, rubbing her nose as Riley coughed and coughed. "This dust is just unbelievable."

Riley covered her mouth and continued coughing so Sadie wouldn't see the surprise on her face from stumbling upon an all-too familiar name in the ledger.

Chapter Twelve

N ow that's exactly how I expected to find you after all these years, Tess Hendrick. Sweaty, dirty, and spitting nails."

Tess straightened up, letting the nails she'd been holding between her teeth drop into her hand. She looked at the woman in a cotton batik skirt coming toward her through the trees. Riley had warned her that Claire Petrenko was coming to Pine Lake for a weekend. Had Tess not known, she wasn't sure she would have recognized her.

Well, she thought, with a strange kick in her chest, *maybe I would have recognized the grin.*

"Claire Petrenko." Tess rattled the nails in her palm. "Come to save my soul after all these years?"

"Oh, I'm sure it's too late for that."

Claire kept striding right at her, and Tess had that feeling that she got sometimes, driving at night on a winter-iced road in North Dakota, seeing the headlights of another truck heading at her from the opposite direction, fearing there wasn't a damn thing she could do to stop a collision no matter how steady she kept the semi on the right side of the double yellow line. Now all she could do was brace herself as her former schoolmate zoomed in for a full-body hug.

Fortunately, with nails in one palm and the grip of a hammer in the other, there wasn't much she could do but stand and wait it out as Claire pulled her tight, laughing, rocking her from left to right while Tess tried not to be as stiff as the boards she was nailing.

"Lord, Tess," Claire murmured, pulling away. "The last time I saw you, you had a pink streak in your hair. I believe you were standing over a garbage can, burning your high school diploma."

"Good to see you, too." Tess took the opportunity to step away and toss the nails toward a box with the others. "Riley tells me you're here for a weekend."

"I've been gadding about the country again, imposing myself on friends." Claire patted her flattened chest. "The good thing about cancer is that people open their hearts *and* their doors."

"I was sorry to hear about—"

"Oh, please." Claire waved a hand. "I've been milking it. Milking it?" She waved to her own missing breasts. "Get it?"

Tess had a close-up view of those dancing brown eyes, close enough that suddenly she could see past the boyishly short hair, the thin cheeks, to the vibrant, laughing teenager Tess used to hang out with, before Tess gave up one set of friends for another. The familiarity sent a strange pang through her, a jolt of unexpected loss.

143

"Hey," Claire said, "don't give me that look. It's a bad pun, but I'm laughing. When I stop laughing, then everyone should worry. So," Claire gazed over the construction site, "when you were raising hell in the Cannery, did you think you'd ever find yourself renovating the Camp Kwenback mini-golf?"

"It's just a project to keep me from tormenting Officer Rodriguez."

"Well, Riley tells me you're doing it for her late grandparents. I think that's a beautiful thing."

"You always did wear rose-colored glasses." Tess bent over to pick up one of the two-by-fours—and to hide a quick flash of embarrassment. "I'd think, after all you've been through, they'd have scratched or cracked."

"Oh, I lost them for a long while." Claire wandered to the pile of lumber, brushed the top off, and gingerly sat down. "But last year Jenna Hogan—do you remember her? Our class, a little thing with a bad leg? No? Well, Jenna showed up at my door and pretty much gave me those glasses back."

"Good for Jenna Hogan."

Tess hefted the two-by-four and brought it to the other edge of the putting green, memories rushing back to her, trying not to think of all the times Claire had shown up at the Baptist church in her Cannery neighborhood with bags of donated clothes or shoes, setting aside a special bag with Tess's name on it. There were warm coats and brand-name snow boots that Tess couldn't bring herself to wear, just because they were given out of pity, out of some rich folk's charity, and Claire knew it.

That was the trouble with coming back to Pine Lake. You couldn't hide here. The past rushed up and punched you right in the face.

"So," Claire said, "I heard you got married."

Tess flinched. She settled the new two-by-four into the trough left when she'd pulled out the old one.

"Maya told me," Claire explained. "I saw her in South Dakota when Nicole, Jenna, and I drove across country last summer."

Tess knew Maya. Maya was an archaeologist on the faculty at Cornell University, a star graduate of Pine Lake High, who happened to be scouting a new dig at the same time Tess was driving trucks in North Dakota. They crossed paths at some greasy spoon diner and Maya, delighted, had planted herself beside her at the counter. The archaeologist had poked, scraped, and brushed at Tess like she was trying to coax a Jurassic jawbone out of tightly packed clay.

"Boy," Tess said, as she knocked the board deeper in the trough, "you Pine Lake girls love to talk."

"Seeing that you're not wearing a ring—"

"It didn't work out. Which you should know, since I heard you saw our farmhouse in Kansas."

Best to just get that out there now, Tess thought. Best to just confess to the greatest sin rather than go through the agony of having Claire Petrenko, in her sweet-faced, calm-as-butter way, inevitably tease the truth out of her.

Claire said, "It was some shock coming on that place."

Tess picked up a rubber-headed mallet to bang the two-by-four deeper. "Because it was in ashes? Or because you couldn't imagine me sweeping that porch, running a tractor in those fields, or baking pies?"

Tess felt the weight of the mallet as she swung it at the two-by-four, smacking it at six-inch intervals to secure it in the narrow trench. She'd met Erik Callahan a few times on Route 29 out of Fargo. A giant of a blond, a Viking without the attitude. He was charming, self-effacing in that farm boy kind of way. He drove trucks to save up for a spread of his own. He had gazed at her across the counter seats like she was a wet dream come to life. They hooked up. Multiple times. She figured it was like some of the other guys she'd connected with on the road over the years—a quick, efficient, purely physical transaction. That's all she'd ever wanted from any man after the trauma of that other bastard. Eventually, she figured, she and Callahan would drift their own ways.

Except they didn't.

"Oh, Tess," Claire said, "did you really make pies?"

Tess kept banging the two-by-four, though it was lodged in good and tight. She kept banging because it made her heart beat harder. It hurt to think about that year, in a different way than it hurt to think about that *other* year. Thinking about Callahan stung in the way your eyes stung when you tried to stare at the sun. One day, she was driving her semi, and then the next thing she knew, she was married and living on a Kansas farm, wringing the necks of chickens, plucking feathers, and cooking them up as the sun poured through the kitchen window. It was like she'd stepped into some sort of prairie novel. A sappy, romantic prairie novel, because in the mornings with the curtains billowing, she'd wake up in the same bed, her head on the massive chest of the same man, his smile slow and wonderful.

The memories tumbled over one another, rocking her, like a High Plains wind battering the cargo of her rig.

"I made rhubarb pie," Tess said, examining her work with more attention than it needed. "I made apple pie, I made blueberry pie—"

"I'd give a lot of money to see you making a pie."

"The marriage was like those pies," she said. "It was piping hot out of the oven, but too quick to cool, and the crust too easily broken."

Once settled and domestic, Tess had felt an uneasiness grow. She knew Callahan was faithful but she didn't like the way his high school flame eyeballed him in the local pub. That woman looked more his type, pleasantly round and well-liked. It didn't help that the neighbors didn't take to Tess's arrival very well, either, some skinny, tatted northern girl who drove trucks and snagged their favorite son. Once again Tess found herself in a place that didn't like her, didn't want her, an outsider again. It only made her get another tat, avoid the church fair, wear leather pants, smoke inside the house.

She had just been waiting for it all to collapse anyway. So she fought with him, tested his patience, saw how far she could push him, waited for him to be another bastard. In the end she realized that the only way to make sure that Callahan didn't leave her was to abandon him first.

Claire's voice, soft and even: "After seeing that farm-house, I worried about you. You always did have a bad habit of setting things on fire."

Tess laughed but it sounded hollow even to her own ears. Of course Claire thought she'd burned the house down. Anyone from Pine Lake would. Callahan certainly did. Right now she felt the bulk of a pack of cigarettes lying in a pocket in her cargo shorts, a pack that had only one cigarette missing. Callahan had always hated when she smoked in the house, so she smoked in the house whenever she was mad at him. She'd smoked one cigarette more than a pack that terrible night, while she paced for him to come home after their argument. She'd woken coughing on the couch hours later, the house in flames.

Even after the arson investigation came back inconclusive, Callahan had always blamed her for destroying his dream.

Which was pretty much what she had done anyway.

Claire's voice interrupted her thoughts. "You know I'm a good listener. If you want to talk—"

"Don't think so."

Still, her mind worked trying to explain, if only to herself, the abrupt turns her life had taken since she left Pine Lake. Two pivotal events came to mind. Once in the moonlight, surrounded by the stench of diesel and strong coffee and bacon grease, with the roar of cars and trucks whipping by on the nearby interstate, when Big Erik Callahan had kneeled in front of her and asked her to marry him. The second was years earlier, quivering after hours of labor, when the doctor placed on her distended belly her infant daughter—Sadie—still warm from her womb.

Both times there'd been a shimmering moment when it felt like a scrim had peeled off her eyes, and she could see the whole, wide world in all its goodness and badness, all its capricious randomness, complicated and full of senseless acts of beauty. Both times her chest had filled with the strangest pressure, and all she could do was gasp, *yes.*

Yes.

Never in a million years could she explain that. Never in a million years would she admit that she'd give just about anything—*everything*—to feel that way just one more time.

Tess tossed the mallet aside and wiped her forearm across her forehead. "Tell me about your cancer, Claire. I take it that you've been through chemo."

Claire, to her credit, waited only a fraction of a pause. "One round of chemo and radiation, too. If I'm deemed healthy enough when I get back to Portland next month, I'll get the thumbs-up to be a guinea pig in a clinical trial."

"Something tells me there's more to the story."

"Of course there is." She let her head drop back, her face in a dappled circle of sun. "But honestly, it's all good."

Tess gave her an eye, but Claire just curved her lips in a mysterious little smile, giving her the serene face of a Buddhist nun.

"Trauma is a kind of mystery, Tess." Claire squinted out to the far trees. "It latches on to you in ways that aren't easy to undo. It's hard to explain to folks who haven't really experienced it. It...changes you."

"Changes you enough to have your head shaved in Thailand?" Tess hefted up some lumber. "Riley told me you did something crazy like that."

"Yes, well, taking Buddhist vows seemed the reasonable thing to do at the time. My sister had just died; I felt a little unhinged. But something tells me you know exactly what I'm talking about."

Tess felt dangerous tentacles of communal experience tighten around her.

"Sometimes I wonder," Claire mused, "how folks who've felt battered by life can be successful at any relationships—friends, family. Husbands. Not that I consider myself to be completely successful—"

"You're kidding, right?" Tess pulled some nails out of the bag, preparing to join the joists. "You just told me that friends have been opening doors all across the country."

"Yes, but that's now." Claire gave her that Buddha smile again. "You didn't see me just after I was diagnosed. My friends pulled me out of a very bad place, Tess. They made me realize I had to stop letting old traumas shape my life."

Tess positioned a nail and reached for the hammer. She was glad for Claire, she really was, for finding comfort in friends.

Tess, on the other hand, preferred to fix things on her own.

"Speaking of trauma," Claire said, "have you seen your mother yet?"

Tess craved a cigarette so hard it made her teeth ache. Something about being back in Cannery Row stirred the need for a hit of nicotine. That, and seeing the house where she'd grown up.

She tapped her fingers on the steering wheel, watching eagle-eyed for the stir of a curtain in the front window. Nothing moved but the lazy twirl of a whirligig in the postage-stamp-size front yard. But Tess knew her mother was in there. Her mother hadn't worked an honest day in the whole of her life. She spent most Tuesday mornings still sleeping off the weekend before.

Tess blew out a long breath and glanced at the clock on the dashboard. This, here, was the power of Claire Petrenko. One simple discussion and Tess found herself compelled to come back to the old neighborhood. On the back of her neck she could sense furtive stares through the windows of other houses. Folks stepped out onto their porches, sweeping, glancing up over the ends of their brooms to eyeball the car. Men came out to sit on the front stoop, to smoke a slow cigarette. It was like she could hear their thoughts because she remembered thinking the same things as she used to peer through the sheer curtains at strange cars parked on the road. Who was this woman in the battered Volvo? A local cop undercover? Someone come looking for trouble? What did she want?

A gut-kick instinct told her to run away.

Her damn heart raced in her chest like it did sometimes at work, when she had to check fill levels on a wastewater tank before pumping some into her truck. As she was climbing those spindly metal stairs up the side of a tank, the Canadian wind swept down over the prairie and battered her against the metal walls. One good gust, one wrong step, and she'd be over the edge falling three stories. Depending on her boss's trucking schedule, it might take a day or two before she was found by anyone or anything but wolves.

Two sharp raps on the passenger-side window and she all but leaped out of her jeans. A woman bent over, peering through the glass, on her face an unspoken question. She mouthed something that Tess didn't hear.

Tess lowered the window and the woman repeated, "Theresa, she's not home."

Tess registered three things at once. One, that the woman knew her name. Two, the woman knew she was looking for her mother. And three, the woman eyeballing her with a tilted smile had the kind of big, blue, slightly protruding eyes of a girl she once knew.

Tess said, "Emma Lu Skye."

Her lips twitched. "I heard you were in town, Hendrick."

Tess glanced beyond her, to the old house where Lu used to live when they were in school together. "Are you visiting your mom?"

"She's gone four years now. The place is mine." Lu raised her brows. "You want to stop sitting in your car like a creeper and come shoot the breeze?"

Tess glanced over at her mother's house, still as death, shingles missing from the roof, the crooked stairs. She'd come here to get this done in a rip off the Band-Aid manner, so she wasn't in the mood to linger.

Lu murmured, "Your mother's working today."

"Working a bottle?"

"No. Not anymore."

Tess laughed. She heard the bark of it echo in the car.

"I'm dead serious," Lu said. "She's three years sober now."

Tess didn't believe it, and the old house was proof. If a woman was sober for that long, you'd think she'd clean the gutters or plant some flowers or slap a coat of paint on the place. The last time that place got a coat of paint was when her father did it. He spruced it up before lighting out for ten acres in Minnesota, leaving her and her mother behind.

Even the paint was slapped on and forgotten.

"She's working thirty hours a week as a home health aide," Lu continued. "She won't be off until late tonight."

"How late?"

"There's no use stalking the place. Your mother isn't returning anytime soon."

Tess thought—a boyfriend of course. The one thing about her mother, she never lacked for boyfriends.

"Join me for a smoke." Lu tilted her head toward the house. "You look like you could use one."

Tess pushed the driver's door open, straightened, and squared her shoulders. Suddenly she was sixteen again, scanning the whole place, eying every dark corner, making sure she knew her surroundings. She strained her ears as she passed the Winters' house, half expecting to hear rising voices, breaking dishes, the slam of a body against a wall, the usual late-afternoon music of Cannery Row. Tess wondered if the brute had finally won custody of his two kids.

She forcibly shook off the memories as she approached Lu's old house, a mirror of Tess's mother's, except this house had trimmed hedges, a straight porch, and what looked like geraniums blooming in hanging baskets. The first step creaked under her weight, just like it had years ago when the two of them used to hang out right on this stoop, before Lu found hockey in high school and Tess found stoners at the Cannery. Tess swiveled and sat on the porch, feeling the sun-warmed boards through the seat of her jeans. Lu offered her a lit cigarette, and Tess hesitated for only a moment before she took it, sucking in a deep drag, feeling the ashy smoke hit the deep part of her lungs. She and Lu used to sit here and watch the world go by, the sun sinking down over the far trees.

Lu said, "Never thought I'd see you back in Cannery Row. When you lit out, I thought you lit out for good."

"Didn't expect to see you here, either."

"Hard to say no to free housing. Why did you come back?"

"Would you believe I'm visiting for old-time's sake?"

"I heard you were driving trucks out in Minnesota or something."

"North Dakota. Hauling waste water from fracking."

Lu whistled through the gap in her two front teeth. "That's got to pay well."

"I get along. You?"

"Working the casino at the res." Lu flicked ash toward the hedges. "Pays well but I work strange hours. Not complaining."

"Where's *she* working?"

Lu chose that moment to take a long drag, so deep that her cheeks hollowed as she sucked. Lu had the whip-thin leanness of someone who preferred cigarettes to food, and the deeply ingrained tics that suggested she'd probably always be a smoker. With her hair cut surprisingly short, Lu's blue eyes looked more prominent than ever, though now they avoided Tess's gaze as Lu took her time blowing out the smoke.

Finally Lu said, "I can't tell you that."

Tess took another hit of the cigarette, felt the woozy head rush of the nicotine. "You know I could find out in a Pine Lake minute."

"If you start asking questions, people are going to start asking questions back. And from what I've heard, you're pretty much keeping to yourself over at Riley's place."

"I'm sure Riley knows where my mother's working."

"But she hasn't told you or you wouldn't be here asking me."

"What's the big secret?"

"Your mother asked me to keep quiet." Lu leaned her elbows on her knees. "I'm your mother's sponsor."

It took Tess a minute to figure out what Lu was saying. It dawned on her as she eyeballed Lu's hollow cheeks, at the way Lu dodged her gaze and found interest in how the ash grew on the tip of her cigarette, and then, with the lightest of flicks, scattered to the wind.

She and Lu had drifted apart during high school, which was pretty much the story Tess had with all the girls at Pine Lake High. Their worries about chemistry tests and whether that boy in English really liked them just didn't measure up

155

on the problem scale when Tess went home every day to find her mother sobbing over the kitchen table clutching the neck of a bottle of cheap vodka, raging about her bastard of a father. Perky invitations to join the track team or come to the Raise Money for Darfur Dance just added to her resentment when she had to spend the evenings doing laundry, food shopping, cleaning up the house, or trying to make sense of the bills her mother let pile up in the mail. When she couldn't handle it anymore, she didn't head off to high school parties. She headed to the Cannery, where one guy offered weed and another offered a certain form of quick affection to help her forget that, when she got home, she'd probably discover her mother boozy and giggling, upstairs in the bedroom with a new boyfriend.

"Started in hockey," Lu said, shrugging. "The high school jocks had a lot of boozy parties. I liked them. Liked them so much I started throwing them for myself on weekdays after I graduated."

"I don't know what surprises me more. That you're her sponsor or that she's finally in AA."

"Did you read the letter she wrote to you?"

Tess's jaw tightened. She remembered receiving the letter. It came in the Kansas mail with the seed catalog and the bills for fertilizer, a sliver of her past sliding into her golden life like a shiv.

"I didn't open it." God knows how her mother had found her after all these years. Tess had made an art out of living off the grid. "In fact, like most things I don't like, I burned it."

"You've got good reason to be angry."

Tess flushed prickly and hot. She wondered how much Lu knew—or thought she knew. Her mother got to be a really good liar toward the end there. Tess wondered whether her mother ever gave her any credit for all those years keeping her fed, clothed, and, in some cases, sober enough to face the police so that Rodriguez wouldn't call social services. Funny thing about that. Her mother always had just enough self-possession to sober up in time. Somehow she knew that if Rodriguez had called social services, then Tess would have found herself living on those acres in Minnesota. That would have been a hell of a lot better for the twelve-year-old she'd been. But then her mother would be left without someone to clean up her messes.

In the end, no matter how drunk, Betty Hendrick always knew how to take care of Bette Hendrick.

"I know you probably don't want to hear this," Lu said, "but it took a lot for her to climb out of the hole she was in."

Tess heard the sound that came out of her, the bitter scoff of contempt. Climbing out of that hole came about twenty years too late.

"That's why she's not here," Lu continued, nodding toward the sagging house. "Lately she's such a wreck she's seeing ghosts."

"Oh, she used to see all kinds of things when she was on the rotgut—"

"It's your aunt she's seeing," Lu interrupted. "She's seeing her own dead sister as a teenager, walking around town as if she's still alive. That's how much it's killing her, Tess. She lost both of you, and the guilt is destroying her."

"Maybe I should dress up in chains when I see her. Rattle them a little and see what happens."

Lu's gaze fell to her blue-painted toenails, and Tess felt a stab of guilt. If Lu was her mother's sponsor that meant Lu might be seeing ghosts, too. For a moment Tess wondered exactly what regrets haunted Lu's conscience.

"She's afraid of you, Tess." Lu took another deep drag and spoke through the smoke. "She's afraid of how angry you are."

"Glad to hear she's finally met her own conscience."

"She's got a lot to atone for, and she knows it."

"I'm sure my mother is doing a fine job of playing the victim. It's a performance I'm very familiar with."

Lu ran a hand through her short-cropped hair, riffling it so that it stood up on end in places. Her thumb flicked at the filter of the cigarette burning low between her fingers. She seemed to be searching the front lawns of the houses for something she couldn't quite find.

"Here's the thing," Lu said. "Your mother knows her limits now. She knows them very well. And she believes seeing you again is the one trigger that'll send her right back to the bottom of a bottle."

Tess sat for a moment while the words sank in. "Are you saying she won't see me?"

"Recovery is a fragile thing, Theresa—"

"Tess." Her back teeth began to chatter as a terrible anger rose up in her. "You call me Tess. My mother killed Theresa long ago."

"She knows she failed you. She knows that's why you left

her." But she knows she's not strong enough to face you, and she doesn't want to take the risk."

Tess looked down and saw her hands curled into fists, the knuckles white, feeling the rage like a red haze before her eyes. "She's still playing the victim."

"Your mother has never forgiven herself for everything she's done, and everything she failed to do." Lu ground the cigarette out on the porch boards, three deep furrows in her brow. "She knows she'll have to live with that pain—"

"I don't give a fuck about her pain."

Tess shot to her feet. She stood on the porch with the sun on her face and the old house in her sight. She stood there staring at the dysfunction she'd lived in from the moment her father crouched down in front of her and asked her what she wanted to do. She could come with him to Minnesota, he'd said, while behind him his lover, her English teacher, looked down at her with that ruler slap of an eye. Minnesota, some far place where she'd have to live with the woman who couldn't stand the way she wrote essays about dead cats. Realizing that, if she went, she'd be leaving her mother alone. Her mother, who couldn't seem to get up in the morning. Her mother, who crawled into Tess's bed every night smelling bad and sobbing about how Daddy was leaving them both.

Tess stepped off the stairs onto the cracked concrete. "I don't know what I was thinking, coming back here. Nothing has changed. I was a fool for thinking it ever would."

Chapter Thirteen

Paging through her notebook, seeing the lists of names and reading the descriptions she'd written from observations around town, Sadie finally came to the realization that her grand plan was a failure.

She slumped in the hard wooden chair, tugging on the binoculars around her neck as she brooded. When she was back home laying out her grand plans, she'd figured that the little town of Pine Lake wasn't Queens, where she could bike the same route every day and not see the same person twice, where about a quarter of her own classroom turned over in any given year. She figured if she stood on a street corner in this Podunk upstate town long enough, she'd probably see the entire population pass by. Certainly someone would pause and look at her and say, *are you related to . . .*

Now she had to admit she'd discovered more information about her birth mother online at home than she had in all her time here.

She squinted toward the computer terminals. There

were only four of them, and every time Sadie came to the library, the sign-up sheets were already filled for hours, mostly by mothers who then sat their kids in front of the monitor to play some stupid learning games. But today, Sadie noticed, there were fewer moms hanging around. There was just one bearded guy who looked like a college student, wearing a pork-pie hat as he slumped over his laptop. So when Sadie noticed a woman gathering her things, she waited a moment for someone else to claim the terminal where the woman had been sitting. When nobody did, she hurried across the room and slipped into the metal computer seat like she belonged there.

She logged into her instant messaging account and sent out a text.

Izzy responded right away.

Sadie! You're alive!

I'm in a library, she typed, *safe in that place we talked about before.*

I was soooo worried about you! Your aunt called here yesterday.

Sadie sat with her hands hovering over the keyboard as a cold, prickly sensation swept through her.

Izzy typed, *She thought you were vacationing with us. My mom got all wiggy. I told her that your aunt was wrong, that you went away with someone from school.*

Sadie typed, *from school?!*

My mom was staring, I had to say something!

Sadie pressed a palm against her stomach where the pancakes and maple syrup she'd had for breakfast churned. She'd been counting on the fact that her aunt would be too preoccupied with Nana to think about her at all.

Sadie typed, *so what did you say?*

I said I couldn't remember the friend's name. I said it was Jones or Johnson or something. Someone in a different class. I had to make something up quick!

Sadie squeezed her eyes shut. Think. *Think.* And when she did, a terrifying question came to mind.

She typed, *What about Nana? Did my aunt say anything?*

Sadie stared at the curser as it blinked once, twice, three times.

Your aunt put your nana in St. Regis.

Sadie made a sound in the back of her throat that she swallowed down before it drew attention. Nana had always hated that place, back when Nana knew what it was. But for the past two years, Nana had had sudden urges to catch the bus into Manhattan to work at the sweet shop she'd managed thirty years earlier. Nana had sometimes talked about her husband in the other room fixing the window locks, when he'd been dead for forty years. The Nana who'd taken her in six years ago had been subsumed by a woman who looked at her with a stranger's eyes and asked, *Little girl, what are you doing in my house?* Sadie told herself that Nana wouldn't even notice where she was.

Sadie?

Sadie typed, *Did Aunt Vi say anything else?*

Not really. Just that your aunt couldn't believe how bad your nana was. That she didn't even recognize her. (((HUGS)))

Sadie's throat tightened. Her aunt knew things had been

getting bad fast. After her last visit, Aunt Vi had looked Sadie in the eye and asked, *Is this too much for you?* If Sadie told her it was too much, then Aunt Vi would have put Nana in St. Regis, and with sighs of martyrdom, she'd squeeze Sadie into that tiny, noisy Ohio house. What choice had Sadie had?

She closed her eyes tight. She couldn't think about this, not right now, not when she might get caught before her work here was done.

Listen Izzy, she typed. *Was my aunt upset that she didn't know where I was?*

Yeah. She sounded embarrassed that she didn't know who you were staying with.

That was her aunt. Always overwhelmed, even during simple phone conversations, when the noise of children screaming in the background tended to draw her aunt's attention away from listening to anything Sadie was saying. Sadie had depended upon her aunt's distraction, in fact, when she first called her aunt to tell her about Nana's little walkabout and roundup by the police. When her aunt began to breathe in short, nervous little puffs, stuttering about flights and schedules and babysitters, Sadie had let her talk. After her aunt finally came around to asking about her, Sadie told her that a friend had offered to take her to their lake house for a few weeks. They were leaving tomorrow, and maybe Sadie should go so she wouldn't get in anyone's way.

Now Sadie wondered if her aunt, having shoved Nana in a nursing home, had finally stopped to think about her sister's child for more than five minutes. She wondered if Aunt

Vi was rifling through Sadie's bedroom, finding phone numbers, making calls, or, worse, alerting the police.

Sadie? Are you mad at me?

Sadie typed, *No, no. You did good! Maybe I'll call my aunt this afternoon. Give her a story so she doesn't go crazy.*

Are you okay? Like, is everything all right?

Yup. I've even got a place to stay that isn't a tree house.

ROFL. Any luck finding you-know-who?

Sighing, Sadie paused a moment before she typed, *I was crazy to think this would work.*

Called it!

But I got to see where my mother lived before I was born.

What's it like?

Lake beaches and ice cream stores and woods everywhere. Sadie twisted in the seat to squint out a far window at the flurry of activity on the library lawn. She raised the binoculars to see more clearly. *There's a band setting up right now outside the library,* she typed. *They do this, like, every week.*

I wish I was there with you! It's hot here and the air-conditioning isn't working. I've got no one to go to the city pool with but my sister and it's boooooorrrrrring.

With a pang, Sadie remembered other summers, taking the bus with Izzy to the public pool, lying out on the concrete, the smell of chlorine so thick you could choke on it.

Izzy typed, *I want to have summer with you! Tell me when you're coming home.*

Sadie curled her fingers into her lap and stared at them, the cuticles bitten to the quick. What was home? The house where she used to live with her nana? Nana would never live there again. Her aunt was probably already sticking a *For Sale* sign in the front lawn. It'd be great to keep on living there, but who ever heard of a fourteen-year-old living alone? Anything was better, Sadie thought, than going to live with her cousins in a family who didn't want her.

Sadie?

I'm not coming home yet, she typed. Sadie glanced up at the clock over the big windows, her mind rushing, that cold prickly feeling washing through her all over again.

Sadie typed, *I have another plan.*

⌇

Sadie sat on her bike across the street from Ricky's Roast until she saw Riley step out into the sunshine. A man in a suit followed her out. He handed Riley something and flashed a white smile. Sadie was relieved when they shook hands and headed off in different directions. After the research she'd done in the library, she needed to have this conversation with Riley alone and *right away*, before Aunt Vi got over her embarrassment enough to call for official help.

"Hey," she said, as she rode up beside Riley, dropping her feet off the pedals to keep pace.

"Hey, you."

"So," Sadie said, "how did your meeting with your mom's friend go?"

"Oh, like every other meeting my mother sets up. Did you know," Riley rushed on, as she raised a hand to show a card wedged between two fingers, "that you could soar to higher spiritual perspectives using up-flow vortices and organic mud wraps?"

Sadie didn't know how to respond to that. Riley was fast-walking, like a city girl, and she was sort of dressed like one, too, her suit jacket flapping, her heels clicking on the pavement. The binoculars bumped against Sadie's chest as she struggled to keep pace.

"Did you also know," Riley repeated, "that meditation labyrinths and relaxation courtyards and treatment terraces are essential to create an atmosphere of natural peace?"

"Ah…"

"Of course you didn't," Riley said, fluttering the card. "You and I, we're un*informed*. But he can tell, because someone of my 'body shape' could sure use a two-week organic juice cleansing—"

"Riley, how much coffee did you have?"

"I had a little too much of something, that's for sure." Riley flicked the card in a public trash can and kept walking. "And right now this body shape of mine is craving some ice cream. Want to join me, Sadie?"

Sadie's heart leaped. "Yes!"

Outside the Creamery, Sadie leaned the bike she'd borrowed against a sycamore tree. She didn't bother to lock it, though she still felt strange leaving it out like that. No one ever locked their bikes around here, and yet the bikes never seemed to get stolen. While Riley went in to order two Pine Lakes Spectacular Sundaes, holding the nuts on one, Sadie saved a tiny table with a tiny umbrella. All around tourists in beach cover-ups wandered in from nearby Bay Roberts to sample the forty homemade flavors or just to plunge inside for a minute to get out of the heat.

When Riley returned, she slid an enormous bowl in front of Sadie, another in front of herself, then plopped down and kicked her heels up on the third chair. "So," Riley said, digging into the fudge with a plastic spoon. "Update me on how the search is going."

"Not good," Sadie conceded. "But I did learn one thing. Your classmates had terrible taste in clothes. What was up with all the plaid?"

"Mountain fashion."

"Nobody tell you that grunge went out, like, *decades* ago?"

Riley pointed a dripping spoon at her. "You wait. You'll be howling about your classmates' fashion sense in ten years."

"No way." Sadie twirled her spoon into the creamy vanilla, the morning's pancakes still sitting like a lump in her stomach, trying to figure a way to bring up a subject that made her queasy. "But honestly, about this project. I think I've been going about this all wrong. I've been wasting my time—"

"A girl your age shouldn't be worried about wasting time. You should be building tree houses and painting your toenails and having swim races to the island in Pine Lake."

Sadie suddenly felt like she was in a Japanese anime and the frame had just panned back to show her alone in a big white space. Painting toenails and swim races? Is that what normal fourteen-year-olds did? Is that what Riley did with her time when she was fourteen years old?

"Unless," Riley continued, "there's some deadline coming up that you'd like to clue me in on?"

"Well, I want to go back to school in September."

"There's a string of words that never left my lips."

"Why? Was your high school bad or something?"

"It's like any school, I suppose. Some kids do great, and some kids don't. One of the women I graduated with is an archaeologist, Maya Wheeler. She's been on the cover of *National Geographic*. But I wasn't much for sitting in a classroom listening to teachers drone on. I'd much rather be out looking for birds or playing softball."

Izzy played softball on the school team, Sadie remembered with a pang. Sadie had tried to join two years ago, but with Nana, she just couldn't make practices.

"I take it," Riley continued, "that you liked your school and you want to go back?"

"I miss my friends. And I don't want to fall behind. The problem is," Sadie said, her chest rising, "if I can't find my birth mother, then my choices of where to live narrow down to zippo."

Sadie concentrated on the ice cream dripping from the sides of the bowl, scraping it with a spoon and then pouring the drippings over the top. She could feel Riley's gaze on her head. Riley wouldn't understand what she was feeling. Riley had Camp Kwenback, Pine Lake, and a large family. No one could possibly understand this unhinged sensation that Sadie felt sometimes, the growing sense that there wasn't a place in the whole wide world where she really belonged.

Sadie often wondered if this dizzy sensation was born the moment her own mother put her into the arms of a stranger.

"Sadie." Riley's head weaved as she sought her gaze. "It's clear to me that you had a loving family once—"

"Once."

"There has to be someone. A distant relative, maybe. Or," Riley ventured, "maybe someone you haven't yet met, but who'd—"

"I'm not doing foster care."

Sadie shook her head so hard she felt a muscle pull in the back of her neck. She *had* stayed in temporary state care once, for two days. Two days she wished she could wash forever from her mind.

"Oh," Riley said, "I didn't mean—"

"It doesn't matter." Sadie dropped the spoon on the sticky table. "I just came from the library, where I did some research. Now I think I've got a better idea."

Sadie breathed deeply, though it seemed every breath took in less and less air. She told herself the answer to this problem was simple. It made perfect sense, as she sat here under the shade of an umbrella outside an ice cream shop, a light breeze rustling the leaves of the tree above them. The solution was easy and logical...if she could just make her throat and tongue and mouth work.

Riley leaned forward in encouragement. "Don't keep me in suspense."

"I just found out," Sadie said, "that you don't have to adopt someone to take custody."

"Oh?"

"In fact, anyone can be my legal guardian." Sadie met Riley's chocolate-brown eyes. "Even someone like you."

Chapter Fourteen

R iley sat frozen in the molded plastic chair listening to the cars lurching over the speed bump, the excited chatter of the kids at the next table, the plink of spoons hitting ice cream glasses—and, above all of that, the ringing in her head of Sadie's words, *even you, even you, even you.*

"It's not a lifetime thing," Sadie ventured, her sneaker patting staccato against the sidewalk. "It's only until I'm eighteen. Hardly more than three years. Legal custody isn't permanent like adoption."

Permanent like adoption. Beads of sweat slid down her neck, but Riley felt oddly cold, all the way to the tips of her fingers.

"The way I figure, you could use the help at the camp." Sadie excavated a chunk of chocolate out of her ice cream. "You've got that tatted trucker setting up that mini-golf. You're going to need someone to sit in the booth and work it."

Sadie slipped the piece of chocolate in her mouth and Riley watched her jaw working it like a marble. She watched the little lump pass from one cheek to the other. She watched Sadie struggle to swallow it down.

"If I lived here in Pine Lake," Sadie continued, clearing her throat, "I'd go to the local public high school. I'd go to the library to study after school, or join clubs. You'd hardly ever see me during the day."

Riley knew she should say something, anything, but she couldn't absorb the magnitude of what Sadie was asking.

"I'm no freeloader, you know." Sadie speared the spoon upright into the ice cream. "I can cook, I can clean, I can make beds, and I can do laundry. You've got lots of laundry. Heck, I can pay bills and run the registration desk when you need to be somewhere else—"

Riley lifted her palm, dizzy. "Sadie—"

"Listen. *Listen.* I've researched this. It's not complicated like getting approved to be a foster home or whatever. It's not like everything you'd have to do to get approved for adoption. For legal custody, it's easy-peasy. I guess this is what my nana must have done when I first came to live with her. All you need is power of attorney so you can enroll me in school and stuff."

"Power of attorney."

"Yes, power of attorney. And you'd get that from my current guardians."

"Current guardians."

"Yeah, they're the ones who took me after my parents died. My parents must have had it in the will or something." Sadie pushed the ice cream away. "Believe me, they'd hand me over to you like I was a hot potato."

Riley felt a pinprick of cold on her lap. She'd been holding her spoon in midair, and now it was dripping melted ice cream onto her skirt. She clattered her spoon onto the table and discovered that she'd forgotten napkins. So silly to forget napkins at an ice cream shop. She never understood why the Creamery didn't keep dispensers right on the tables.

Riley dove into her purse to find a tissue. The effort gave her something to concentrate on that wasn't Sadie's anxious face. The effort gave her something to concentrate on other than the fact she knew exactly how Sadie felt. How many times in her youth did she ache to fly away to any place where she might just belong?

Tess had been right. The minute Riley discovered Sadie in that shed, Riley should have called the authorities.

Oh, God.

Riley rubbed at her skirt, rubbing, rubbing, rubbing it all over her, making a bigger mess than before. But that's what Riley Cross always did, right? It was never intentional; she never *meant* to cause harm. She'd spent a lifetime trying to keep everyone happy, even if it meant avoiding making changes or decisions. For thirty-odd years, she'd just bobbed right along, afraid to churn the waters, uncertain even in the face of facts, unable to give up the possibility of choice, until, like a tsunami, events knocked her ass over tit. Thus she let her marriage linger for years knowing she never wanted kids. Thus her divorce papers were still sitting, unsigned, on the registration desk. And whenever she *did* dare to make a decision—like leaving her job, like taking on the albatross of Camp Kwenback—the world rolled its eyes at her, holding its collective breath in anticipation of disaster.

And here she was, sheltering a runaway, giving Sadie rising expectations that the girl could find a stable home and live in blissful domestic harmony when that was the most impossible thing in the world. Riley tossed the sticky tissue on the table and pressed the butt of her hand against her forehead. She wished Claire hadn't left Camp Kwenback this afternoon, boarding a train to visit a New York City friend. Riley could use some of Claire's wisdom, because right now Riley was overwhelmed by all the reasons this absolutely couldn't be. Sure, Riley might be able to overcome the fact that she'd be a terrible excuse for a guardian, but how could she ever explain something like this to Declan? If Declan ever heard that Riley was taking legal custody of a teenage girl, it would make everything she'd told him a lie.

It would rip his heart to pieces.

Then her gaze fell upon the spray of pamphlets in the tote by her feet, the ones that addressed the foggy, difficult, inevitable issue of her immediate future, and she pounced on the lesser problem.

"See this, Sadie?" She tugged out a pamphlet and shook it so that the paper crackled. "It's a resort in the Catskills."

Sadie, stone-faced, barely grazed it with a glance.

"Today I met the man who runs this place." The front of the flyer was a logo of a naked silhouette against a yellow sun. "He wants to tear down the swing sets and turn the cabins into massage rooms. They want to clear-cut ten acres of woods and landscape a golf course."

"Was I just speaking Swahili before?" Sadie's lips whitened. "Because this conversation just took a weird turn."

"This man told me," Riley persisted, "that he'd bring Camp Kwenback into the twenty-first century by making part of the lake a nudist beach."

"They know there are snapping turtles in that lake, right?"

"He said a nude beach is a major draw. He said people want to do yoga at sunrise. He said people want mud wraps and juice cleanses."

Sadie went quiet and looked at Riley like you'd look at an old lady mumbling to herself on a park bench. "I don't have a problem with a nude beach," Sadie began carefully. "I don't really want to look at naked old people, but that's your business, and you gotta do what you gotta do to—"

"I don't want to do this."

"Okay."

"No." Riley shook the pamphlet. "I mean I *really* don't want to do this."

Her grandparents were dead, and Camp Kwenback was dying, and Riley's heart was shriveling up with it. She'd tried to revive the place in her halting, half-assed way, and look where that had gotten her. She was about to witness her biggest failure—and here was Sadie, fragile, vulnerable Sadie, asking to be a part of it all.

You just can't build a solid life on a rotting foundation.

"The point I'm making," Riley ventured, "is that, come winter, I won't have a home, a job, or a future. I won't have the means to take care of—"

"What you're trying to say," Sadie retorted, shooting to her feet, "is *no*."

Riley watched the walls slam down behind those pale green eyes, the layers and layers of defenses, each one more opaque than the last. Riley's heart leaped to her throat, because the sight reminded Riley of the name she'd found in that ledger and the suspicions blossoming in her mind.

"Sadie, I'm—"

"Thanks for the ice cream." Sadie swept her backpack on her shoulder. "It was a stupid, stupid idea anyway."

⁓

Riley needed to talk to Tess.

She hugged a light sweater to her body, the floorboards creaking as she paced barefoot in the darkened lodge. She'd spent the early evening shuffling papers by her computer, surreptitiously watching her runaway from over the top of the registration desk as Sadie played chess with Mrs. Clancy. Sadie had acted as if nothing had changed between them, but Riley could tell that she was hurting. Squatting with her feet on the seat of a wooden chair, Sadie looked like a red-tailed hawk, solitary and untouchable, observing the world from on high through a hooded gaze.

Now Riley paced alone in the main room, waiting for Tess to return from wherever she'd disappeared to, wondering— not for the first time—if she was crazy to have such suspicions. She just couldn't get out of her head the way Sadie's face had shuttered this afternoon. Tess looked exactly the same way whenever Riley dared to venture a question that bordered on the personal. Sadie had even removed herself from the conversation—just as Tess had done so many times, in her case pleading fatigue, an aching shoulder, a migraine. Maybe it was just something all traumatized runaways did.

But then there was that *other* issue. Tess's name in the Camp Kwenback ledger, the dates fitting perfectly. Riley's mind flashed white whenever she dared to consider the possibility—*no*. Tess was a difficult woman to know, but she wasn't cruel. After all this time, Tess would have said something.

A flash of light swept the room. Riley glanced out the window and saw headlights hover at the end of the drive, then fade out. A moment later, she heard the faint slam of a car door and saw the shape of a woman's silhouette stride toward the construction zone that would soon be the renovated mini-golf.

Riley slipped her feet into a pair of canvas sneakers and stepped out onto the porch, closing the door behind her. Cicadas sang in the trees, their buzz rising as she descended the stairs to the graveled parking area. A cloud passed across the moon, darkening the world to indigo. Bracing herself for a difficult conversation, she head out across the driveway, her steps muffled as she stepped into the woods.

All she could see of the old mini-golf were a tumbling pile of shapes, rolls of artificial grass, stacks of two-by-fours, and the rusty dismembered parts of metal clowns and sun-bleached windmills. The new mini-golf was covered by tarps against a brief afternoon rain. As she came closer, she heard the scrape of plastic tarp being yanked and saw its shiny wrinkled creases catching starlight before falling to the ground.

Then the cloud cover thinned and moonlight fell through the clearing, illuminating the scene. Riley drew in a long, slow breath as the lumps between the trees resolved into figures. Silver light limned one furry upturned face and caught another bear's raised paw. The pale moonlight gleamed on a vest, winked on a stubby tail, and painted the raised leg of a ballerina bear. Grouped to face each other, the bears stretched out their arms as if leaning back in a dance, while smaller bears peeked out of the shadow of their elders, heads tilted, and their faces wide with toothy grins.

There they were, Tess's tribute to Bud and Mary, the old wooden bears dancing under the moonlight.

Riley paused, drinking in the sight of the bears, as well as the sight of Tess as her friend stood motionless, contemplative, unguarded. Then Tess brushed her bangs off her brow and raised her face to the sky. Her profile, bathed in moonlight, stood in stark relief.

And suddenly Riley knew what it felt to be a soaring bird hitting the clear surface of a glass window.

Not seeing, until the end, what had always been right in front of her.

Chapter Fifteen

W hy didn't you tell me?"
         Tess startled as Riley's voice came out of the darkness. She shoved her hands in her back pockets just as Riley emerged from the woods.

"I wanted it to be a surprise." Tess tilted her head at the collection around her. "I knew the dancing bears was Bud's favorite story so I figured I'd set it up this way."

Riley's face was pale, pulled in an expression Tess couldn't quite read. Her friend was clutching her sweater close although the night was balmy. For a heartbeat, Tess wondered if she'd misread Riley's signals when Riley first gave her the green light for this project—she wondered if she'd overstepped her bounds. She was acutely aware that Bud and Mary were *Riley's* family, and Tess was just a temporary intruder.

Riley said, "I'm not talking about the bears, Tess."

"Oh?"

"I'm talking about Sadie."

Tess blinked, and for a moment her mind went blank, until she realized what Riley must be referring to.

"I guess she told you about our discussion at Bay Roberts." Tess cocked her hip. "I didn't take that girl for a snitch."

Riley paused. "You talked?"

"I did most of the talking. I tried to knock some sense into her, but that girl's stubborn like I've never—"

"Then you didn't tell her."

"To go back home? I sure as hell did."

Riley took a deep breath. "I saw the ledger, Tess. Grandma kept great records. You stayed in Cabin Ten during the year Sadie was conceived."

Tess tried not to flinch as the words sank in. Her thoughts stumbled, skittered, raced. She could say her mother had gone on another bender. She could say there'd been another fire in their Cannery Row house. She could say that her mother had shacked up with another fly-by-night boyfriend. It should be simple to stand here and dream up a reason she'd stayed at Camp Kwenback for those weeks while Riley was off at college.

Any half-truth would do.

"You and Sadie have the same nose," Riley said into the silence. "You both have the same jaw—"

"Does Sadie know?" The words flew out of her, launched by terror.

"No." Riley tightened her grip on her sweater. "I didn't figure it out until just a moment ago."

Tess felt her whole body deflating like air flooding out of a balloon.

Riley whispered, "So it's true then."

Yes.

Yes, it was true, even if the word wouldn't pass her lips. This secret had shielded her and Sadie for so long that even thinking the truth started a roaring in her mind, like the shudder of a tin roof under the assault of high plains winds.

Riley whispered, "What happened?"

Tess stiffened her spine. "Figure it out. I got pregnant. I had a baby. I gave her up."

"But she's here now." Riley gestured to the dark shape of the lodge through the pines. "She came here just to look for you—"

"Not me," Tess interrupted. "She's looking for someone who bakes gingersnap cookies. Sadie's not looking for a tatted-up big-rig driver who lives out of her cab."

Tess threw her arms wide to show the scars she had dug into herself on the outside to match the ones within, the inscription crawling up the inside of her arm in Latin, *My tears would drown the world, as my inner fire would reduce it to ashes.*

Riley's voice, breathy, uncomprehending. "But why else did you come back to Pine Lake?"

"To make sure she gets home safely."

"But she doesn't have—"

"Yes she does. I've been trying to tell you this all along." Tess caught herself, forced her voice to be calm. "Sadie *does* have a family, an aunt and uncle who live outside of Cleveland. They're good people. They have an acre of land and four kids, Sadie's cousins."

"How do you know?"

"I've been watching her since the day I gave her up."

Tess wished she could suck up that slip and swallow it whole. She turned away from Riley and curled her fingers into the mama bear's shoulder, bracing herself, seeking an easy way to explain. She'd been keeping tabs on Sadie and her adoptive family for years. One Christmas season she'd even parked outside Sadie's grammar school on Long Island and watched her mother hustle Sadie into the Catholic school. Sadie had dressed up as a sheep for the Christmas pageant. As Sadie skipped inside, she bounced her head back and forth so that her sheep ears danced.

Tess squeezed her eyes tight. She'd always wondered if it would have been easier to give her baby up if Sadie hadn't been born a girl.

"I don't understand," said Riley, pacing in the pine needles behind her. "How could you watch her without anyone knowing?"

"The Internet. Social media." Tess forced her feet flat on the ground, the better for balance. "Her grandmother should have monitored her better. Sadie got online young. Sadie knows me as Mindy from Minnesota, a goth with an interest in origami."

"So...you know Sadie's aunt and uncle?"

"I know who they are. Sadie has known her cousins since they were born. Her aunt and uncle took Sadie in after her parents died, and then, a couple of months later, she was sent to live with her grandmother in Queens."

"She told me they don't want her. She told me," Riley repeated, "that they'd hand her off to me like a hot potato."

"What the hell does that mean?"

"Sadie asked if I'd be her legal guardian."

Something struck Tess in the shoulder, and Tess grabbed where it hurt only to realize she'd staggered a few paces back and bumped into Winnie. She breathed hard, feeling the first creeping tendrils of jealousy, knowing they were unworthy, undeserved, even as they tightened around her heart. Her head told her that her daughter was no fool. Sadie grasped the worth of Camp Kwenback just like Tess had all those years ago. Sadie saw a kind-hearted protector in Riley, and her heart had led her right. Tess told herself that the situation could be worse, that there were a lot more difficult places to grow up than in Camp Kwenback, doing homework in the main lodge, swimming in the lake, and playing among these dancing bears.

Tess forced her voice to be even. "Sadie knows a good thing when she sees it."

"Come on, you know I can't be her guardian."

Jealousy was like acid in her mouth. "Because Sadie already has a legal family."

"Plus she has you."

"I'm no guardian."

"That can change."

"I signed a consent form." The words were branded in her mind. *I fully realize that I relinquish forever any and all rights as parent of said child.* "When you sign a consent form, you legally abandon a child."

Riley made a strange, choking sound.

"Sadie's the adopted daughter of a couple of nice, honest apple farmers," Tess insisted. "Let's keep it that way."

"No."

Tess felt a kick of anger. "What would you tell her then? That she's the spawn of a messed-up trucker with a juvenile criminal record and a failed marriage?"

"I would tell—"

"Should I tell her she's the granddaughter of an alcoholic?"

"—her the truth."

"The truth?" She shuddered at the word. "The *truth*? Should I tell Sadie that she only exists because pharmaceuticals failed?"

Tess remembered those pills she'd choked down, among many pills she'd taken that day, the ones they told her she should take, the ones that would reduce the possibility, and she'd taken them because, on that day, that was what she'd wanted and she'd been a shaking mess.

"Sadie knows that." Riley's voice was flat and hard. "Every adopted kid knows that. We're the lucky ones."

Tess couldn't look at her. In her mind, she saw Sadie's face, red cheeks buried behind a hood in the cold of winter. She saw a girl in striped stockings kicking her legs on a swing in the grammar school playground. She saw a tween slinging a backpack over her shoulder, striding out of the little house in Queens. She saw grainy social-media pictures showing experimentation with brown eyeliner.

Her blood ran cold sometimes, thinking about the fragile series of events that brought Sadie into this world.

"Should I even ask how all this happened?" Riley pushed away from a bear, the small button at the top of her sweater caught between agitated fingers. "In high school, you wore the birth-control patch like it was a badge of honor."

"My father's support payments stopped after my eighteenth birthday. Some weeks I had to choose between dinner, medicine, and vodka." The tendons in her shoulders tightened. "That was an unlucky week."

"But you went through with the pregnancy."

She hadn't known she was pregnant until four months later. When she found out, she had slapped her belly right in front of all the nurses, calling the fetus a little parasite.

"Once I knew," she said through a tightening throat, "I made an adoption plan."

"An adoption plan." Riley tugged violently on her sweater button. "Everyone uses such careful words these days. Our mothers made an 'adoption plan.' There was a 'transfer' of custody. But you know what? At the bottom of all that is the truth every adopted kid I know slams ourselves against, over and over, until we're mentally bruised and bloody: Our birth mothers willingly gave us away." Riley glared at her. "*You* gave Sadie away."

"That's not fair."

A flash of guilt shot across Riley's face.

"I did it," Tess said, "to protect her."

She spoke the words with a stiffening of her spine but she wanted to crouch down and hide her head between her knees. The truth was that Tess hadn't wanted to hand Sadie over to the Tischler family, in the end.

But if she told Riley that, she'd have to tell her *why*.

Sometimes Tess felt that her life was a huge scale and she spent every moment of her day struggling to balance it. In the hospital she wanted it all to be over. She wanted that baby out of her body and out of her life. She wanted to be back on the streets with her fly-by-night friends, looking for some happy-happy. But the instant Sadie eased out of her body, bloody and slippery, her daughter's cry shot a hundred thousand hooks into her heart. Tess knew with a force like a bright light, *This is my daughter.* She remembered bracing herself on her elbows, gasping for breath, unable to take her eyes from the creature moving in the doctor's gloved hands, realizing with a shock that the arms now stretching out for that child were her own, that she was reaching for the baby that only moments earlier she'd been counting down the minutes to be rid of.

"Tell her, Tess." Riley's voice, hard in the night.

Tess heaved like she'd run for miles. She'd wanted Sadie so much after she was born. She'd wanted to protect this little girl the way she herself had never been protected. But as the days passed, and the adoption counselors asked hard questions as they pressed her to sign the papers, the doubts and insecurities multiplied. How could she ever take care of this child, alone, unemployed, homeless? Was she even capable of loving her? She'd screwed up every decent relationship she'd ever had—with her old Pine Lake friends, with her asshole boyfriends, with her hopeless mother. Would she screw things up with this fragile girl? So she'd given Sadie away.

But Tess feared that at the bottom of that decision lay an

ugly complicity, a complicity that chipped off a piece of her heart whenever she dared to face it.

Maybe what she'd done wasn't for the best.

Maybe it was just easier.

"Tess," Riley said, softer now. "Tell her."

"I can't."

"Yes, yes, you can."

"Sadie will hate me."

"Sadie won't be happy you took so long to say something, but she won't—"

"Your mother put you up for adoption. Don't you hate her for it?"

"No."

That "no" ended on an up tone, and Tess knew there was more to the story. She waited for it while the cicadas sang in the trees, the volume of their song rising.

"I didn't hate her," Riley continued, digging furrows in her arms. "Not at the beginning, when I didn't know her. Not until she told me she didn't want me. That she didn't even have a daughter."

"Maybe she said that to protect you."

"Protect me? From what?"

"I don't know. But I'd like to meet the birth mother who managed to escape guilt."

Riley flipped her hand in dismissal. "Well, maybe you and my birth mother can discuss that over tea one day. In the meantime, you've got a chance to make this right. This secret is a hollow in Sadie, don't you understand? Sadie will fill it up with a million nightmares—"

"Or she can fill it up with dreams." Tess glanced to the lodge in the distance. "Dreams of mothers who smell like gingerbread, and—"

"Damn it, Tess, what kind of woman are you to skulk around here, keeping such a secret from your own daughter?"

She wanted to speak, she really did. The urge was overwhelming, a tide dammed up just under her sternum. But every time the truth rose, it slammed against the constriction of her throat. She'd kept all of this inside for so damn long. She couldn't open her mouth. The hinges of her jaws had seized.

She wouldn't tell this story.

"Tell her, Tess." Riley stepped in front of her, all angry brown eyes. "Because if you don't, I will."

Chapter Sixteen

Sadie woke up in the middle of the night. She lay blinking on the bed, listening to the cicadas singing, crickets chirping, and, from the deep woods, the sound of an owl hooting. But the sound that woke her up hadn't come through her open window—it came from the creaking floorboards in the hallway outside her room.

Sadie swung her legs over the side of the bed. Nana used to putter around the house in the middle of the night, and Mrs. Clancy had proved no different. Once Sadie had caught Mrs. Clancy rattling the locked handle of the lodge's sliding back doors. Since then Sadie had been alert to late-night noises. Sadie knew well that all it would take was one little distraction, one little mistake, for there to be a real disaster. After all, had Sadie not been in such a dumb hurry to get to school one morning, she wouldn't be here in Pine Lake right now, doing crazy-ass things like begging a stranger to take her in.

She poked her head outside her door but the hall was

empty except for the spill of moonlight pouring in from the far window. Sadie stepped out and padded barefoot down the stairs and into the dim main lodge. She caught sight of Mrs. Clancy standing by the front window. The moonlight flooded through her nightgown, setting it aglow.

Sadie made loud footsteps as she crossed the room so she wouldn't startle the older woman. "Hey, Mrs. Clancy," she said, "is there a party going on out there?"

Mrs. Clancy turned and put a finger to her lips. She summoned Sadie closer and pointed out the window.

"Look," Mrs. Clancy whispered, "the bears are dancing."

Sadie squinted into the darkness but saw nothing but starlight glinting off the roof of Riley's car. Everything beyond the tree line was a blur.

Mrs. Clancy pressed her palms together and drew her shoulders up in excitement. "Remember how Mr. Cross used to tell us that this would happen someday? How the bears would come alive by the light of the moon and dance together under the stars?"

Sadie looked at Mrs. Clancy, sleep ruffled, giddy. Nana's hair was that same pure white, wispy and thin, like cotton candy. No matter how many times Sadie had combed it, she couldn't keep it neat. Sometimes she caught Nana pulling at it in agitation, gathering puffy piles in her lap.

It was going to be hard on Mrs. Clancy, Sadie thought, when Riley lost this place for good.

"You're not looking." Mrs. Clancy curled strong, bony fingers around Sadie's wrist. "Can you see them?"

"Not really. But—"

"Here, look through these." Mrs. Clancy grasped for something against her chest and then struggled to pull a pair of binoculars over her head. "You'll see the bears as plain as day down in that little clearing."

Sadie obliged, if only to get Riley's precious binoculars out of Mrs. Clancy's hands. Tossing the strap over her head, Sadie lifted the binoculars to her face and nudged the dial to put them in focus—

—and, oddly enough, there was something out there, a pile of shapes by the mini-golf area. She rotated the dial until she saw the collection of figures—yes, they were bears—some with their arms raised toward the sky.

"How Bud loved to collect those bears." Mrs. Clancy rubbed her hands together, a dry rusk of a sound. "Bud always denied it, you know. He used to say that *they* found *him*. He'd tell me how he'd come upon one on a trip farther upstate, and it would remind him of another one that he'd owned. He just had to buy it, never mind Mary shaking her head. They were like lost family, he said. He was just bringing them back together."

Sadie's finger paused over the focus dial as she saw something else in the moonlight—two human figures moving among the bears. They were too far away, and the light was too dim, to make out faces. But Sadie could guess that they were Riley and Tess.

She lowered the binoculars. She told herself Riley and Tess could be out there talking about ex-husbands or money troubles. Maybe Tess had just lost her car keys around the construction site and that's why she had crouched down.

Maybe Sadie was just full of herself, thinking that they might be talking about her.

Then Sadie remembered the flare of alarm in Riley's eyes when Sadie had uttered the words *legal custody.*

Mrs. Clancy leaned in close. "Do you see them, Sarah?"

"Yes," Sadie said, jerking the binoculars back to her face. "They're the bears from the barn."

"Why, yes, of course they are."

"I guess that woman Tess must be using them to make the new mini-golf."

"Well, that woman best catch them quick before those bears disappear into the woods."

Sadie watched Riley and Tess pacing and stopping, crouching and standing, while a sick feeling settled in her chest. No way were they out there just talking about the weather. Sadie didn't have to be a psychic to know that right now they were making plans to hand her over to the authorities.

"Poor Riley," Mrs. Clancy mused, pressing so close to the window that her words made a circle of fog on the glass. "Bud's not going to like that she left the barn door unlocked and set the bears free."

Sadie didn't bother to correct her. Why would she bother? Mrs. Clancy lived in a nice place, where people took care of her and wooden bears really did dance to life in the moonlight.

"It's late, Mrs. Clancy." Sadie took Mrs. Clancy's hand in her own. "Let's let the bears dance in peace."

"I'm so glad I finally got to see that." Mrs. Clancy let

Sadie turn her toward the stairs. "I feel like I've waited all my life to see that."

Sadie walked her through the main lodge, past Bob the Bear, whose balding tummy bore the burden of so many wishes, past the moose antlers that, during Christmas, were covered with tinsel, or so she was told. She walked Mrs. Clancy through the room that had held wild parties, where Riley's great-grandparents had served moonshine in little white teacups and the place had been raided four times by the police.

Such pretty stories, Sadie thought, as something dark and ugly curled inside her. Maybe Riley would feel less torn apart about losing Camp Kwenback if she just took a good hard look at the truth. These were really some *other* family's stories. Riley's real family story was a big mystery, and Riley had gotten so close to it that she'd run right back to her adoptive family.

But Sadie was different. She knew that the family she'd grown up in wasn't really hers. Her mom and dad had loved her, but they were dead and gone now. Her aunt and uncle had rejected her. Just like her biological mother had rejected her.

Just like Riley had rejected her.

When she turned eighteen it wouldn't matter who her birth mother was. At eighteen she could forget *both* families, and she'd forget Riley and Camp Kwenback, too, and she'd run away far enough from everyone and everything she'd ever known. She'd fly away someplace new, so she could make up her own stories.

Sadie let go of Mrs. Clancy's hand just outside the door of the older woman's room. "Good night, Mrs. Clancy."

"Good night, my dear." She patted Sadie's arm. "I'm so glad you're here to take care of me."

Mrs. Clancy closed the door behind her. Sadie stood in the hallway, her heart a stone suspended in her chest.

She had to make a new plan. There was no way around it. Nobody was ever going to take care of *her*.

Chapter Seventeen

Tell her, Tess."

Riley gripped her arms so hard she knew she would have bruises later. Something angry was curling up within her, something harsh and unforgiving for the woman standing defiant before her, unwilling to acknowledge the most fundamental of human responsibilities and confess the truth to the child she brought into the world—and then gave away.

Riley watched Tess pace a few steps and then crouch down. The muscles in Tess's shoulders flexed, and from this vantage point, Riley recognized Sadie's own narrow-boned frame, the same curve of neck and shoulder. The fact that Riley hadn't noticed this earlier only made her angrier.

"My grandparents didn't know, did they?" Riley said, already knowing the answer to the question.

Tess shook her head once.

"If they'd known," Riley said, "they would have let you stay. They would have moved mountains to help you keep—"

"I didn't know I was pregnant when I was staying here."

Riley paused and did a mental calculation. Tess was probably in her third month by the time she left Pine Lake. "How could you not know?"

"I had other things on my mind."

"I'd like to know what was more important than a pregnancy—"

"Would you?" Tess shot to her feet. "It must be hard to imagine life in Cannery Row from the vantage point of your backyard swing set."

Riley went mute.

"By the time I realized the truth," Tess continued, "I was far away from here, living on the street, and it was too damn late to do anything about it."

The anger curled a little tighter inside Riley. She did another mental calculation. Since Tess hadn't been able to terminate this pregnancy, Tess had to have been past four months when she supposedly found out, at a point where the baby would have been moving inside her.

The gaps in her story were growing deep and wide.

"I found out by accident, when I went into the hospital for a cut on my hand." Tess stared at her open palms. "It was deep and wouldn't stop bleeding, otherwise I'd have ignored it. In the hospital the nurse gave me a look-over and asked how far along I was. Far along for what? I asked. Then I called her a bitch for thinking I was knocked up just because I was homeless." Tess rubbed those palms together, like she was trying to grind pine tar off her skin. "Is this what you want me to tell Sadie?"

"I want you to tell her the truth."

"The truth is ugly."

Riley dug her nails into her biceps as she began to tremble with something more than anger. She understood that there were times when a woman couldn't keep her baby, especially a young woman with no one to lean on in the world. She understood that the adoption system was set up to take care of the innocent child. She also understood that the separation that resulted from adoption wasn't clean, wasn't joyous, wasn't without repercussions, that both birth mother and adopted child bore lifelong scars that pulsed, itched, ached.

"The truth," Riley said, "is that Sadie's a miracle. Women have choices. So my existence, and Sadie's, too, they're both miracles."

Tess didn't say anything, hiding behind her bangs.

"You've been watching her." Riley stepped closer, the dry pine needles crackling under her feet. "You've spent some time with her. You know what a smart, level-headed, even-keeled young woman she is. Your *daughter*, Tess. Your flesh and blood."

"That had nothing to do with me. She's made that way because of the family I placed her with."

"Then let's talk about that family you placed her with. Their deaths, the way she was bounced around to her aunt and uncle and then her nana's house, and then having to take care of her grandmother—"

"Take care of her grandmother?"

Riley saw the surprise in her eyes. So Tess didn't know

everything. "Her nana has dementia. Sadie has been taking care of the older woman for years."

"Dementia?"

"Sadie would still be there, in that house, if her nana hadn't gone wandering. She wandered straight into the hands of the authorities, and Sadie's cover was blown."

Tess bent over and put her hands on her knees. She seemed to be having some trouble breathing. The sight gave Riley hope that she was finally breaking through Tess's tough-girl shell.

"The family you put Sadie with is dead," Riley repeated. "Her nana is in a home of some sort. You're her only family now, the only one—"

"They were vetted." Tess's voice was harsh. "I chose them from a dozen families."

"That's in the past. Now you can make this right."

"Nothing can make this right."

Riley closed her eyes and willed patience. Why else was Tess here, if not to make things right?

The answer came to her like a bolt of lightning. "You think she'll reject you."

"She's smart, so I know she will."

"You're *afraid* she'll reject you."

Afraid like Riley herself had been afraid, when she wrote the first letter to her own birth mother. Anxious like Riley had been when she picked up a pen to compose the second. Black spots in front of her eyes, terrified, when she picked up that phone to dial her birth mother's number.

Riley had never considered the possibility that a birth

mother, seeking first contact, could be just as fearful as an adopted child.

"You're such a Girl Scout, Riley."

Tess's voice was full of disdain, and Riley felt a prickling of defiance toughen the tendons of her neck.

"My father left me behind when I was twelve years old," Tess retorted. "He left me alone with an alcoholic to take care of. That alcoholic later sold me out for a cheap bottle of vodka. You think there's anything a fourteen-year-old can say to hurt me?"

"Yes."

"Then you don't know me very well."

Riley balked at that, but she didn't deny it. Yes, they hadn't hung out in high school. Yes, they'd only had a few weeks together in total. Summer weeks, too, outside of the strictures of school. But she'd never believed that their relationship was no more than a camp summer thing, preserved in amber. She'd always thought they'd shared something special—Camp Kwenback, Bud and Mary, a certain sensibility that Riley hadn't found among any of her other Pine Lake girlfriends. More than once since Tess had returned, Riley had glimpsed the puckish, imaginative girl she'd played with in their youth beneath the attitude and the barbs.

But even as Riley convinced herself she was right, the doubts came rushing in, as they always did. The queen of good judgment Riley was *not*. Maybe she was just fooling herself about the woman who stood before her, like she had fooled herself about so very many things. Maybe the years—

and the mileage—had changed Tess so much that the softer creature Riley had once known had grown a shell of its own.

Well, if Tess wasn't going to take responsibility for Sadie, then Riley was determined that someone else would.

Riley asked, "What about Sadie's father?"

"Sadie doesn't have a father."

More denial. "Everyone has a—"

"If Sadie's lucky, her father is dead or rotting in prison."

The words struck Riley hard. She took three steps away from Tess, unnerved by the harshness of her voice.

Riley ventured. "Do I know him?"

"No."

"Did he...was he abusing you?"

"Seriously?"

"Then why—"

"Why? Why what? Why did I leave Pine Lake?" Tess crossed her arms. "I left because Rodriguez wouldn't let it go. That damn cop came to Camp Kwenback all the time, bringing all the ugly here, hounding me to get involved in the investigation, when I just wanted to put it all behind me."

Investigation.

"Sadie doesn't need to know her father," Tess said. "Ever."

Tess turned away again, moving like she was caught in a box of her own making. Walls, walls, walls on all sides, she kept running into them, turning to find another. She planted her fists on her hips but they didn't stay, they slipped off, and her spine bowed like she couldn't bear the weight of the words.

Riley's heart began to pound. "Tess, Sadie is going to ask—"

"She won't. Because I'm not telling her who I am." Tess jabbed a finger at Riley. "And after you hear my story, neither will you."

Chapter Eighteen

Tess knew right away that her mother had brought some-one home. Light poured through the windows onto the porch, and through the cracked glass of the front window—through the rag she'd stuffed there—she could hear the bluesy sounds of Nina Simone. Irritation needled her. She'd spent the evening working a rush job with a freelance con-tractor, unrolling insulation into an airless attic, itching as she crawled into small spaces to tuck it in between the rafters. Chaff and fluff stuck to her skin, and she was bone-deep exhausted. She needed a good night's sleep, not the hassle of dealing with one of her mom's drunken parties.

The front door was ajar despite the December chill. Tess shoved it open and heard the clink of a bottle neck hit-ting glass. Her mother and some guy were sitting on the old couch, sharing the depression where the spring was broken. In one glance, Tess took in the bottle of no-name vodka, the dirty glasses, and the ashtray overflowing with cigarette butts.

"Theresa!" The strap of her mother's bra sagged on her arm. "Come in and meet my new friend."

Mom brought men home all the time, usually skinny, bleary-eyed, half-pickled, toothless types that Tess would find snoring on the couch the next morning. They had names like Bud and John and Mack. Her mother had already forgotten this one's name, but when the burly stranger turned his gaze on Tess, he swallowed her up in one gulp.

Hackles rising, Tess kicked her work boots onto the rug by the door. "The cops will be here in ten minutes if you don't lower that music."

"Oh, don't be like that, Theresa—"

"Mrs. Skye is watching from across the street."

"That sour old prune?" Her mother playfully ruffled the guy's shaggy blond hair. "I can handle her."

"Hey"—Tess raised her palms—"I don't want the cops here, *he* doesn't want the cops here, do you want the cops here?"

With a sigh, her mother stretched back to tweak the music down a notch. The stranger ran his hand up her mother's skinny chest to grab a boob while he grinned at Tess.

Tess gave him a gimlet stare, the one she usually reserved for assholes like Rodriguez. She'd been looking forward to a shower, maybe even a nice long bath, but considering the sullen, sharp-eyed stranger drinking on her couch, that wasn't going to happen. So she grabbed the banister and made a lot of noise going up the stairs. She washed up as best she could while her mother's laughter rose above the music. Ever the watchdog, she waited for danger sounds—broken glass, raised voices, footsteps on the stairs.

Tess hated that her mother could laugh so easily when trouble was all around her. On the kitchen table lay a pile of unpaid medical bills from when her mother had fallen on the concrete sidewalk last winter trying to make it home from a bar. Six stitches, ten months of payments, and her mother down there spending the last of her alimony on vodka.

Tess wondered if this guy would use a condom, and then wondered why she even gave a damn.

She slipped into her bedroom and shot the bolt. She'd been working twelve-hour days trying to prove herself to the contractor who'd chosen her over the Mexican, Ecuadoran, and Guatemalan day workers shivering behind Target, figuring, as he'd told her, that boobs didn't matter as much having your own tool belt and speaking plain English. She figured she'd be asleep by the time her head hit the pillow.

She woke up to the sound of shattering wood and a hand compressing her mouth and nose.

"Tess?"

Tess started in the moonlight. She blinked at the sight of Riley crouched beside her, her face tense and pale. Something prickled on her hands, and she lifted them up to find them sticky with pine needles. She breathed in the resinous scent, sharp in her nose, overwhelming the memory stench of cheap booze and onions and something fermenting, old beer or cabbage. She told herself she was sitting on the ground with Bud's bears casting shadows all around her. She was here, in Camp Kwenback, safe.

And there was Riley, staring at her, waiting for the story Tess wasn't supposed to tell.

Tess said, "My mother brought him home from some dive bar. He'd bought them a fifth of vodka to share."

Not a fucking word and this will go easy.

Tess had kept a bat lodged between the bed and the wall—she'd put it there after their house had been robbed the prior year. While he pressed against her mouth with one hand and fumbled with his belt with the other, she stretched her arm out in an attempt to grab it. The head of the bat slipped against her fingertips and knocked against the bedpost. That got his attention. With a grunt he lifted his hand from her mouth, grabbed the bat, and threw it to the other side of the room. Then he cracked his knuckles against her skull.

She saw stars, bright stars before her eyes, and not the glow in the dark ones she and her father had stuck on the ceiling when she was eight years old.

Riley whispered, "Where was your mother?"

"Passed out on the downstairs couch with her hand around the neck of a bottle."

Tess couldn't move for a while after he'd hit her, blinking until she made out the cold, blue light of the streetlamp shining through her bedroom window. She could hear the clink and clatter of his studded belt as he tossed it to the floor, the whirr as he unzipped his fly. A metallic taste slid down her throat. Later she'd find out it was blood from where she'd cut the inside of her cheek. The thought kept passing through her mind—*I have to stay conscious*—even as he shoved her T-shirt up, mauled her breasts, then flipped her over.

But she should have fought harder, even if her only weapon was her fingernails. She should have struggled until he'd left her bloody and half dead. She should have left scars on his face, dug her thumb into his eye and felt the jelly of it pop, instead of growing increasingly paralyzed by the thought that he might have a knife, that he might carve her into pieces, that he might kill her for kicks.

Later, in the hospital, they told her she had a concussion, a cracked rib, two black eyes, abrasions on her wrists, and in her vagina, and a slight tear in the rectal wall.

The sudden coolness she felt on her forearm was Riley's hand.

"After he took off"—Tess's teeth ached from the memory of biting through her bonds—"I drove myself to a hospital in Albany."

"But you called the police first, right?"

Her throat constricted again, and this time the tightness radiated up to her ears. During the trip to Albany, her whole body had begun to shake. She'd gulped air like there wasn't enough of it, though it flowed freezing through her open window as she did eighty on the highway. She'd nearly driven off the road in the pink light of dawn, so she'd pulled over so fast gravel popped up and pinged beneath the chassis. She'd laid her bruised forehead against the steering wheel as shock gave way to shame gave way to fury, in a mix that threatened to smother her.

She'd pulled out her phone, not really knowing what she was looking for. Looking for a friend, she supposed, as she scrolled through a contact list full of weed dealers and cannery potheads and contractors who'd take her on only for day work. Her fingers paused over the phone number of Camp Kwenback, hovered there as she thought of Bud and Mary, their welcoming faces, their smiles, their clean beds—and the thought of stumbling bloody into the lodge like some apocalyptic zombie, once again bringing dirty drama into their lives.

And then, suddenly, there was Rodriguez's name. Sometime in the past few years, maybe after a perp walk in plastic cuffs when he caught less than an ounce of weed on her or when he'd confiscated her phone during a raid on the Cannery, he'd added his number into her contact list, along with a note.

Someday, Hendrick, you're going to need this.

"I called Rodriguez," Tess confessed. "He came to the hospital."

She'd been wearing nothing but a hospital gown and the nurses had just finished violating her with the rape kit. She heard Rodriguez's voice outside the curtains. When he came in, she couldn't look into his face. He'd given her crap for so many years, warned her of what became of wayward juvies. She hadn't wanted to see the grim, self-satisfied *I-told-you-so*.

He pulled over a stool. He flipped open his notebook and started asking questions in a low, gruff voice that she couldn't read. She looked at him from under her lashes for some hint of accusation, or weary sarcasm, or the pity she dreaded most of all. He fixed his gaze on his pen as he wrote, so all she saw was the spot on the back of his head where his dark hair whorled. He forced her to corral her swirling thoughts, to think linearly, to remember details. *Think hard. This is important.* She remembered the crescent scar next to her rapist's eye, the chain-link tattoo around his neck, the split in the lobe of his left ear. Rodriguez read over everything, cold as a fish, like he was writing a speeding ticket. His coolness unnerved her and then made her furious. She taunted him with details, told him to write *that* down. He told her he'd only write that down if she wanted him to. He told her there'd be someone coming around soon for her to talk to.

She'd tensed when he stood up. The skin was tight around his eyes, but looking at those eyes was like falling into a pit. She told him to go fuck himself, because if he had reached for her or said a single kind word, they would have had to put her in a padded cell.

"If Officer Rodriguez knew," Riley murmured, "that means every cop in town must have known. Rodriguez was a junior officer back then."

Tess pressed a thumb against the upper inside corner of her eye socket, where the usual stabbing migraine had begun. "I don't know how he did it, but he kept it quiet. He promised me he'd distribute the report on a need-to-know basis."

"My grandparents never said a thing. Not a word, not a whisper, nothing."

Riley began to rock, pushing herself with her toes, burying her head on her knees. Tess wondered if she'd said too much, wondered if, when Riley raised her head, Tess would see the horror of the whole story reflected back at her.

Tess never wanted to see that horror in Sadie's eyes.

Riley asked, "Did Officer Rodriguez ever find him?"

Tess shook her head.

"But he's still looking, right?"

"The statute of limitations for rape has run out in this state."

"But there must have been security cameras at the bar—"

"The bastard probably slipped over the border before I was released from the hospital," she said. "Rodriguez made me talk to a sketch guy, kept coming back to talk to me, but the bastard just disappeared into the world."

"It's all making sense now. You leaving Pine Lake so abruptly, your mother going off the rails." Riley sucked in a quick breath. "Your mother must have blamed herself. She must have been devastated."

An ugly laugh lurched out of her. In the weeks after the rape, as she slept long nights and longer days in the cabin, letting Mary feed her blueberry pancakes, sitting next to Bud, smelling his pipe as he rocked by the fireplace, she had bathed in their warmth and ignored the rest of the world. Tess had assumed that her mother was helping with the investigation. Even on her worst benders, when her mother accused her of stealing her vodka, her money, her food stamps, her boyfriends, when her mother called her a fucking spoiled princess, a greedy Daddy's girl, or a lying whore, Tess had learned to let the words roll off her back. That was the bottle speaking, the devil on her mother's back. Like every other time, the liquor would wear off and Tess would find her mother weeping at the kitchen table, begging for forgiveness.

Tess said, "Do you know what my mother said when Rodriguez returned to the house to get an official statement? She told Rodriguez that I'd made the whole thing up." Tess ran her fingers through her bangs, not caring about the pine needles sticking to her palm. "She claimed I was trying to steal the house from under her by sending her to rehab. I believe her exact words were that I was a lying, greedy bitch."

"But…but you were beaten. Your bedroom door must have been broken into pieces."

"Never get between an addict and her booze."

Her mother didn't visit her at Camp Kwenback. Her mother didn't recant her statement. And as the weeks went by, Tess refused to go to follow-up appointments, medical or otherwise. *I'm fine. Really, I'm fine.* She stopped talking to Rodriguez. She felt as if she were burrowing into a very dark place, until the difference between the brightness of Camp Kwenback and the darkness of her mind became too much. That's when she left Bud and Mary. She told them she was going to her father's house in Minnesota, when really she was just *going.*

Riley said, "Everyone blamed you for leaving your mother."

"Of course they did. No"—Tess raised a hand to stop Riley from speaking—"don't say you're sorry. *I'm* not sorry."

"But—"

"It was a relief." Tess laid her head back and blinked at the stars. "In the end, it was for the best that my mother didn't help. I'm glad the bastard was never found."

Riley turned incredulous eyes on her. "Tess, he still needs

209

to be found. He needs to be convicted, thrown in jail, and marked as a sexual offender—"

"That's not so simple."

"But there's physical evidence—"

"There's evidence that I was knocked around and we had sex. If he has any kind of defense lawyer, he'll claim the sex was rough but consensual."

Riley seemed to have swallowed her tongue.

"I'm sorry to be the one to clue you in on the ugly side of the criminal justice system, Riley. I'm not exactly a lily-white defendant, some sweet creature who played softball at Pine Lake High. I've got a juvy record as long as my arm. And the only other witness—my mother—is an alcoholic who swore to a cop that I'd made the whole thing up to send her away to rehab. Do you think we could get a felony rape conviction from he-said-she-said?"

"But... that's what happened."

"Even if he were caught, he'd plead the charges down to some nth degree sexual assault misdemeanor. He'd get off with maybe eight months' time."

"But he'd have a record—"

"Which would likely be barred from other criminal cases. All that effort, useless."

Tess squeezed her eyes shut and remembered the months that followed, when she'd run away from everyone and everything she'd ever known. She'd hopped trains and slept in stations, her days a blur of motion, the start of the restlessness, the bad times. The pregnancy came as a shock, but at least it got her off those streets. And when Sadie was born and lying in her arms, she couldn't help but think, *Here's another victim.*

No. Tess's jaw tightened. Sadie would not be a victim.

Not then, and not now.

"So now you know." Tess squinted toward her car, debating, jonesing for a long, deep suck on a lit cigarette. "Now you understand why I can't tell Sadie I'm her mother."

Riley didn't say anything. A cloud passed over the moon, casting Riley's face in shadows, but not before Tess got a glimpse of it, stricken, but unconvinced.

"I had to cut all ties between us." Tess tried to loosen the tightness in her chest, her own body's lingering resistance to confession. "It was the only way to protect her from that bastard, just in case he was ever found."

"He's a rapist," Riley said. "He'd never have any connection to Sadie."

"Men get custody of their natural children all the time." Tess thought of her old Cannery Row neighbor, Mr. Winter. "Even wife-beating bastards can steal their kids away—"

"But not rapists."

Tess felt a smile twitch at the corner of her lips. She looked beyond the spiky tips of the pines, thinking how nice it must be to live in Riley's world.

"In thirty-one states in these United States of America," Tess said, "rapists can claim parental rights to their biological children."

The rest of the story tumbled out of her in pieces. After she'd given Sadie up, she'd run. She tried the runaway circuit for a while, but her heart kept stretching back to the daughter she'd left behind. She couldn't bear wondering if the rapist had been caught, if he'd somehow found out about Sadie, if he'd gone to court to challenge the dismissal of his parental rights. Tess knew the name of the family who'd taken Sadie in, she knew the state they lived in, she knew she needed money to track Sadie. So she swallowed her pride and did something she'd sworn never to do—she showed up at her father's house in Minnesota.

There she recuperated, worked odd jobs, collected enough cash to get herself a car. There she suffered her step-mother's wary eye and her father's guilt for as long as she needed to save the five grand to pay for the course to get a commercial driver's license. The moment she found a company that'd hire a woman driver, she lit out, went as far away as she could from anyone she knew.

That's when her home became the cab of whatever rig she was driving. That's when the most permanent thing in her life was a drop-box in Bismarck.

The bastard would never find her this way.

And he'd never find out about Sadie.

Tess started at the feel of Riley's hand on her arm. Riley had edged close enough that their hips were bumping. Riley looked off to some dark distance, but Tess could see a gleam of tears in her eyes, and her jaw working like she was trying to find the right words.

"I get it now," Riley finally said. "I understand why this has been so difficult. Why you feel you can't reveal yourself to Sadie."

Tess let out a breath that she hadn't known she'd been

holding. She let it out and felt her spine bend as she pressed her forehead to her knees.

"But, Tess, there's still one thing I can't wrap my head around."

Later Tess realized she should have seen this coming. The question struck her so hard she felt jackknifed.

"After all that happened," Riley asked, "how could you love his child?"

Chapter Nineteen

S adie had a plan.

She wandered through the aisles of the grocery store, picking up boxes of granola bars and putting them back, trailing her fingers along cartons of individual serving portions of vanilla pudding, feeling the weight of her basket shift on her forearm as two Granny Smith apples rolled around inside.

Last night, staring at the ceiling in her room, that plan had finally come together. She would get up early, dress, and fill her backpack tight. She would wait until she heard Riley leave through the sliding back doors to go bird-watching in the woods. Sadie would sneak into the barn, take the bicycle, and pedal into town. When Sadie didn't come down for breakfast, Riley would assume she was sleeping in. And while ignorant Riley was taking care of things at the lodge— maybe even calling the cops to come on over and pick up the runaway—well, that runaway would be double-checking the train schedule at the station, shopping for snacks, getting some cash using Nana's ATM card, and slipping onto the 10:30 a.m. train to Manhattan.

Now she frowned at a bottle of mayonnaise, wondering why she was weighing it in her hand. She didn't feel guilty about skipping out of Camp Kwenback without saying good-bye. No, she didn't feel guilty about stealing the bike, either, because she intended to leave it leaning against the big oak in front of the library, where Riley would eventually find it when she realized Sadie was gone for good.

Riley had been nice to her for a while, Sadie granted her that. Good to her in the way someone was good to a stray cat. Best to feed it for a little while and then hope it'll wander away to find a permanent home.

Preferably in Ohio.

Now she found herself staring at a bottle of Tabasco sauce, wondering why she'd pulled that off the shelf. No one seemed to be paying her any mind, but she felt like everyone's eyes were upon her nonetheless. A lone young girl with a too-heavy backpack carrying a basket full of mayonnaise, barbeque sauce, and black olives couldn't help but be suspicious. She didn't even like olives.

Riley liked olives.

Her throat went dry, like it did sometimes when she was coming down with a cold. A prickling started at the back of her eyes. What was she thinking, anyway, running around in this goose chase, staying here in this hick town for so long? She didn't even like this little grocery store with its green cardboard bins of mountain berries and precious little mason jars of local honey with the honeycombs still in them. She couldn't stand all these happy, shiny folks wandering through in flip-flops and terrycloth cover-ups. That library with its showy green lawn was so tiny that, if she hung around here, she'd read through every book within the year, if the clanging bells of the church across the street didn't drive her crazy first. The place was as fake as Disney World, right down to the stupid hipsters at Ricky's Roast and the fat tourists at the ice cream store and the bearded hikers digging into lunch at Josey's. And without Izzy, what fun would she have dipping her toes into the water of Bay Roberts or sitting in the great room at Camp Kwenback choking on the smoke of a hearth fire while it rained?

Sadie clattered the bottle of olives back on the shelf. Nope, it was the 10:30 a.m. train back to Nana's house for her, just as she'd planned last night. She would live there on her own, whether her aunt liked it or not. She'd show Aunt Vi that she could handle money, find a job at a restaurant, she figured, or a pizza place, someplace that would feed her as well as pay her. Her aunt would be a pushover, signing any forms that would release her from any responsibility for her sister's adopted child. And then Sadie would have all the proof she needed to file with the court for youthful emancipation.

Emancipation. She rolled the word around in her mouth and tried to ignore that this was the part of the plan that had cracks. You had to be sixteen to go before the courts to ask for emancipation, a detail that kept rising out of the corners of her mind. And there was always the possibility that she'd arrive home to find a *For Sale* sign pitched in the little front yard of Nana's house. Her aunt would probably want to sell the old house so she could use the money to help pay for the St. Regis nursing home.

And yet…there were easier ways to be emancipated that didn't involve depending on the stupid law. There were other trains she could catch. She knew no one would give a damn if she just hopped the one that came first and set off for places unknown. Maybe it was better to leave the disaster of this broken life behind and then go make another of her own. The train that kept rumbling through her mind was the freight train that used the tracks just south of town, a freight train that, according to that Hendrick woman, headed to all kinds of points west.

She reached for another jar as someone shuffled around the aisle. Sadie looked at the jar with great interest, even though she didn't know what she was holding. The jar felt cold. It was full of ghostly white vegetables floating in water or oil or something. She couldn't read the label through the blurring of her vision.

A rubber sole squeaked against linoleum in a way that made her shoulders flinch, and then Sadie heard someone gasp. Sadie didn't bother to look up to see who'd stopped just a few feet away from her. She just figured she'd startled the woman who came around the corner and found a fourteen-year-old staring at a bottle of…Sadie twisted it…artichoke hearts. Whatever the heck they were.

Until she heard a tremendous crash.

Something wet sprayed her ankles. Sadie skittered back. She grasped the handles of her own basket, relieved that it wasn't hers that had fallen. A vinegary smell rose up from the puddle on the floor, a pool of liquid peppered with green glass and what looked like sliced pickles. Sadie looked up and saw an older woman standing frozen in place, pressing her hand against her mouth.

"Here," Sadie said, setting her basket on the floor away from the puddle. "Let me help you with that."

Sadie used the edge of her sandals to push a path through the broken glass so that she could reach the fallen basket. Nana hated loud noises; they always sent her into a panic, so maybe the shock of the spill had unnerved this woman, too, because she didn't move. Sadie crouched down at the woman's feet, tilted the basket level and examined what remained within—a few withered apples from the bargain bin, off-label cereal, a couple of cans of soup on sale, and a quart of tonic water.

Sadie thought, *Living on Social Security*. A voice on the loudspeaker announced, *Clean-up in aisle four*.

"You'll need a new box of cereal." Sadie rose up from her crouch and held out the basket. "It's got some pickle juice on it. But everything else looks okay."

An odor of neglect billowed from the armholes of the woman's faded cotton dress. The woman's hair was dyed that brassy shade of red that never looked real, and she was staring at Sadie with so much crazy that Sadie wondered if she had dementia like Nana. The older woman took a tentative step toward Sadie and inadvertently kicked a chunk of green glass into a spin across the floor.

Sadie reached out and seized the woman's arm, to stop her from slipping in the puddle. "Are you okay?"

The woman's gaze widened. She mumbled something under her breath, something weird like *you're not a ghost*.

Sadie said, "Ma'am?"

Sadie peered at her more closely and noticed—past the collapse of wrinkles and the bloodshot whites of the woman's eyes—that there was no dementia here, no fogging of the senses, just an alert, oddly troubled woman who couldn't seem to believe what she was seeing.

Odd. The woman had bright, gray-green irises.

Green eyes with a starburst of rusty-brown filaments.

The overhead lights seemed to dim. The floor felt slick beneath her sandals. Beyond this woman's green gaze, the world turned fuzzy and began to spin.

"Ladies." A guy with a mop rolled his bucket close. "If you'll just let me by, I'll clean this up—"

The woman blinked, startled. She yanked her arm out of Sadie's grip and stepped back. A word stuck in Sadie's throat—*wait*—but the older woman kept moving. The woman's wet sneakers squeaked as she swiveled and rounded the end of the aisle.

Sadie moved to follow.

"Whoa there." The young man held out an arm, keeping her in place. He pointed at the glass at her feet. "You'd best go around the other way."

"But that woman—"

"Don't you worry about that old crow, she's just fine," he said. "Old Mrs. Hendrick is always breaking something."

Chapter Twenty

The first time Tess opened a hatch atop a dirty water storage tank, the fumes hit her like a bomb blast. Her grip on the steel rails had been the only thing that prevented her from tumbling over the catwalk three stories to the ground. Since then she always wore a gas mask when checking the water levels, even though the mask was heavy and suffocating. It protected her from caustic fumes and toxic vapors, but wearing it, she saw little through the scratched Plexiglas, heard less, and smelled nothing.

Sometimes it felt like she'd spent her whole life muffled in that gas mask, filtering out the ugly.

Now, lying flat in the backseat of her car where she'd spent a restless night, she turned that gas mask over in her hands as the morning light sifted through the pines and winked through the bug-like lenses. Even through the closed window she heard the screech of the jays and the *chiva-chiva-chiva* call of some mouse bird Riley had once pointed out to her. The backseat smelled faintly of oil and old leather.

Though she lay still, her thoughts careened far and wide in new and dangerous directions.

A sudden knock on the window startled her. She arched her neck and saw a Camp Kwenback coffee mug, then beyond, a familiar face surrounded by a cloud of red hair.

"Rise and shine, pumpkin." Riley raised the cup. "It's a new day."

Tess made a snort of a sound, more out of habit than snark. She uncurled her legs and pushed herself up to a sitting position, raising her voice so Riley could hear her through the closed window. "I love the customer service around here."

"I aim to please." Riley stepped away from the door as Tess pushed it open. "That couldn't have been comfortable, sleeping there all night."

"I needed a womb."

Riley barked a sudden laugh. "That's not what I expected to hear."

"I'm used to sleeping in the cab of my truck." Tess unfolded herself and then stretched her arms above her head to remove the kinks. "My cab is a lot more comfortable than the backseat of this car, but at least it had that familiar, pod-like feel."

Riley held out the mug. "After I left my husband and moved in here, I slept a few nights in the tree house by the beaver dam." She gestured to some far point beyond the woods. "I was eaten to death by mosquitos, but I also located the hiding place of an eastern screech owl."

"Priorities."

"It was a reminder of what I most love to do."

Tess raised the cup. "Industrial strength?"

"Brewed just for you, black, no sugar. Come inside and have breakfast with me."

Tess hesitated. She glanced past Riley toward the lodge, feeling a deep-body prickly sensation. After last night's confession, Tess wasn't sure how she felt about laying eyes on the object of that confession, sitting on a café chair swinging her legs.

"Sadie's not in the lodge." Riley shrugged. "She took the bike into town about half an hour ago. I saw her leave."

Tess buried her face in the cup so her relief wouldn't show. "So," she said, swallowing the hot brew, "what's on the menu?"

"Blueberry pancakes."

Riley's smile crinkled all the way to her eyes, like Mary's used to, as crazy as that was. Tess's first urge, like always, was to hide any expression of gratitude. Instead she stopped herself, paused, and then mumbled a half-volume thanks.

"You're welcome." With a wink, Riley swiveled and headed toward the lodge.

Tess fell into pace beside her, thinking it was so much easier to hold people at arm's length and pretend that little things like blueberry pancakes in the Camp Kwenback kitchen didn't matter. The sharing of her darkest secret had shifted her friendship with Riley in new and still uncertain ways. The path beneath her feet was rutted and uneven, and Tess told herself that's why she felt like she hadn't quite found her balance.

"So," Riley said, kicking up some gravel as she walked, "did you give any thought to what's next?"

"Finish the mini-golf?" Tess gripped the cup with two hands, less to prevent spilling than as a crutch. "Go back to my job hauling fracking wastewater across North Dakota?"

Riley didn't bite. Tess pulled a face. Wise-ass remarks didn't do any good deflecting curiosity if the recipient didn't react.

"Yesterday I was convinced I'd go back," Tess heard herself saying, "but now I've got a problem. I've worked as a big-rig driver for so long that all the High Plains truckers know me. It's a career; it pays a decent wage. But it means I spend most of my nights sleeping in my cab. The closest thing I have to a home is temporary housing I rent during the downtimes. The most stable thing in my life is a drop-box in Bismarck."

"Do you love the job?"

Tess thought about dragging twenty-foot hoses, climbing the spindly steel catwalks in a sweaty fireproof suit, the High Plains winds buffeting her truck as she blinked, bleary-eyed, down flat highways, shoveling out in sub-zero weather during a snowstorm.

She said, "Let's just say it keeps me in tats and jeans."

"Then quit."

"Just like that."

"It's incredible how it feels," Riley said, "to leave a job you don't love. I think it's the one decision I've made that I haven't once regretted."

"Starvation might be an issue."

"Yeah, I've pretty much been living on a large helping of guilt with a side of failed expectations. That's what my mother has been serving up anyway."

"Hey, a silver lining—that's one of the few family dysfunctions I managed to avoid."

"You want it? You know, just to complete your set?"

Tess laughed, and she heard Riley laughing, too, and the combination was a singular, striking harmony.

Tess found herself blinking. "The thing is," she said, clearing her throat, "it's not a good time to be a jobless high school graduate these days. And I'd need a job if I were to—"

The words stuck in her throat. She couldn't believe what she was about to say. She felt like she'd tiptoed into a minefield she'd planted for herself.

Riley's voice was as light as air. "You're pretty good with your hands, Tess. I suspect there's always work for someone who can use a hammer and a saw."

Tess blurted, "Did you know I used to raise chickens?"

"Get out."

"My best broody hen was a Golden Laced Wyandotte. She'd do a staggered hatch of six eggs at a time and not lose a single one of them." She had no idea why she was telling Riley all this. "The Buff Orpington was pretty good, too, a nice producer."

"I think I just experienced a seizure because I didn't understand any of that."

"I'm talking hen breeds. We preferred the Silkies. We'd have dozens of fresh eggs every day of the week. We sold the ones we didn't eat ourselves."

"You really did live on a farm in Kansas."

"I also had an organic garden covered in chicken wire to keep out the critters. In season I'd pick peas in the morning, shell them in the afternoon, steam them, and serve them to Callahan at night when he came home from the fields." Tess snorted a laugh. "Isn't that a pretty picture."

And it was, for a little while, idyllic and calm, except she always felt like it was somebody else's picture and she was just taking up space in the frame.

"I hate to break it to you," Riley said hesitantly, "but we're not in Kansas anymore. I'm not sure you could raise chickens for a living around here."

"No, no." Tess's sandals scuffed on the graveled path. "The point I'm trying to make is that domesticity was an experiment of mine. Eighteen months of matrimony ended when that farmhouse all but burned to the ground."

"I'm so sorry, Tess."

Tess swallowed a breath. She'd expected Riley to ask if she'd done it. She'd even gone tense, waiting for that verbal shiv between the ribs. After all, Riley was present in the crowd all those years ago when Tess, on a dare, set the insides of a metal garbage bin on fire. But Riley hadn't asked that question, and now the silence was like a ringing in her ears.

"I know it was my fault, any way you look at it." That night, she'd built up a head of fury that gave off more heat than the red tips of the cigarettes still smoldering when she'd fallen asleep on the couch. "Let's just say there's a good reason I don't smoke anymore."

"I'm glad of that, though I'm sorry—"

"Last night," Tess interrupted, not wanting to hear another murmur of sympathy, "after our talk, all I could think about was those months in Kansas. Settling down with Callahan should have been wonderful. And it was, for a while. But raised the way I was, Riley, growing up in Cannery Row with my mother...I'm just not so sure I can ever live any kind of normal domestic life."

"But," Riley said, mounting the stairs of the porch, "you spent the night in your car thinking about it, didn't you?"

Tess leaned against the stair railing, feeling like she was back in the hospital again, chewing over the same arguments. She remembered holding her wispy-haired baby girl, swaddling her in soft cotton blankets, telling the adoption counselor she'd changed her mind, she wanted to keep her daughter; there must be a way she could keep her. The adoption counselor asked her how she intended to support the child, where she'd live, how she'd work, and who would watch the baby while she worked, how she would pay for diapers, formula, clothes, a crib, toys...and Tess remembered tensing up as the questions came at her. Sadie must have felt it, too, because she'd started crying. Tess jiggled her, trying to get her to stop, and then the nurse marched in. The nurse looked at her and the counselor looked at her— flat eyes, knowing eyes, weary eyes—and Tess, exhausted, hormonal, shattered, did what she was expected to do. She handed Sadie into more experienced hands, knowing she could never be any kind of decent mother.

Tess took a deep breath, feeling the cool morning air right down to the bottom of her lungs. Maybe things could be different now. She felt different after last night's confession in the shadow of Bud's bears. She imagined she felt a little like the flatbed of her rig after a thirty-ton trailer had been lifted from her semi, the joints and axles rising light and groaning in blessed relief.

The sound of a car rumbling up over gravel drew their attention.

"Huh," Riley said, glancing at the approaching black-and-white. "It's awfully early for a police officer to be making a house call."

"It's never too early for Rodriguez to harass me. I wonder what this is about now." Tess's heart did a stuttered beat. "Didn't you say Sadie took the bike into town?"

"Yes." Riley looked at her. "So?"

"So no Sadie, and here's a cop coming up the drive."

Possibilities hit Tess like buckshot. In her mind she saw an SUV canted on the shoulder, blue smoke rising on the side of the road, a bicycle wheel in a ditch turning above a twisted frame.

"Mothers," Riley murmured, shaking her head. "They always think the worst."

"I'm not—" Tess cut herself off and then flushed as she dipped her knees a fraction to see into the backseat of the police car as Rodriguez turned into a parking spot. "She's not in the car."

"Of course she isn't. Rodriguez doesn't know anything about her. And Sadie is very good about following the rules of the road. Stop worrying, Tess." Riley raised her voice as Rodriguez exited the car, "Good morning, Officer."

"Morning, Riley."

"You're here awfully early," Riley said. "Should I be worried?"

"Contrary to popular belief, I'm not always the bearer of bad news." Rodriguez gave Tess an eye. "Occasionally I lead little old ladies across the street. Once in a while I actually save kittens."

"Just don't bring those kittens here." Riley gripped the binoculars on her chest. "They're the number one killer of birds, you know."

"I'll keep that in mind." Rodriguez turned his eyes on Tess. "I've got something to discuss with you."

That anvil-jawed face gave away nothing. Tess said, "Is something wrong with the precinct phone?"

"Some things are better discussed in person. Besides I wanted to catch you before you skipped town. You have a bad habit of doing that."

"Last time I checked, you weren't my parole officer." Tess leaned back and scraped her coffee cup on the porch rail. "Or have you just come by to confess your undying devotion?"

"Put away the shiv, Theresa. You'll want to hear this."

Riley put a steadying hand on Tess's arm. "Can I get you some coffee, Officer?"

"No, but I would like a moment alone with your smart-mouthed friend here, if you don't mind."

"Riley can stay." Tess slapped her hand over Riley's before Riley could mumble an excuse. "I want Riley to stay."

The embarrassment she'd expected didn't rise like she thought it would. She eased her death grip on Riley's fingers but she did not let her go. She would think about why later. New adrenaline flooded her veins because, as far as she knew, there was only one piece of unfinished business between her and Rodriguez.

"All right then," Rodriguez said. "If you're sure."

Then Rodriguez did something that made Tess more nervous than seeing him break down a door at the Cannery. Rodriguez *hesitated*. He adjusted the waistband of his regulation blue pants. He sighed. Then he crossed his arms and gripped his biceps and took great interest in scraping the gravel under his shoes.

"After your recent visit to my precinct office," he began, as he lifted one foot onto the second stair, "I decided to dig into things."

"Things."

"I don't like cold cases. They clog up the system. The files grow, take up too much space."

Tess's jaw tightened. "Didn't I tell you to back off?"

"At first I just researched the statutory limits to be sure I wasn't mistaken that they'd passed."

"Come on, Rodriguez. You have that rulebook memorized right down to the footnotes."

"My instinct was right. It turns out there was some legislation at the state level about that statutory limit issue. Just a few years ago."

"So you're you a lawyer now?"

Riley squeezed her arm, and Tess tried to restrain herself.

"The world changes," he said. "Technology advances, and the laws change with it. Now there's a DNA exception to the statutory limits."

Her older, wiser self, conscious of Riley standing next to her, tried to keep her mouth shut, but there was no restraining the mouthy fifteen-year-old within her. "You know, Rodriguez, you could have just asked me on a date, and we could clear up all this sexual tension."

"The new law allows us to test old evidence. The new tests give better, more accurate results. The combination of the law and technology activated a whole slew of cold cases—"

"I love it when you talk dirty."

"Do you ever take anything seriously, Tess?"

The use of her name stunned her. She didn't like the way he spoke it, didn't like the way it sounded falling off his lips. That was her new name, that was her new life. Rodriguez was her old life. And in her new life, there was only one thing— one young girl—who she cared about enough to take seriously.

Riley removed her hand from Tess's arm and laid it firmly on her back.

Well, Tess thought, maybe two.

"Victims have rights, too," Tess said, the stair creaking beneath her as she shifted her weight. "You told me that once."

"You gave me permission to investigate this case a long time ago."

"When I was half conscious in a hospital bed. There's no statutory limit on that kind of permission?"

"Victims of sexual assault"—he paused, his gaze flickering to Riley, checking her face for acknowledgment—"often don't pursue prosecution out of some misguided sense of guilt or shame—"

"Now you're a shrink."

"Some cases I wouldn't pursue. I'd let them go cold and keep them in a box in the basement." That anvil jaw shifted. "But I knew Theresa Hendrick when my badge was still shiny. Theresa's a tough young woman who has lived a tough life. She is strong enough to handle this."

"You don't know anything about me, Rodriguez."

The words came out of her like fire but they were a lie. She knew it, and worse, he knew it. This cop knew more about her than her own classmates at Pine Lake. He'd arrested her when she'd stolen tampons from Ray's. He'd brought her back home to the cluttered house and met her drunken mother, who'd answered the door braless in a tank top, clutching a can of some off-label beer. He'd caught her half naked with a boyfriend in the Cannery. He'd sat next to her hospital bed where she'd lain, bruised and battered, describing the man who raped her.

Maybe that's why she was always pushing him away.

He said, "Once I realized the statutory limits could be circumvented, I went back to the evidence files to see if any further investigation was even possible." A muscle twitched in his cheek. "It turns out we still have your old rape kit."

Tess flinched. She remembered the sore swabbing, the plastic zip of her clothing into marked forensic bags, including her favorite cotton-soft sleep shirt, stained with blood and semen.

"The chances of any retrievable DNA from a fifteen-year-old kit were low," he continued, "but so was the chance of Theresa Hendrick showing up in Pine Lake so many years after the crime."

Her heart tripped. "What, a girl can't come home and see her friends?"

"C'mon, Hendrick, I know how impossible it is for you to ask for real help. Why the hell else are you here, lying low in Camp Kwenback, visiting me under false pretenses in the precinct, other than to help in the prosecution?"

Sadie. Tess closed her eyes, willing away the first stab of a rising migraine. Rodriguez had jumped to conclusions. She couldn't challenge those conclusions because she couldn't tell Rodriguez about Sadie.

"So I did," he continued, "what I had to do. I sent the rape kit to an upstate crime lab to be retested. I called in an old favor and appropriated special funds in order to have it expedited."

"Don't you have any hot city hall embezzling crimes to investigate? Bar fights to prosecute? Stoners to rout out of the Cannery?"

"Some cases stick in a cop's mind." His nostrils flared as he flattened a hand on his bent knee. "Some cases make a cop wonder if he couldn't have done something earlier to prevent them from ever happening."

She felt a strange vibration and realized she was shaking. She stared at the trembling palms of her hands, thinking about one night when he'd dragged her home. She remembered his face when her drunk of a mother opened the door. She remembered him holding her back by the arm as she tried to shoot into the house and seek safety in her upstairs room. She remembered him several days later, pulling up to her on the street, talking to her momentarily sober mother, lingering on the porch, finally handing her his card.

You're going to need this someday.

She'd torn it into pieces, put the pieces in an ashtray, and set them on fire.

"They found DNA, Tess," he said. "It's not perfect, but it's good enough to run through a criminal database."

Her blood left her extremities, her body went cold, and she felt the pinprick of numbness in her fingers and toes.

"This morning," he added, "we got a hit."

Tess took a step back and stumbled up the porch. She didn't want to hear this. She resisted the childish, irresistible urge to slap her hands over her ears, to strike them and strike them and strike them so she wouldn't hear the name of her rapist. And once again she was in her childhood bedroom with the sound of the bolt giving as he broke open the door, and there he was looming over her, wiping his mouth with the back of his hand.

Tess's voice shook as she backed up against the door. "I told you not to do this."

"We've got him, Tess." Rodriguez's brow rippled. "He's in jail on another assault charge, but he's up for parole in a few months."

A *few months*. She looked wildly at Riley's stricken face, willing Riley to make him stop.

"We can prevent him from doing this to any other woman," Rodriguez persisted, "when you press charges, face him in court, and tell the truth."

Everybody was so convinced that truth was always a good thing—but it was a lie that saved Sadie. Sadie grew up in a bubble of happiness with a loving family, having all the clothes and food and protection that she needed as she had grown into the young woman who'd shown up at Camp Kwenback—because Tess gave her up to let Sadie live with a lie that wasn't born out of an act of bloody violence.

She said, "I'm leaving."

Rodriguez lifted his foot off the last stair and stood, legs splayed, blocking her path down the stairs. "You ran once. That didn't solve anything."

"You can't force me to testify."

"You'll let a rapist go free?" He skewered her with an eye. "You'll let him go free to do this to another woman?"

"You always were a bastard, Rodriguez—"

"You won't disappoint me." He shook his head, convinced. "Not in this."

She couldn't seem to breathe. Rodriguez wouldn't move, and he was so big, looming over her. Riley gripped her arm from behind, and Tess tried to shake it off, but Riley only shook her harder.

"Tess," Riley said, yanking. *"Tess."*

Tess whirled on her, ready to shout, but Riley wasn't looking at her. Riley was staring down the gravel road. Tess's heart skittered as she turned around and saw Sadie coming up the road, leaning over the handlebars of her bike, pumping hard, the gravel grinding under the rubber of her wheels.

By instinct Tess pressed down on the stair beneath her right foot like she was pressing down on the brake. By instinct her right hand sought the ball of the gear shift, grasping, her thoughts stuttering ahead to the coordination needed to downshift to slow all sixty-two thousand tons of her eighteen-wheeler down. Her fellow big-rig drivers had warned her about this all the time. You work in this business long enough, they said, you'll be caught up, you'll feel a tremendous hit. Sometimes Tess felt that her whole life she'd spent roaring seventy miles an hour down a snow-dusted road with her headlights illuminating only the next one hundred yards or so—tense for those white lights to flash on something—a hitchhiker, a herd of elk, a ghost—too late for her to downshift, too late for her to stop.

Because Tess knew by the furious way Sadie skidded to a stop at the bottom of the porch, by the way she ignored the police officer; by the way she planted her feet on the ground and eyeballed them.

Sadie *knew.*

Chapter Twenty-One

W hy didn't you tell me?"
Sadie crossed her arms and ignored the police officer. Riley had probably called the cop to take her away, like some collarless dog caught pooping in the front yard. But Sadie didn't care about police officers or foster care or any of that right now. She was too focused on ignoring the blonde standing next to Riley. She was too focused on watching Riley, who'd stilled like a rabbit Sadie had once startled while walking in the woods.

Riley said, "I don't know what you're talking about."

"You know what I'm talking about." Sadie tried to shift her gaze to the woman in black but she just couldn't. It was like there was a doorstop on her eyeballs, preventing them from turning in that direction. "You both know what I'm talking about. You and *her*."

Riley took a step down the stairs. "Sadie, why don't you come inside—"

"You know where I just came from?" Sadie settled her

weight on the far back of the bicycle seat. "I was doing a little shopping, thinking how very *nice* you've been to me these past weeks, how much I was going to miss being someplace where someone gave a damn about me. Then guess who I bumped into?"

Riley poised on the bottom stair, stricken, the Tess-woman pacing beyond her.

"Old Mrs. *Hendrick*, that's who." Sadie couldn't seem to stop bobbing her head. It was like that plastic Elmo figure that her mother used to keep on the dash of the car. "Old Mrs. Hendrick stared at me with those buggy green eyes, dropping a jar of pickles like she'd just seen a ghost."

The blonde made a quiet, strangled sound while Riley stared at Sadie with those troubled eyes. And Sadie worked it all out quickly, adding that choking noise to all the other evidence until she couldn't deny that every clue led to what she'd been too afraid to believe.

Tess Hendrick really was her birth mother.

Her mind pivoted away from that truth, a one-hundred-and-eighty-degree screaming mental swivel. No way on earth was that nosy, tatted oil-trucker her mother. That prickly jerk had been living in the same inn with her for all this time, doing her best to push her away. Sadie wished she was young enough to pretend she didn't see it, pretend she didn't know what she now knew, wished the trucker would stop pacing and say something.

Then the cop, who'd been standing there like a stone, said, "Someone tell me what's going on—"

"It's none of your business." Sadie didn't have any trouble glaring at the cop, though a shiver of prickles spread across the back of her neck. An odd expression passed across his face, a quiver of what looked like confusion. Maybe he'd seen her around town, marked her as a runaway already. She didn't care. He was a stranger, and he had nothing to do with this. He could just butt the heck out.

Then she focused on Riley, because Riley had known, Riley should have told her, Riley she'd trusted.

"You lied to me." Her mouth felt hot.

Riley opened her mouth to say something but nothing came out.

"I thought I could trust you." Sadie gripped the handlebars, feeling an urge to back away and then pedal out of here. "You knew all this time, and you didn't tell me anything."

"I didn't know until last night." Riley shared a look with the blonde, now sinking into a crouch at the top of the stairs. "I would have told you if I could. But this isn't my secret to tell."

"Yeah, I get it. You kept to the girl code." Sadie lifted her fingers in air quotes. "You two were just protecting each other. Pine Lake High, rah, rah, rah."

She hated that Riley had such a quick excuse, such a reasonable one, too, because Sadie remembered seeing the two of them pacing around the bears by the mini-golf in the middle of the night. She didn't want to believe Riley didn't know until just then. She didn't want to believe that Tess could have kept this secret so long. Sadie looked down at her knuckles, turning white where they crushed the pink rubber of the bike's handles.

She wished there were just one person in the whole, wide world she could really, truly trust.

"Tess," Riley said, over her shoulder, "why don't you walk down to the boathouse? You two can have a little privacy there."

"Who says I even want to talk to her?" Sadie felt panic rise within her. "Who says I'm hanging around to listen to whatever she's got to say to me now, when all she's wanted to do all this time is get rid of me?"

She'd envisioned this so differently. She'd imagined calling her birth mother first, maybe hearing the sound of a dog barking in the background, the sound of food sizzling on a skillet, the rumble of a husband's curious voice. She imagined the surprised pause, the voice that held a catch of tears, a confession that she'd always known this day would come. Sadie imagined a sudden invitation to visit, an offer of a weekend to meet the extended family, a plane ticket paid and forwarded through the mail. She imagined a meeting in a bright, white airport where she'd dress right, in nice shoes and a swirling dress with her hair pulled back. In her mind, when she saw her birth mother—a soft woman with sad eyes and a trembling lip, because she was sure she'd recognize her immediately in the crowd, as if a light shone only on her— she'd open her arms and start running.

Sadie heard the creaking of the floorboards as the blonde jerked up, swiveled, and walked into the inn, and Sadie could only guess that she kept walking through to the sliding back door and then down to the boathouse by the lake.

Sadie stared at the door, breathing hard. Riley placed her

hand on her shoulder. Sadie jerked, trying to knock it off, but Riley just held on all the tighter.

"Remember in the attic," Riley said, "when I told you my story?"

Sadie remembered fragments of that afternoon, the dust motes swirling in the light coming through the window, the smell of pine resin, the musty book full of old photos, and most of all, the pain in Riley's voice as she talked about her birth mother's rejection.

"Even in the best of situations," Riley said, "a conversation like this is going to be difficult. Maybe you should put it off until you're feeling strong and clear-headed—"

"Why? Am I not going to like what she's going to say?"

Sadie tripped into Riley's melted-chocolate eyes in the hope of seeing some real assurance; some guarantee that Tess had a good reason for skulking around Camp Kwenback without saying a word. But Sadie knew how to read people. She understood what it meant when someone stared at you while a muscle flickered in the corner of their eye and the edges of their smile quivered. For all of Riley's mustered confidence, her hand trembled upon Sadie's shoulder.

"You've had a shock, Sadie," Riley said. "You can choose to wait."

She heaved in breath after breath, and it wasn't because she'd raced back from town. She knew she didn't have any real choice. Yeah, she could back up and turn the bike down the path and race away, but that cop was watching this whole scene like he was taking notes to be tested on it later. It wasn't likely she'd make it to the train station to catch the 10:30 a.m. to Manhattan without him driving up, lights twirling, to seize her for the usual do-gooder interrogation.

"I'm not waiting." She swung her leg off the bike. "This is what I came all the way up here for."

She left the bike in Riley's care as she turned toward the beaten path around the side of the lodge. She walked as if both her legs had fallen asleep, stumbling, weaving a path toward the boathouse she could just see through the stand of birch trees. One part of her hoped the blonde wouldn't be there. She hoped that the coward had scrambled up to her room to pack rather than face her after so much time. If that were the case, then Sadie could shrug it off like it didn't matter that her birth mother had rejected her not once, but twice. At least she could avoid this confrontation that her birth mother didn't want anything to do with anyway. She could head back to Queens with Plan D in her mind and never give her trust to a stranger so easily again.

Her heart did a little double trip when she squinted and caught sight of the figure in black pacing on the boards.

Suddenly every step was a strain. When Sadie finally reached the shade of the boathouse, she avoided the blonde's eyes. A breeze rustled the trees, sweeping through the open area, bringing the odor of muddy banks, a vague smell of fish. Two paint-chipped boats were roped in two bays and knocked up against the pilings. She walked toward the closest bay where she leaned against one of the posts.

Birds shouldn't be singing. The water shouldn't be gurgling against the banks. The sun felt warm on her hair, and it all just made her mad.

The blonde wandered into the shadow of the next bay, her arms crossed, her gaze on her own toes like she was checking her nail polish. "Did she say anything to you? My mother? At the grocery store?"

"Doesn't matter what your mother said," Sadie said. "I want to hear everything from you."

Already the blonde was trying to get Sadie to make this easy, to breeze over the details she might already know.

"Everybody's telling me she's sober now." Tess scraped her flip-flop against the boards. "I haven't seen her so I don't believe it. She was never sober when I lived here."

Sadie remembered the vague scent of neglect that clung to Mrs. Hendrick, but she hadn't smelled any alcohol on her. If this woman was looking for sympathy, Sadie would rather give it to the devil.

"So," Tess said, "you're probably wondering why I wrapped you as a baby in a Camp Kwenback towel."

Sadie bumped against the post. She had a hundred million questions, but that particular one she hadn't intended to ask—at least not right away.

"That's what led you to Pine Lake, right?" Tess asked. "The strange thing is, that's exactly what I didn't want to happen."

Sadie felt splinters tug on her T-shirt as she sank against the post like she'd been hit right in the chest with a dodge ball. So there it was, an admission that her birth mother hadn't ever wanted Sadie to find her at all.

As if Sadie needed more proof.

"I ran away from Pine Lake twice when I was younger

than you." The woman gripped her arms hard. "The first time I didn't know where I was going. I just headed out through these woods. I stumbled upon this place by mistake when I saw the light through the back windows. I crept up and peered through and saw Bud sitting by the fire reading the paper. I saw Mary with her feet up on the table, talking on the phone. Bud and Mary—Riley's grandparents—they took me in, no pesky questions. Just like Riley did for you."

Sadie tightened her jaw because that sounded like her own story. She'd trudged blindly through these woods, too, on the day she'd hopped off the train. She remembered being worried she'd never find her way out of the woods until she saw the line of broken-down cabins, and beyond, the spill of golden light out of the lodge and a redhead sweeping the back porch with a real broom.

"Riley's grandparents let me sit around by the fire and do nothing." Tess squinted down at her feet. "Mary served me hot chocolate and corn chowder and gingersnap cookies until I couldn't eat any more. The best thing about that visit is that, for weeks, I didn't have to clean floors or go grocery shopping or do anything but come home from school, do my homework, and run wild in the woods. They even made my bed." Tess took great interest in rubbing one flip-flop against the other. "I felt like a kid instead of the nursemaid I'd become. Riley tells me you know how that feels, too."

Sadie's shoulders tightened. So Riley had told Tess about Nana, too. Well, Riley sure had been free and loose with Sadie's secrets, as free and loose with them as she'd been tight-lipped about Tess's.

Her anger focused to a pinpoint that threatened to burn a hole in the floorboards at her feet. "If you liked Riley's grandparents so much," she retorted, "why did you go steal a towel from them?"

"That towel wasn't the first thing I'd filched without paying." The Tess-woman shrugged. "I didn't have a lot of sense back then. And though I didn't know it at the time, when I stole that towel, I was pregnant with you."

Sadie's gaze wandered to Tess's belly. She couldn't envision anything growing under that wall of muscle. And she didn't feel any sort of umbilical cord bond tugging at her, like she'd always expected to feel, even as she hated herself for searching for it.

"Rodriguez, the cop you just got all mouthy with," Tess said, still nattering on about nothing, "he kept coming by Camp Kwenback where I'd holed up. He made all the guests nervous, and I didn't like doing that to Bud and Mary. So I left Pine Lake and took that towel with me." The blonde's voice hitched in a funny way. "I stole that towel, Sadie, because I needed to remember that there were two people in the world who gave a sh"—she paused, her jaw working— "who *cared* about me. And they weren't even my biological parents. I bet you know how that feels, too."

"You don't get to ask about that." Sadie kicked a leaf off the edge of the bay into the water. "You don't get to talk about my parents."

Sadie's mind suddenly flashed to when she'd sat on the pink carpet of her bedroom with her back propped up against her bed, wearing her penguin pajamas, and her mom sat close beside her with the book *Goodnight Moon* open on her lap, reading in her singsongy voice only to stop at every page and ask Sadie, "Where's the mouse now?"

Where's the mouse now?

"Ah." Tess's voice was low, soft. "So it worked."

"*What* worked?"

"The towel." The blonde dropped her arms to her sides. "I wrapped you in it hoping your adoptive parents would be as good to you as Bud and Mary had been to me."

Sadie pushed away from the pillar and shot down the length of the bay as if she could walk away from that confession, too soft to be believable, too strange to consider. It echoed in her ears as she toed off her canvas sneakers and laid them on the warm boards. She plunked down, peeled off her socks, and tucked them into her shoes. Then she ignored the splinters that pierced the skin behind her knees as she dropped her legs over the edge.

She focused on the feel of the cool water flowing past her skin as she moved her legs to create eddies of current, trying to slow the rushing of her thoughts and to lower the burn of her anger. Her toes were ghostly blobs, barely visible from the surface. Here, in the narrow end of the pond, the water was the color of the cream soda Nana loved, always served with her lunchtime grilled cheese.

Sadie heard the Tess-woman moving around, though she pretended to ignore her. On the opposite bay, the blonde followed her cue, kicking her flip-flops aside, yanking up the ends of her skinny jeans, struggling to roll them above her knees. The woman made no noise as she dipped her feet in the water. The woman made ripples that Sadie jerked her feet out of the water to avoid.

Sadie's mind screamed, *She is not my mother*, while another part of her brain noticed things she didn't want to see. Like how small-boned Tess was—if you could see beyond the muscles and the disappointingly small boobs. Sadie figured that probably meant she was stuck with these tiny bumps that hardly merited a sports bra. She forced herself not to look for more than a couple of seconds at a time because, whenever she did hazard a glance, she saw something else they had in common—small feet, knobby knees, a sprinkle of dark moles on the skin of her lower legs.

Then another so-called fact bubbled to her consciousness. "I bet you weren't even a teenager when I was born."

A pause. "Is that what your mother told you?"

"She said you were young. Being a teenager is young."

"I was young, barely into my twenties when—"

"She said you just wanted a better life for me than you could give me. But someone in her twenties is old enough to work. So that was another lie, wasn't it? My own mother, lying to me."

"She probably felt it was easier than the truth."

"What's the truth? That you gave me up because I wasn't convenient?"

"The truth is more complicated."

"Try me."

Tess turned her face away and squinted down the narrow end of the lake. "I placed you for adoption," she said, "because I was convinced that I'd turn out to be as bad a mother to you as my own mother had been to me."

Sadie's bullshit meter tweaked into the red zone. "I haven't seen you even drink a single glass of wine with Riley, and I've seen you two hanging around outside by the picnic table like BFFs. You're seriously telling me you gave me up because you thought you'd be a drunk like your own mom?"

"Mothers cast long shadows, Sadie."

Sadie flinched at the use of her name. "Well, you were right about one thing. You are a bad mother."

The floorboards of the other bay creaked as the woman shifted her weight.

Sadie ventured, "You've been following me all these years, haven't you?"

"I have."

"How did you know I'd end up here, right now?"

"Call it an educated guess."

"Based on what? I didn't know I was coming here myself until Nana took a long walk through traffic, like, months ago."

"You're not always careful what you say online."

Sadie's heart did a thudding skip. She remembered her aunt's warning when Aunt Vi gave her a Christmas gift of a used computer. Sadie remembered the lecture about being safe on the Internet, not talking to strangers, not arranging meet-ups with people she didn't know, not telling anyone where she really lived. At the time it was a lot of babble in her ears that she only half registered because of the excitement of connecting things and plugging the computer in. Aunt Vi wanted the computer so she could video-call to check on her, but Sadie had just been thrilled to be able to join the online party everyone else in her school was a part of.

Now she mentally ran through her list of friends on the forum for adoptees, realizing she didn't know even half of them. She always hit "confirm" whenever someone tried to friend her because who didn't want to have lots of friends?

Now she felt exposed, one-upped, like she was lying naked in the bright sun. "You've been watching me like a spider."

"It's lucky I did."

"Lucky?"

"Running away from home is a stupid thing to do. One wrong move and you could have found yourself shooting heroine between cargo cars in some Midwestern depot."

"Is that what you did when you were pregnant with me?"

"Not while I was pregnant."

A breeze riffled the leaves in the trees in the silence, and the blonde turned her face away.

"Well, maybe I'm smarter than you." Sadie slipped her fingers under her thighs, warming them between the boards and her skin. "It's wrong what you did. Creepers watch girls like that, you know. Pedophiles do that."

"Mothers do that."

"You're *not* my *mother*."

Her mother used to walk her to the school bus, hand her a lunchbox with homemade oatmeal raisin cookies, kiss her on the head, and then wave good-bye. Her mother used to blow cool air on her knee scrapes before slathering them with antibiotic lotion and stretching a superhero Band-Aid over them.

Then another thought came to her. "Did you know when my parents died in that accident?"

"Not right away." The Tess-woman plucked at a string on her jeans. "It was harder to keep track of you back then. I didn't find out until you'd already been settled with your nana."

"Would you have come running to claim me otherwise?"

"I knew you had a family. Aunts, uncles, cousins—"

"Oh, just admit it. You didn't want me."

"I saw you one Easter at church."

Sadie started at the change in subject.

"You were in fifth grade. You played a wailing woman," Tess said, "during the Stations of the Cross."

Sadie remembered the blue cloth she'd wrapped around her head, remembered crowding against her friends, the whole church watching.

"And I saw you in your sheep costume one Christmas," Tess added. "You were on your way into your grammar school for the nativity play. You kept shaking your head to make the ears flop."

Sadie's lungs seized. She remembered that costume. Her nana had sewn it. She'd let Sadie push down the foot pedal of the old sewing machine while she stitched the seams. Sadie mentally shook herself and shoved the memory away. She didn't want to spoil that memory with the thought of some stranger lurking behind a car.

"You're not going to believe me," Tess said, "but I didn't want this to play out like—"

"Right."

"I'd hoped to tell you the whole story someday when you were older."

"Screw that."

"I was a woman who didn't expect to be pregnant, and I didn't even know about you until I was pretty far gone."

"Oh, so you couldn't abort me then." Sadie took some satisfaction in seeing Tess flinch. "Well, I know you're no church-going Catholic, so someday you'll have to explain how you managed not to know you were pregnant for so long."

"Let's just say it had something to do with sleeping be-tween cargo cars in a Midwestern train depot."

This time Sadie flinched.

"What we really should be talking about," Tess said, her voice low and even, "after you're finished unleashing all that anger on me—"

"I've got a reason to be pissed—"

"—is what you want to do going forward, now that you've met your sad, creepy excuse for a biological mother."

A noise lurched out of her, a noise that was a laugh but wasn't a laugh at all. "I guess I'm not going to be invited to stay in your nice house in your good neighborhood."

"I had that once. A farmhouse in Kansas. Complete with chickens and enough land for a dozen kids to run around on."

"It's nice what you can achieve when you're not saddled with a kid."

"But since my marriage imploded," she continued, "I've mostly been living out of man camps and the backseat of my car."

"What the hell is a man camp?"

"It's a bunch of prefab trailers in North Dakota that house oil rig workers. It's a pretty rough place."

"Was my father an oil rig worker?"

A cloud passed across the sun, darkening the lake, casting a sudden chill. Sadie glanced up and saw the gray underbelly of it, bringing with it the faintest smell of rain.

"No, Sadie," Tess said, "he wasn't."

"Was he some guy you were all moon-eyed over, who took off the moment he found out you were pregnant?"

"Do I look like the kind of girl who goes moon-eyed?"

"Izzy tells me her mom and dad are probably still together because they adopted her," Sadie said, wondering why her heart was pressing up her throat, wondering why she was babbling so much. "They wanted kids and they got her, so they were happy. She's Chinese, and in China they have a one-child policy. Her biological parents didn't want her because she was a girl. So," she continued, reaching the limit of her breath, "let's just say I've heard some pretty bad stuff about parents not wanting their kids. So I can handle the truth if my father didn't want me."

If Sadie could make a language out of choking sounds, it would probably sound very much like the noises Tess was making right now. Choppy little half words, swallowed down before they were spoken. Sadie dared a glance from beneath her lashes and saw that Tess had drawn her feet out of the water, crossed them at the ankles, and now she'd buried her head in the vee between her knobby knees.

Sadie said, "I've got a right to know who my father is, you know."

"It's not easy to tell you, Sadie."

Once, when she was little, her parents had brought her to the Jersey shore. She'd raced right down the shoreline with her mother calling out behind her. She raced right to the edge where the water thrust up the slight incline of the sand. And, ankle deep, she remembered the pull of that water on the backs of her ankles, the way her feet suddenly sank like quicksand into the ground, and how, when she looked up, an angry white spray of a wave knocked her right in the belly, dragging her with the undertow a few feet farther, into someplace cold and full of choking sand.

"It was one night." Tess turned to meet Sadie's eyes. "I don't even know your father's name."

Tess's gaze was steady and straight, but Sadie understood what it meant when someone stared at you stone-faced like that, like it hurt not to move a muscle, like it was costing her to stay silent. Sadie understood that what the woman had said was at best a half-truth, at worst, a complete lie.

Then angry words gathered in her throat, but they didn't come, they wouldn't come, because Sadie wouldn't let them come. She felt overwhelmed, undone, numb. And suddenly she shot up to her feet, bare on the hot boards, the whole world around her warped like she was blinking at it through a fish-eye lens.

She'd been happy once, when her mother and father

were alive, when her mother used to come in in the mornings and wrestle her into tights, and her father used to swing her up in his arms whenever he came home from work. The world had been full and safe until suddenly it wasn't. Suddenly she was living at her aunt's house, a place of noise and confusion. She hadn't been happy, she hadn't been wanted, but at least her aunt hadn't lied about how she felt, at least Sadie had always been sure of where she stood. She'd dealt with that, finagling her way to Nana's house where everything had been good again—cream soda at lunch and black-and-white movies in the evening. Nana, while she still could, taught her how to talk with confidence on the phone and use the ATM. When Nana couldn't, Sadie just adapted, making her own lunch, cleaning her own clothes, washing her own hair and Nana's, too. She was happy then, too, in a way. Nana had always smiled up at her after she brushed her hair, her white face had been beaming and calm, and the two of them had been together. Yes, she'd done well enough, went to school, had friends, and realized there was nothing she could do about her situation. But no matter what happened, Sadie definitely could take care of Sadie. Sadie would find a way to make herself happy.

"Sadie?"

But all those social workers, the guidance counselors and the principal, even Izzy, they had all been right about this. She should have waited until she was eighteen. By coming here she'd opened Pandora's box, and now she didn't know how to shove all the demons back in. Maybe there was something magic about waiting until that age because now, having found out what she'd come looking for, there was a ringing in her ears and a numbness in her tongue and she wasn't sure if she could stop herself from keeling right over the edge of this bay into the murky water.

"*Sadie.*"

The voice was sharp, clear, right up against her ear, and Sadie startled but couldn't look at the figure looming up just to her right, like there was that doorstop on her eyes again. Funny, all her life she'd wanted to stare into the face of her birth mother and see herself in those features. Now that birth mother stood so close she could feel her breath against her shoulder, hear the wheeze in her throat, and she couldn't bring herself to turn because she was afraid of exactly what she'd see.

And she thought about something for a minute. Her aunt's house hadn't been that bad for the few months she'd lived in it, if you could forget the noise and the mess and her cousins getting into her stuff and pulling her hair and throwing peas. Suddenly it seemed like such a small thing, to have cousins who didn't know better than to throw peas.

"I want to go home." Sadie turned her back on the Tess-woman and headed out of the boathouse. "I'm going home."

Chapter Twenty-Two

I bet North Dakota is looking pretty good right now."

Rodriguez's voice came from the shadows. It startled Tess so much that she felt—all at once—the hot sun on her head, the cool water around her ankles, and the hard boards beneath her. She was at the boathouse, alone, without Sadie. For all her fervent wishing, she hadn't turned back the last two hours. She could no longer pretend that everything that had happened had just been a dream.

"So, Rodriguez," she said, her voice raw, "do you still think I should press charges against the bastard?"

"I didn't come down here to talk about that."

At the sound of his low, rumbling voice, Tess's vision blurred. *He knew.* Of course he knew. Riley must have filled in all the blanks. His knowledge intensified the hot-breath shame of being Theresa Hendrick, the Cannery Row troublemaker who'd been caught sticky-fingered at Ray's, smoking weed with shiftless twenty-two-year-olds, the ungrateful daughter who drove her mother to the bottle, then abandoned her by leaving town for good.

Tess Hendrick, the hard-hearted bitch who handed off her own daughter to complete strangers.

Rodriguez said, "Teenagers are a tough breed."

A small voice inside her blurted, *You've been harassing them so long, Rodriguez, that you should know*, but she couldn't risk speaking because she was trembling too much.

"I've got two of those monsters at home," he said, "so I know what I'm talking about."

She peered down the narrow end of the lake so he couldn't see her face. Tess remembered the picture in his office, a couple of young boys frolicking in the leaves. Two natural sons, raised by their natural parents, probably in a neat colonial home with a white picket fence. Rodriguez the good cop would do things right. Rodriguez would do things by the book.

"One of them has a really bad habit," he said into the silence. "Every time I catch him breaking the rules, every time I force him to face consequences, he threatens to go live with my ex-wife."

Can't say I blame him, she thought, even as her mind caught on the word *ex-wife*.

"Teenagers can't help themselves," Rodriguez persisted. "Their brains aren't fully formed. They act on impulse. They do what's easy, instead of what's right."

It wasn't only teenagers who did that. Here she was in her thirties and maybe her brain wasn't fully formed yet, because she still didn't know if she'd done the right thing. Was it really better for Sadie to think that her biological mother was a liar, rather than know that the father she'd never met was a rapist?

"Do you ever wonder why I pulled you out from among your Cannery friends all those years ago?"

Tess squeezed her eyes shut, wishing Rodriguez away along with the last two hours. She didn't want to play interrogate the delinquent game, because he was too good at it and the memory he'd invoked rose unbidden—of the group of neighborhood dropouts ruffling her hair as they let her join them in the old abandoned factory, of the vinegar smell of the place, the strange echoes, and the red glow at the end of the joint they shared, the one that made her feel floaty, the one that helped her forget what she'd run away from. She remembered the door swinging open, too, and the way Rodriguez threw her against the wall.

"I took you aside," he said, "because you looked as shell-shocked as Sadie just did, when she pulled up in front of that porch. You looked about as shell-shocked as you do now."

Tess wrapped her arms around her knees and drew them closer, though no matter how tight she held she couldn't make herself disappear, or erase the memory of Sadie's hurt, accusing eyes.

"I see in Sadie what I saw in you all those years ago. You both think the world is fucking you over because you're bad, you're not worthy, because you don't deserve anything better. Meanwhile, inside, you're both screaming for someone to—"

"So," she interrupted, just to make him stop, "you had some kind of superhero complex, is that it?"

"I followed you around to watch over you. You understand that. It's the same reason you've been following Sadie."

Tess absorbed the hit and blinked up at the trees, wondering why she was sitting outdoors yet there didn't seem to be enough air to breathe.

"You deserved better back then, Tess," he said. "You still do."

"Sadie deserves better." Sadie deserved a bed to sleep in, cousins to play with, a backyard to read in. That's what they should be talking about, not this nonsense about teenagers and ancient history. "That's why Sadie's going back to Ohio. That's where she belongs."

"And you're going back to North Dakota."

The muscles in her shoulders tightened. Rodriguez was a bastard to stand there and unpeel her like this. In her mind she'd already packed her bag and thrown it in the trunk of her Volvo. In her mind she'd already headed west, passing at high speed the green signs that marked the change of highways from here to Bismarck, and maybe farther, maybe north to Manitoba. There were lots of remote places where big-rig drivers were in great demand, where she could disappear into the world, so Sadie would never have to worry about running into her sad, creepy excuse of a biological mother again.

"I came to Pine Lake to make sure Sadie didn't end up on the streets like I did." The muscles of her jaw clenched. "Now she's going home to her people. Mission accomplished."

I'm not running away.

"Riley tells me she has some concerns about the aunt."

"Better an aunt who doesn't want her than a biological mother Sadie doesn't want."

"The aunt doesn't want Sadie? You *know* this?"

Tess's vision blurred and no amount of blinking put into focus the curving shoreline at the narrow end of the lake. She'd meant to ask Sadie about her aunt, but they never got that far in the conversation. Tess had been more concerned that Sadie would somehow find out about her father. Sadie needed to be kept in the dark, and Tess had been determined save her yet one more terrible shock. In the process of keeping that in mind, she'd subsumed all other concerns.

Tess heard the crack of one of Rodriguez's knees as he crouched down, so close that she imagined she could feel the warmth of him behind her.

"The way I see it," he said, "you've still got a whole lot of unfinished business here in Pine Lake, Tess."

Her heart pattered oddly in her chest. She felt the first throb of a migraine above her right eye. "You know damn well how hard it is to convict a rapist. You know damn well that rapists rarely serve more than a couple of years—"

"I'm not talking about that." He laid a hand on her shoulder and held firm as she tried to flex from under it. "That's unfinished business for another day."

She shook her head. Thinking about sitting in court talking about the rape was somehow easier than remembering all that she'd left unspoken with Sadie. Like the confession she'd wanted to make. The confession that she'd never loved anything—anyone—even a fraction as much as she loved her only daughter.

He said, "You are not your mother, Tess."

The words cut deep.

"You were never like your mother," he repeated, tightening his grip. "Despite all the terrible things that happened, you never abandoned your daughter."

"I did—"

"Never," he repeated. "And my gut instinct tells me you're not going to start now."

Chapter Twenty-Three

I'm coming with you."

Riley startled, banging her head on the raised trunk lid of her car. Tess came up beside her and swung a rucksack into the space Riley had just cleared. Her friend hid half her face behind a pair of sunglasses, but Riley recognized that set of jaw. She'd seen it just a moment ago on Sadie.

Riley said, "What do you mean, you're coming with us?"

"To Ohio. Today."

"But Sadie thinks it's just her and me on this trip." Sadie had darted back to the lodge about ten minutes ago, claiming she'd forgotten something in her room.

"I know," Tess said, "but I'm going anyway."

Riley eyed her unmoving friend. Emotions were running high at Camp Kwenback. Yesterday, after Riley had promised Sadie she'd take her back to Ohio, Sadie had retreated to her room and refused to come out. Tess, on the other hand, had retreated to the mini-golf, hammering away by the light of her car headlights, not eating a bite of the food Riley had brought out to her, muttering something about needing to take care of unfinished business.

Riley sank against the car. "I don't know if that's a good idea."

"I have to meet this aunt. I have to know I'm leaving Sadie in good hands." Tess pulled off her sunglasses to reveal the dark smudges beneath her eyes. "Please, Riley." Her throat worked. "We might not get another chance."

Riley's stomach tightened. Her heart broke for both of them because she knew what it was like to be an adoptee yearning for a birth mother, and now she knew that there are birth mothers who yearn just as deeply for their children. But the issues between these two were wide and deep. If they were stuck in a car for a nine-hour trip to Ohio, they might find a way to communicate. Or they might leave deep, bloody wounds on each other like two wild turkeys caught in a cage.

Then the front door to the main lodge banged open and Tess slipped her sunglasses back on. Sadie bounced down the stairs, her ponytail bobbing. She stumbled as she caught sight of Tess, then she swiftly looked away.

Riley pushed away from the car. "Got everything now?"

Sadie waved her toothbrush and then rounded to the passenger seat, where she'd insisted on stashing her backpack. "Can we go?"

Riley hesitated. If Sadie went back to her aunt and Tess took off for North Dakota, the chances that these two prideful people would ever have a relationship were slim to none.

Riley blurted, "Tess is joining us."

Sadie's head popped up. "What?"

"She's coming along." Riley heard Tess swivel in the gravel and shuffle a few steps away. "To Ohio."

"When did this happen?"

"Just now."

"Who said she even gets a vote?"

"Sadie—"

"Do *I* even get a vote?"

A wave of emotion passed over Sadie's face, the same angry, hurtful betrayal that she had revealed yesterday in this parking lot when the truth came out.

"Listen," Riley said, lowering her voice, "Tess quit her job to come find you. She drove across half the country to make sure you were safe." Riley tilted her head to her friend pacing circles in the gravel. "Do you think there's any changing that mind?"

Sadie's gaze shifted past her. The expression on Sadie's face rippled like the patterns on the surface of a wind-swept lake.

"I don't have any choice, I suppose." Sadie gestured toward Tess's car. "She's got her own car; she's just going to follow us no matter what I say."

"She's coming in my car."

"Hell no." Sadie's ponytail flew as she shook her head. "She can take her own car. She'll be halfway to North Dakota by then, or wherever the hell she lives, and she can just keep on driving."

"Sadie, I'll be driving eighteen hours out of the next

thirty-six. You don't think I could use another driver to take a turn at the wheel?"

Sadie's jaw hardened. "I shouldn't have let you talk me out of taking the train."

"C'mon, Sadie, I couldn't put you on a train alone—"

"It's not like I haven't done it before."

Riley closed her eyes, willed patience. "Both Tess and I want to make sure you make it to your aunt's house safely."

"I don't want to talk to her."

"She's not exactly a blabbermouth."

"I'm telling you I'm *not* going to talk to her." Sadie bent her head to slip into the passenger seat. "Let's just get this over with."

⌒

Hendrick women, Riley discovered, kept their word. Except for Riley pointing out landmarks along the highway, asking if anyone needed a bathroom break, or attempting lame jokes about songs on the radio, the first four hours of the trip were made in ever-thickening silence. Sadie didn't open her mouth until a fast-food picnic lunch at a travelers' rest stop—and only after Tess set off to stretch her legs by the dog run.

"So," Sadie said, pulling out her ear buds as soon as Tess was out of earshot, "how much longer is this awful ride anyway?"

"It only seems long, Sadie, because it's done in silence."

"Are you going to answer my question or do I have to go dig up a map and, like, make calculations?"

"We won't be at your aunt's house until the early evening at best." Riley eyed the food spread across the picnic table. "Are you going to eat those fries?"

"Not hungry."

Riley reached for a fry and dipped it in ketchup. "Why don't you tell me something about this aunt and uncle of yours before we knock on their door?"

"Other than Aunt Vi is furious after you and that cop made me call her yesterday?"

"You lied to her. You can't blame her for being angry."

"If you'd gone along with my cover story, she would have never known I'd made it all up."

"You'd make me part of the deception."

"So? It's not like you haven't lied to me before."

Riley took a deep breath and contemplated a response. In truth, Riley hadn't had time to lie to Sadie. But considering everything the girl had gone through over the past twenty-four hours, Sadie's flippant comment just didn't seem worth disputing.

So Riley decided to change the subject. "Tell me how your aunt and uncle are related to your mom and dad."

"Aunt Vi is my mother's sister. She and Uncle Bill had triplets a couple of years before my parents died."

"Wow. Triplets."

"Three boys. Using something called the turkey baster method, according to Nana, when she was just starting to forget how to put the brakes on anything that came out of her mouth. Boy, don't I wish I never looked *that* up on the Internet."

"Ah."

"My aunt and my mother both had trouble getting pregnant. My mother chose adoption to make a family. Aunt Vi chose to spend a fortune to have kids who would carry on her oh so precious genes."

Riley chose to ignore that ripple of bitterness, too happy that Sadie was finally talking about something. "Triplets are a lot of responsibility."

"Yeah, well, she didn't stop there. She had Ruby just before my parents died." She picked up a French fry and whirled it in her hand. "Izzy was right."

"Izzy was right about what?"

"She said it was stupid to come to Pine Lake." Sadie squinted down the sweeping lawn outside the travelers' rest stop to the cars whizzing by on the highway. "Maybe I got exactly what I deserved. Some nose-pierced, smart-mouthed trucker for a bio-mom who can't wait to run back to a home she doesn't have."

Riley's breath stopped. "That's harsh."

"Is it? She's been riding my butt since the minute she saw me. The only reason she came to Camp Kwenback was to rush me back to my aunt."

"Or get a runaway off the streets—"

"That's an excuse. She's not exactly telling me to come live with her, you know." Sadie made a snorting noise. "She can't wait to push me back to the family she dumped me on, all those years ago."

"Sadie, I know the news was a shock—"

"Oh, don't even go there."

"It was a shock to me, too. Never in a million years did I think Tess had a child, never mind that you were that daughter."

"Right." *Riiiiight.* "You two, best of friends, and she hid it for how many—"

"We were friends, good friends, when we were younger. Things changed when her father took off with our grammar school English teacher."

"Oooh, small-town drama."

Riley thought of the transformation, a girl who once loved to splash through the marsh and hunt for frogs, to the one six months later dying her pale hair black, sporting a spiked neck choker, and giving her an eye like a dare. "It didn't feel like 'small' drama to Tess."

"You know what?" Sadie tossed a fry toward a cluster of sparrows. "I don't give a damn about her problems."

"I get that," she said, "but if you just take a moment, take a deep breath, and step back from the situation—"

"Is that what you did after you spoke to your birth mother? You just"—Sadie curled her fingers into air quotes—"stepped back from the situation?"

Riley stared at the battered wood of the picnic table and tried to remember exactly what she did after she spoke to her birth mother on the phone. Her husband had been there, staring at her, talking to her, telling her how sorry he was. The microwave timer was beeping. It kept beeping and beeping and beeping until her husband left to go hit the keypad to stop it. When he came back, she must have told him it was okay, she was okay, but she wasn't. She'd felt numb, dissociated, like she'd mentally been wrapped in cotton.

When she'd finally emerged from that muffled cocoon, whole months had already passed, and for a long time she felt ungainly, off-center, like a broken-winged bird.

"Uh-huh. Just what I thought." Sadie shifted her weight. "You can't pull that over on me, Riley. I know your story, remember? I know you didn't just 'step back from the situation.'"

"I tried to."

"Oh, sure you did. You came home to Pine Lake the first chance you got, right? You came running back to your family and your hometown."

"Sadie, it was almost a year after I contacted my birth mother when my grandparents died and left me Camp Kwenback."

"Maybe it didn't happen right away, but the minute the opportunity showed itself, you seized it, didn't you?"

Riley opened her mouth but she couldn't think of what to say because that sounded pretty right.

"I'm telling you"—Sadie patted her chest—"that if you felt back then like I'm feeling right now, right this minute, then all you wanted to do was run back *home*. Or at least to the next best thing—to someone you trusted."

Riley rejected the explanation even as it needled her. "I trusted my husband."

"You left him, too."

But not because of that. It wasn't his fault that, after the phone call, she found herself mentally upended, contemplative, questioning, reexamining every one of those steps and wondering how they led her to such restless discontent.

"Well," Sadie added, "I don't know much about guys. I've only kissed a boy once, at the St. Patrick's Day dance in seventh grade, and it was so sloppy that I had to wash afterward."

"I assume," Riley said, struggling to put the conversation back on track, "that what you're telling me is that you're going to Ohio because you can trust your aunt."

"Oh, I trust her. She tells me right out when I'm a pain in her neck. That's the good thing about family. Living under the same roof, you can't keep a lie for long."

Riley rubbed her brow, wincing. How long had she lived in that Upper West Side apartment with her husband, maintaining the lie that she wanted to have children? How many years did she muffle her own discontent, happy to follow Declan's lead because Declan was strong and smart and good and handsome, and when she followed his lead, it was all good...until the day she spoke to her birth mother.

She shook herself. This wasn't about her. This was about the young woman brooding on the bench beside her, the young woman who didn't know the full story of how she came to be. But Riley knew the full story. With that in mind, she tried to think of some way she could talk around it to make Sadie understand.

"Yesterday, how much did Tess tell you," Riley ventured, "about the days after she found out she was pregnant with you?"

"Only that she didn't know until it was too late to get

rid of me." Sadie twisted on the bench and lifted her knees to her chin. "And something about shooting heroin between train cars in a Midwestern depot."

The words took Riley's breath away.

"What?" Sadie exclaimed. "She didn't spill that little detail yesterday? While you two were hanging around the mini-golf talking about me?"

"I knew things were bad during those years...but she didn't go into detail."

"She saves that for her 'scared straight' talks."

"That shows just how overwhelmed she'd been by—"

"Oh pul-ease."

"Sadie, I'm trying to make a point." Riley watched a couple of sparrows fight over crumbs on the grass by their feet. "You know what it's like to feel overwhelmed. You've had plenty of reason. When your parents died—"

"You don't get to talk about them."

"When your parents died," she repeated, "do you remember how you felt?"

"I was only eight years old."

"I bet you felt dizzy, nauseous, like everything was beyond your control, rolling right over you."

"So I'm supposed to think a pregnancy did that to some tough, tatted chick?"

"It wasn't just the pregnancy." Riley bit at her thumb, skittering around the details. "Her mother treated her badly. Tess couldn't believe, after all the years she took care of her, that her mother chose alcohol over her."

"See this." Sadie raised a hand close to her squinting eyes

and rubbed two fingers together, imitating the world's smallest violin.

"So," Riley pressed forward, "imagine Tess in a dorm in some Ohio adoption agency, waiting out the days of her pregnancy, counting down the minutes until she could get out of there, and then you were born." Riley hesitated, not quite sure how to explain what Tess had told her about that moment. "You were born," Riley said, "and Tess told me that everything changed."

Sadie made a long, scoffing raspberry.

"Tess told me that the pregnancy was one thing, but birth was something different. Suddenly she didn't want to go back to that train depot, to the false friends, to the false happiness, to everything she'd been jonesing for before. She told me that she'd been dead all those months. And yet, suddenly, there you were, emerging from her very much alive. Do you understand what I'm saying?" Riley reached over and put her hand on Sadie's knee. "You saved Tess."

Sadie yanked her knee away. "Then why the hell didn't she save me?"

⁂

Sadie didn't think she could stand the silence anymore. It felt like she'd been sitting in this car for a month, bracing an unopened bottle of water on her thigh. She had one foot kicked up on the dash, and she was angry that she had nothing to do but gaze out the window at the wooded verge flying by and wonder why her biological mother just sat in the back, silent, like some kind of tatted oracle waiting to be consulted.

Enough.

"So," Sadie said, slapping the bottle of water against her thigh, "you're coming to meet my aunt."

The hum of the tires changed pitch as they traveled across a bridge, bumping, bumping, bumping. Neither woman answered at first. Out of the corner of her eye, Sadie saw Riley flex her fingers against the steering wheel and then glance in a sort of panic in the rearview mirror.

The Tess-woman said in a flat voice, "Yes, Sadie, I'm going to meet your aunt."

"She's not going to like you, you know. Aunt Vi hates tattoos. Says they make a girl look cheap. So what are you going to do when you meet her? Are you going to beat her up?"

"Of course not—"

"Are you going to threaten her if she doesn't act nice to me?" Sadie twisted in the seat, peering at her from around the side. "And what are you going to threaten her with? Taking me away?"

The blonde didn't even look up, absorbed with tugging a string dangling from the end of her cutoffs.

"Aunt Vi would love if you took me away," Sadie said, "but that's the problem. You aren't offering to take me in."

The woman's shoulders rose and fell. "If I had a—"

"Even if you did," Sadie interrupted, not wanting to hear any more lies, "I wouldn't go with you anyway."

The Tess-woman flinched, and because of that Sadie didn't turn away like she was intending to, having said her piece, because that looked like a real flinch and she hadn't expected that at all.

"I just want to make sure you're safe at home," the blonde said, speaking the words like she'd memorized them or something. "I just want to see that you're settled in a decent place."

"Too bad you couldn't give me a decent place." There was something growing hot in Sadie's chest, something burning that swelled. "Too bad you were too busy sleeping around with strange men and not thinking about the consequences. Heck, I passed eighth-grade sex ed, and even I know better than to do that—"

"Sadie!"

"Riley, maybe you can stop being her mouthpiece for five minutes," Sadie retorted, "and let her talk for herself."

Tess murmured, "It wasn't like that."

"It wasn't like that? Some guy you were with for one night and didn't know his name?" Sadie nudged her seat belt off her shoulder and twisted so she kneeled backward on the seat, gripping the headrest in her hands. "Do you even know what my father looks like? Or could I be, like, the child of any number of random guys?"

Riley barked, "Enough."

"It's all right, Riley." The woman's voice was irritatingly quiet, and she sat as calmly as a social worker. "It's an honest question. Yes, Sadie, I know the man who made me pregnant with you."

"You sure?" Sadie pulled a curl from her own ponytail. "He got hair like mine?"

The Tess-woman swallowed, and it looked like she was swallowing down a really big pill. "You've got hair like my aunt," she said. "If I had to guess, I'd say my mother was shocked to see you in that grocery store because you look like her sister, who died when she—"

"Yeah, yeah, great story, but you're just changing the subject. What I want to know is what part of me looks like my father."

"I don't remember him clearly enough."

Sadie saw the way Tess met Riley's gaze in the rearview mirror, saw the odd expression that passed over Tess's face, sensed some story being woven tight between them.

"You're lying." That ball of heat in her chest was starting to burn. "If he was just a nobody, you wouldn't act all weird every time I ask about him."

Tess rubbed her forehead. "This conversation isn't easy—"

"I'm going to find him someday, just like I found you," she said, determination rising. "I'm going to come back to Pine Lake and look in yearbooks again, and newspapers. I'll ask about who Tess Hendrick hung around with back before I was born. Maybe I'll even talk to that cop friend of yours and see what he knows—"

"Sadie," Riley interrupted, "haven't you learned anything about doing this before you're ready?"

"Oh, I'll be ready this time. I'll be eighteen or maybe even twenty, but I'll track him down just like I tracked you

down, Miss Eighteen-wheeler. I've got a right to know my father—"

"Don't call him that." The woman turned away but not
before Sadie saw her face collapse. Sadie raised herself up
off her knees because now she knew she was onto something.

Riley said sharply, "Sadie, sit down."

"I'm fine."

"It's dangerous—"

"You just keep your eyes on the road, Riley."

"I think"—Riley tugged on the waistband of her shorts—
"we've all done enough talking for now."

"You're the one that set up this little car ride, right?" Sadie
glared at Riley. "You're the one who wants us to talk—"

"It's all right, Riley." The Tess-woman's voice was smaller
than before. "I'll answer her questions."

"Will you really give me a straight answer?" Sadie asked.
"Because I'm half of that man, whoever he is. He's in my
blood and my bones and my brain, and I've got a right to
know who he is. Just like I had a right to know who you are,
no matter how bad that ended up."

"He's not a good man, Sadie."

Sadie's heart leaped. "He's alive then."

Tess's brows drew together under the swoop of her bangs,
and the woman found something interesting to stare at on
the car floor, but she didn't say anything, and Sadie figured
not answering at all meant that she was right.

"So what does that mean, exactly," Sadie said, her mind
tripping over possibilities, "that he's not a 'good' man?"

"Hey," Riley said, her voice weirdly high, "why don't we pull over at this next stop up ahead and take a breather—"

"Seriously, though," Sadie leaned over and the headrest bit into her throat, "is he what made you into such a hard-ass, Miss Hendrick? Was he a bad boyfriend, beating on you or something?"

"Yes." The word came out with a spray of spit. "Yes, he beat me," she repeated. "He beat me bad enough to put me in the hospital."

Then the woman drew her legs up on the seat to hide her face between her knees. Riley made a strange sucking noise between her teeth so Sadie glanced over and saw the stricken expression on her face, too.

An odd thought came to Sadie, a thought that caused her mind to slow down, her thoughts to skitter in strange directions.

"You're lying to me," Sadie said. "You're both lying to me."

Tess's eyes were swollen. "I've never lied to you, Sadie."

"But you told me before that my father wasn't your boyfriend."

"He wasn't."

"You told me that you were with him only one night."

"Yes."

"Now you're telling me he beat you. That he put you in the hospital."

Tess hesitated, and a honk startled them all. Sadie gripped the back of the seat as Riley swerved the car out of the left lane in time for a truck to zoom by her. Sadie watched the panicked way Riley glanced at the controls and then eased her foot off the gas. Sadie saw the worry on Riley's face as clearly as she saw the tears.

And all the considerations that Sadie had barely formed—of a faceless father who went on to become a professor or a baseball player or an accountant like her real father and just never knew about the child he'd helped conceive a child he'd welcome if Sadie somehow showed up on the doorstep of his big suburban house—they all crumbled as her thoughts slid to something she balked to consider.

"You told me," Sadie said, her throat going dry, "that you don't know his name."

The blonde was silent.

"You told me," she whispered, "that you don't remember his face."

And then all the pieces of what she knew and what she didn't know swirled in her head—the nameless father, the one single night, the violence that put Tess in the hospital, the secret told in the moonlight to Riley, the angry cop confronting a shaking Tess—and it all coalesced into an ugly, incomprehensible whole she wished she could forever push out of her brain.

It couldn't be true. The Tess-woman would tell her it wasn't true.

Sadie blurted, "You were raped."

Chapter Twenty-Four

S-s-stop the car."

Sadie tumbled back into her seat. Her whole body went numb cold, and it wasn't because of the air-conditioning blasting out of the vent near her shoulder. She wanted to stand up, pace, move, escape. There wasn't enough air. It flooded through the vents but she couldn't breathe it in. Black spots winked before her eyes, and her stomach dropped as a burning began right under the bone in the middle of her chest.

She said, "I'm going to throw up."

The car made a sickening swerve that swished the contents of her belly. The whole car vibrated as it rumbled over the warning strip. Sadie was thrown back against the seat as Riley pressed on the brake. The car churned up dust as it came to a lurching stop on the shoulder of the road.

Sadie blindly grasped for the handle, shoving it open so fast that she tumbled out. She heard a shout as she fell hard on the ground. Gravel bit into her knees. Her body heaved, a hard heave that made her arch her back as she struggled to all fours. She managed to crawl a few steps away from the car before the chewed-up contents of a hamburger and fries launched out of her, spraying down the grassy slope.

She heard two car doors slam, a confused patter of feet, a twist of a cap, a gurgle of water. She heaved again, a tightening of her diaphragm that strained her throat but brought up nothing but bile. Someone pulled her ponytail out of the way and slapped something wet and cold on the back of her neck.

"Breathe, Sadie."

The shock of hearing the Tess-woman just above her made her flinch. She heard a sharp intake of breath as the pressure on the back of her neck eased. Riley murmured something, and then Sadie sensed the touch of a different hand on her neck. She heard Tess move away.

"I should never have asked," Sadie said, her mouth burning. A whoosh of air flooded over her as a truck zoomed by on the interstate. Rocks bit into the palms of her hands, and streams of cool water dripped down her neck to make a pattering of dark spots in her shadow. "It's like when you kick over a rock. You always find something slimy."

A water bottle loomed in her vision. Riley said, "Drink."

Sadie checked the state of her stomach, waiting for another surge of bile. She leaned back, shook the gravel off her hands, and then grasped the bottle. It was slippery with condensation.

The water swished in her mouth, acid-tainted. She turned her head to spit it out. Then she gulped the fresh water down, watching as—a dozen steps beyond Riley—Tess stumbled and then dropped to her backside like she'd lost control of her legs. The blonde caught herself by throwing out a hand.

Sadie heard herself stutter, "I'm a rape baby."

"Don't." Riley seized her knee. "Don't call yourself that."

The words echoed through her head like the shriek of a fire alarm through the halls of her old school.

"Three things," Riley said, stepping into the line of her vision. "There are three things you have to remember."

"I don't want to talk anymore."

"I'm not asking you to talk. I'm telling you to listen."

Sadie pressed the bottle against her sweaty forehead, closing her eyes, suddenly very tired.

"First," Riley said, "never *ever* refer to yourself as a rape baby."

"It's what I am."

"It's not what you are." Riley gripped her arm then shook it, forcing her to open her eyes. "The rape is something that happened before you were born."

"And I'm what came of it."

"What makes you think it matters," Riley said, as she tugged Sadie back into the shadow of the car, "how we came into this world?"

"Who the hell is we?"

"You, me. Adoptees." Riley sank down beside her. "We have this great secret in our lives, a mystery we're compelled to solve, right? Maybe we make that mystery more important than it deserves to be."

"So, what, are you a rape baby, too?"

"Maybe."

Sadie caught her breath.

"My birth mother never told me her story. I never got that chance." Riley's gaze shifted to where Tess was leaning on an elbow. "After hearing what Tess told me, it got me thinking that maybe my birth mother had a reason to put me up for adoption. Maybe she was even trying to protect me, in a strange, brutal way."

"Did you hurl?"

"Hurl?"

"When you spoke to your birth mother," Sadie said, jerking her chin to the unloaded contents of her stomach, "did you throw up?"

"Later. When my husband wasn't around to witness it."

Sadie picked at the edges of the damp label of her water bottle, trying to stop her breath from sawing through her throat, trying to absorb what Riley was saying, but all thinking stopped at *rape baby*.

"The problem with calling yourself names," Riley said, "is that the words will stick. They'll burrow into your brain until you can't think straight anymore, then you'll fix on the stupid idea that you're less worthy than other people—or worse, not worthy at all."

"I don't feel like that." It was a lie because there was a dark haze around her vision now, a black void that threatened to swallow her up, and a strange reluctance to look in the direction of that woman. "Are you sure you didn't smoke something funny before we left Pine Lake?"

"There's proof. You're the exact same smart-mouthed girl now as you were when I found you in the generator shed trying to keep warm."

That seemed like ages and ages ago, a hundred thousand years. "Can we just get back in the car and get this whole trip over with?"

"Not yet." Riley's brows were drawn so hard that a deep line appeared between them. "This is important, Sadie. My run-in with my biological mother was years ago, but it taught me one thing. I'd spent my whole life pleasing other people at all costs. You know why I did that, I know you do."

So they'd like you. Sadie peeled off the label of the water bottle as a new burn began in her belly. *So they wouldn't abandon you.*

"A lot of people do crazy things because they don't feel they deserve any better," Riley said. "This isn't just about adoptees like you and me. The first step down the wrong road is to pin yourself with the label 'rape baby.'"

A wave of sensation rolled over her, an itching that irritated her skin and made her fingers curl, that made her want to dig her nails into her arms and legs and belly and sides and scratch off a layer.

"What matters," Riley persisted, "has nothing to do with biology. What matters are the choices you make, and how you treat the people you love. Like how you sat with Mrs. Clancy and played those board games. Like how you went to the library and did the research you needed—"

"Research I wish I'd never done."

"You set a goal, and you achieved it. That's my point. We are what we *do*, Sadie. Not what we are born into."

"Maybe it's different if you're born from a rape—"

"It's not." Riley shook her head so hard her ponytail whipped the side of the car. "It's no different even if your biological mother is like mine, who wishes I'd never been born. There was never a baby born on this earth, Sadie, that didn't deserve to be unconditionally loved."

The water bottle slipped out of Sadie's hands. She watched it roll through the dirt. Then she pushed herself to her feet, stepped over it, and kicked at the scrubby grass. Her ears rang, a high-pitched whine that threatened to block out the sound of the pinging gravel, the whoosh of the cars as they zoomed by. Out of the corner of her eye, she saw the blonde look over her shoulder at both of them.

"I look like him, don't I?" Sadie looked down at her own hands, spread her fingers, and found them trembling. "She avoided me as much as she could these past weeks. Like she couldn't bear the sight of me, like I reminded her of everything bad that happened."

"Oh, Sadie, Sadie, you've got this wrong in so many ways."

"From the moment she arrived," Sadie said, her voice rising, "that woman has been scheming to get rid of me."

"Not because of how you looked. Tess just wanted you to be off the streets and safe at home."

Sadie's heart hardened. "Of course you'd defend her."

"I defend her because I understand her." Riley rose to her

feet. "Some people come off real gruff. They're even more gruff when they're around the folks they care about—"

"Gruff? She's spiked like a stegosaurus."

"She's got good reason. Everyone she has ever cared about—both her father and her mother—have betrayed her."

"Boo-frickin'-hoo."

"So she acts like it doesn't matter, like nothing can cut through her skin, like everything is a joke. In fact, she acts exactly like you're acting right now."

Sadie crossed her arms in front of her chest even as the memory came, unbidden, of the blonde making the same gesture at the boathouse yesterday.

"I can't believe I didn't notice how similar you two are earlier." Riley startled her by brushing her cheek with one quick finger. "The shape of your jaw, your nose, your shoulders. Both of you took care of a family member, without question, without complaint—both of you so devoted—"

"She wasn't devoted enough," Sadie heard herself say, "to have kept me."

"She was devoted enough to figure out the identity of the family who adopted you. She's still loyal enough to follow up on you. She was devoted enough to give you away because she truly believed that would be the best for *you*."

"Every birth mom says that—it's the perfect excuse." The ringing in her ears was starting to cause a pounding behind her eye, and weariness overwhelmed her again. All she wanted to do was get away from here, get home. "You said there was a third thing."

"What?"

"You said I had to remember three things. I heard 'don't call yourself names' and 'you are what you do.' Let's finish this. What's number three?"

Sadie watched Riley's soft chocolate-chip eyes as her gaze skittered to her friend again. Part of Sadie wanted to swivel on one foot and storm up to her biological mother and yell at her for *not* telling her everything—or yell at her *for* telling her everything—her brain couldn't decide.

"Sadie..." Riley stared at the ground as if the answer to all life's mysteries resided in the pattern of scattered gravel. "I don't know if I can tell you this."

"What, are you afraid of breaking a promise?" The muscles of her shoulders clenched. "Breaking a promise isn't much worse than lying."

"I wouldn't be breaking a promise, and I sure wouldn't be lying," Riley said. "I know Tess wants to say this directly to you, but with the way things are right now, she's afraid she'll screw it up and make things worse."

"Then don't tell me anything else." Sadie walked to the car door and yanked it open. "Let's just go to Ohio, okay?"

"When I found out about all this, I asked Tess how she could love you."

Sadie flinched.

"Tess was in labor for thirteen hours," Riley said. "They wanted to do a cesarean section but she refused, because she knew that surgery meant a longer recovery. She didn't want to spend one more minute in the hospital than she had to. She said..." Riley hesitated, grimaced, and then released a shaky sigh. "She said she couldn't wait for the day that you were born. So she could leave."

Dark spots winked before her eyes. She tightened her grip on the passenger-side door to keep herself on her feet

"Thirteen hours in labor," Riley repeated, tracing patterns in the dust with the toe of her sandal, "and then you were born."

Sadie noticed the sudden lack of cars on the highway, the silence of the deep woods, the distant roar of other highways, other cars, and more than that, a silence among them, a space that echoed in her ears, which peeled open despite herself to hear the story every child wanted to hear, the story of the day she was born.

"Tess didn't intend to look at you when they put you on her stomach. She was sure—convinced—that you'd look just like him."

Sadie's hand slipped off the grip. She tumbled onto the passenger seat with a painful bounce. She became conscious of the other woman, a smear of darkness she could just see out of the corner of her eye, looming closer.

"But there you were," Riley said, raising her face to the sky, "kicking and squeezing your hands, and there was a ropy cord still connecting your bodies together. Then Tess looked at you stretching your face up like you were trying to open your eyes and see her. The first thought that flew into her head—unbidden, unexpected—was that she had a daughter."

The intensity in Riley's brown eyes willed Sadie not to look away.

"It didn't make any sense, she told me. It didn't make

any sense at all. She'd been so angry during those months. Angry at what happened. Angry at her mother, who hadn't done anything to prevent the assault or even to help the police find him afterward. She was angry at Officer Rodriguez for harassing her at Camp Kwenback. Most of all she was angry at herself, for losing control of her own life." Riley leaned in. "But there you were, Sadie, lying on her belly in that big, white room, and she said it sounds crazy but she realized instantly that you weren't him, and you weren't her, either. You were somebody completely new, a tiny thing with a shriveled-up face and bowed purple legs, and you were covered in blood and she'd never seen anything so beautiful in all her life."

A dozen snarky thoughts flooded through her mind—*those must have been some good drugs*—but she couldn't speak them, for her tongue was numb and swelling.

"Sadie."

Riley was on her knees in front of Sadie with her head lifted like Sister Madeleine did whenever she kneeled before the statue of the Blessed Virgin Mary to pray for the souls of her third grade math class.

"Tess let you go," Riley said, taking her hands, "to sever the link between the senseless thing that happened and the beautiful daughter that came of it."

Sadie's heart pounded and her legs quivered and her shoulders shook and her whole body felt hot and cold at the same time. Beyond Riley that dark shape took another step closer until that other woman stood only a few paces away.

"But Tess loved you the instant you were born," Riley whispered. "And Tess has loved you every day since."

Chapter Twenty-Five

S ADIE'S HERE!!!"

Riley stepped off the stairs as the front door to Sadie's aunt's house swung open to a chorus of squeals.

"Geronimoooooooooooooooo!"

Four dark-haired blurs launched out the front door, whipping by Riley and Tess to head straight for Sadie. Riley winced as the four cousins tried to knock the girl to the scrubby lawn.

"Mikey, get her down."

"I'm trying. You gotta grab her by the arms!"

"Push," said the third, "just push."

"Huh! That'll be the day you knock me down," Sadie said, weaving in place. "No one can knock Sadie down."

Over their heads, Sadie gave Riley a weary, baleful look. The boys grunted and pushed and seized handfuls of her T-shirt. Sadie held her ground enough to reach over and muss the hair of the smallest attacker, a five- or six-year-old girl clinging to the back of one of her brothers.

The little girl piped up, "Mum says you're going to live with us! Is that true, Sadie?"

"Looks like it."

"I cleared you a bed in the attic! I put Jo-Jo there and some blankets and all my books."

"Thanks."

"And I've got a kitten. Of my own!"

"That's awesome, Rubes."

Riley thought Sadie sounded exhausted but resigned. During the last hundred miles in the car, Riley had been encouraged by Sadie's thoughtful calm. It was Tess she worried about now, Tess standing behind her bearing the dazed, bewildered look of a bird that had flown full speed into glass.

"I see you've met the monsters." A woman squeaked open the screen door and held out her hand. "I'm Violet," she said. "You must be Riley."

Violet was a tall woman a little bit older than herself, wearing a cotton skirt and an orange tank top, braless, without a stitch of makeup on her face. Riley gripped her hand. "Pleased to meet you. This is"—Riley hesitated—"my friend Tess."

Riley could tell by the look that passed across Violet's face that Sadie's aunt wasn't as pleased to meet Tess. Riley sometimes forgot how physically intimidating Tess could be to those who didn't know her.

"Sorry we're late," Riley said. "We ran into some rush-hour traffic coming past Cleveland."

"Are you hungry?"

"We stopped for fast-food about an hour ago." Riley

glanced at Sadie, still struggling to keep upright, her clothes being pulled in all directions. "I hoped we could have a talk while Sadie gets settled in. Something happened during the trip that we think you need to know about."

Vague worry passed across Violet's face "All right, then. Boys, get off your cousin, now." Vi pulled the screen door wide as the boys redoubled their efforts to knock Sadie over. "MIKEY, MARK, MITCHELL, ENOUGH."

Riley blinked as her ears rang.

"Ruby," Vi continued, "show Sadie up to the attic where you made our little vagabond a bed."

"Who's a vagabond?" Sadie tried to disentangle herself from the boys.

"You are, kiddo." Aunt Violet gave her wink. "You had yourself quite an adventure. I want to hear all about it. Later."

Sadie straightened her clothes and then passed Tess and Riley, rolling her eyes as she trudged after a bouncing Ruby up the stairs. The boys pushed one another and then chased themselves around the side of the house.

"I'll make us some tea." Vi raised a brow and glanced warily beyond, to Tess. "Or will I be needing whiskey?"

A crossed-armed Tess didn't seem capable of a response so Riley said, "Tea will be fine."

The house had that vague smell of cat. Just walking through the den, Riley eyed two of them, perched on top of what appeared to be a guinea pig cage. Shoving toys aside with the edge of her foot, Vi cleared a way through the den and the narrow hallway cluttered with sports equipment to a small kitchen in the back.

"Bill—my husband—isn't home right now," Vi said, shoving the faucet on to fill a teakettle as Riley took a seat by the breakfast nook. "He's off on a job on the other side of the state. I can't tell you how grateful I am that you two drove Sadie all the way here. If I'd tried to take these monsters with me for a ride that long, I'm not sure all of them would have survived."

"Sadie did mention that you had triplets." Riley glimpsed them just outside the kitchen window, bent over a rabbit hutch.

"Bunch of hooligans." Vi pulled three cups out of a cabinet and shoved them on the table, where they slid across with a gritty sound, like there was a layer of old sugar underneath. "Where's your friend?"

"Oh, probably checking out your animals," she lied. "She loves cats."

Violet gave her an odd look. Riley didn't know what else to do but smile. She figured Tess was probably taking stock of the place. Riley had noticed that the house was unkempt, the paint dinged and chipped, scratches on the cabinets, pale crayon marks on the walls, but she sensed that it didn't so much give off an aura of dirtiness as it did of well-used chaos.

Tess might think differently.

"If you don't mind," Riley said, pushing past the awkwardness, "I have a couple of questions about when Sadie first came to live with you. She was sketchy on details, and I wondered—"

"You can ask," Vi said. "But frankly, I don't remember much."

Uneasiness twitched inside Riley, like the pull of a muscle between her ribs.

"What I mean," Vi said as she sat down across from her, "is that the details of those months when Sadie first lived here are hazy. I had four kids in diapers, three of them starting to walk when my sister and her husband died." Just then the back door slammed open and the three boys came tearing through the mudroom, yelling all the way through the kitchen and then out through the front door. "Some parents fill up these books about their kids' first year, marking the first step, the first rollover, the first tooth. Me? I just tried to keep them fed and changed enough so I wouldn't unintentionally starve one or the other to death. Sadie arrived in the middle of that panic."

"Sadie mentioned that she had some trouble adjusting when she was here," Riley said.

"Oh, Sadie hated it here." Violet pulled a grimace. "Part of it was from the shock of her parents' death. She'd wake up screaming, sleepwalking, and acting out in school to the point that the school guidance counselor was calling me and recommending therapists."

Therapists.

"Sadie wasn't here a week," Violet continued, "before she ran away."

Riley didn't have any explanation, really, for the slow sinking of her heart.

"Honestly, I don't blame her." Vi looked out the window to where the boys had turned on a water hose. "Heck, *I* wanted to run away. There were babies crying all day and all night."

"Where did she run to?"

"She was trying to get back to her parents' house on Long Island. Yes, from here, from Ohio." Vi ran a hand through her hair, and Riley noticed that her fingers shook a little. "She scared the life out of me. She ended up spending a couple of nights in some group foster care home." Vi stood up at the sound of the water gurgling in the teakettle, but not before Riley saw her chin quiver. "For two days I was sure I'd killed my sister's only child."

Violet turned off the flame under the kettle and then opened a cabinet. A box of tea bags tumbled out onto the counter and fell to the floor. Violet ignored the fallen box as she stood in front of the open cabinet, flexing her hand over the handle, staring at the contents within but making no selection. Violet said softly, "I suppose what you really want to know is why I sent Sadie to Queens to live with my mother."

Just then Riley noticed a shadow standing in the doorway from the living room. Tess stood framed there, just outside the light, grasping her own arms. She looked twitchy and red-eyed and unhinged.

Riley stood up to fetch the fallen box of tea bags from the floor. "Please sit, Violet—"

"You have to understand." The teakettle rattled as Violet picked it up from the stovetop. She poured water into the teacups, leaving a trail of boiling water from stove to table and then back to the stove again. "When my mother heard about Sadie being so unhappy here, she insisted that Sadie live with her. Sadie couldn't pack her bags fast enough. At the time there was no reason to fight."

Riley went mute, sensing the rush of a coming confession. In the shadows of the living room, Riley saw Tess digging her fingers into her arms.

"Back then, my mother was as healthy as a horse. Oh, she'd forget to pay a bill now and then. She lost her car once, in a parking lot, had to call the police because she was convinced it had been stolen. My sister Rose had been taking care of those incidents. Protecting me, I guess." Violet fell so hard into a chair that the legs scraped across the linoleum. "By the time I realized how bad my mother had become, years later, Sadie refused to come back to Ohio. She didn't want her whole life upended again."

Riley tightened her grip on the cup, willing Tess to stay out of sight.

"I visited Queens as much as I could," Violet continued. "I handled the bill paying from here. I tried to coordinate my visits with school conferences but…" Vi gestured to the window where her three boys, fully dressed, were now soaked to the skin from playing with the water hose. "I did what I thought was best for that girl. She's my sister's only child— she may as well be my own blood. I would never, *ever*, hand her off to a stranger."

Something fell in the living room, the clatter of something heavy tumbling to the hardwood floor. Violet's anxious gaze shot toward the shadows where Tess stood amid a cluster of fallen hockey sticks, bracing a hand on the wall, looking as if one more emotional wallop would knock her flat.

"I'm just going out back," Tess waved to the backyard. "To have a smoke."

After Tess left, Riley turned back to see in Violet's expression a growing realization that there was more going on here than two good Samaritans driving home a wayward child.

"Am I in some trouble or something?" Vi's expression turned to alarm. "Why are you asking all these questions, anyway? Are you two social workers?"

"We're not social workers." Riley sank back in her chair. "Do you remember when we spoke on the phone yesterday? When I told you that Sadie came to Pine Lake looking for her birth mother?"

"I remember."

"Well...Sadie found her."

Violet's gaze shot to the backyard, beyond the frolicking boys, to the blond, tatted woman now leaning against the back fence, holding a cigarette in a shaking hand.

"Those therapists the school counselor recommended?" Riley murmured. "I hope you kept their names."

꒰

It was nearly nine o'clock at night by the time Riley saw the tips of two cigarettes extinguish in the backyard by the darkness of the fence. Tess and Violet strolled into the light cast through the kitchen window. Violet called for her boys and directed them into the house, where they stormed in slapping wet footprints on the kitchen floor. Violet excused herself to put the boys in their bath upstairs, said her good-byes, then promised to shoo Sadie down from where she was playing with her cousin's kitten so she, too, could say her farewells.

As Riley and Tess exited the house, an evening breeze ruffled the grass. Katydids chirped in the trees. Tess kept her back to the door, her face in shadow, nudging the wheel of a bike left abandoned on the front lawn.

Riley ventured, "Aunt Vi was not at all what I expected."

"No witch's hat," Tess murmured. "No warts."

"For a while in the kitchen there, I thought you were going to lunge at her, like, with a machete."

"The thought did pass my mind."

Riley put her hand on Tess's shoulder. "Sadie will be fine here, Tess. She gave us only part of the story."

Tess let her head fall back to look at the stars. "I'm not one to judge a mother for doing her best for a child."

Under her hand, Riley felt the tremor that shuddered through her friend and found herself wondering if her own biological mother had also buried her sorrow this deep. For some folks maybe it was just easier that way—easier than admitting guilt or the truth that the decision, for better or worse, still hurt.

Then the screen door squealed open.

"Aunt Vi told me you're leaving now." Sadie stepped onto the porch and let the door slam behind her. "I thought you were staying the night."

Riley dropped her hand from Tess's shoulder and noticed two things—the tense timbre of Sadie's voice and the way Sadie's gaze lingered on her birth mother.

"You've got a full house here," Tess said. "And you probably can't wait to see the back of me anyway."

Sadie didn't deny it. She shoved her hands in the back

pockets of her shorts, and the motion reminded Riley so much of Tess that her heart squeezed.

"I spoke to your aunt Violet," Tess said. "I want you to know that I gave her my cell phone number and my drop box address in Bismarck—"

"Yeah, yeah, okay."

"If you ever want to talk," Tess said, "tomorrow or next week or next month or even next year—"

"I got it."

"—I'll be there to answer. I'll be there to tell you whatever you want to know. That's a promise, Sadie."

"Okay. Bye."

Tess swayed a moment, looking stunned at being so abruptly dismissed, but Sadie made no move to come closer or to say anything else. The girl just stood there on the porch and then scraped at something on the stairs with her sandal. Tess flashed Riley a defeated look before turning to walk to the car.

Riley took some comfort in the sight of Sadie lifting her head again, of Sadie's gaze following Tess into the darkness.

"I have something for you." Riley opened her purse and poked around inside. "I want you to have these."

Sadie's eyes widened at the sight of the Leica binoculars. "But those are your favorite."

"You squint all the time, did you know that?" Riley held them out as Sadie came down the stairs. "These will help for now, but I told your aunt Violet that she should make you an appointment to get your eyesight checked."

Sadie wrinkled her nose. "Glasses?"

"You'll rock them. I know you will."

Sadie looked unconvinced. She frowned down at the binoculars, idly unwinding the strap.

"Sadie—"

"Yeah, yeah, I know."

"Listen, you can call me whenever—"

"I heard this speech already."

"Day or night." Riley's heart started to race. "I mean it."

"Mm-hmm."

"And if at any point, you'd like me to pass a message to Tess—"

"Can you stop talking about her?" Sadie said the words as if she were just weary of the subject. "Just for one minute?"

Riley nodded. Sadie needed time and space to sort out her feelings. Riley couldn't push, even if she did wish for some sweeter resolution for Tess, now probably rocking in a fetal position in the car.

"Promise me one thing." Riley tilted her head toward the house. "Don't run away from here, okay? Give your family a chance."

"Like I have any choice." Sadie swung the strap of the binoculars over her head. "I'm way past Plan D, remember?"

"You do have a choice. We all have choices."

Riley's voice wavered. She resisted an urge to reach out and chuck up Sadie's chin, like Sadie was nine years old or something. Right now, Riley ached for Sadie all the way down to the arches of her feet. She wanted to scoop her up, cradle her close, and then set her someplace warm and dry where Riley could always watch, protect her, keep her safe.

Then something went loose inside her, a soft tug that released a warmth through her body. It wasn't the womb pull of maternal instinct she'd once expected to feel, that fecund hormonal rush that made people yearn for an infant. No it couldn't possibly be, because the young woman standing before her was no fragile baby. Sadie was strong but she was still a lost nestling, bristling and unsure, looking for a safe place to stay until she learned to fly on her own. Riley understood how important it was to fly on one's own.

The idea descended upon her with all the gentleness of a loon gliding onto a lake. The idea came, and hard upon it came doubts and fears—that it was too difficult, required too many sacrifices, and couldn't be done without destroying everything she'd been fighting so hard to keep—but what had she been fighting to keep, really? Maybe Camp Kwenback was just the physical manifestation of a perfect childhood, of perfect families, of a perfect life. Maybe she'd clung too long to her husband's vision of the same. Maybe what she should have been doing all along was to stop trying to fix someone else's broken nest and instead have the courage to create a new one of her own.

"Sadie."

Sadie looked up at the sound of her voice, all wide green eyes, and Riley's heart rose to her throat. There was this thing about choices. You think the hardest part is making one—taking the wavering temperature of your heart, weighing the pros and cons, choosing to destroy old dreams in order to build new ones—but you'd be wrong. Making a choice was only the first step.

Sometimes it was the easiest.

"If you decide you don't want to live here," Riley said, as she put her hands on Sadie's shoulders, "then come and live with me."

Chapter Twenty-Six

Tess recognized her rapist right away.

Standing behind the one-way glass staring at her attacker, Tess felt an odd vertigo along with a tingling in her fingers. She smelled a phantom scent, diesel and old beer and something fermenting. Then she heard a shuffle of footsteps and sensed someone coming to stand directly behind her. *Rodriguez.* His unexpected presence at this lineup gave her something solid to focus on as the five men in the next room turned as a group to show their profiles.

Nearly sixteen years had passed since that monster had busted through the door to her childhood bedroom. She had shoved that memory in a box in the attic of her mind, in the hope that someday, maybe, she'd stumble upon it with a sense of surprise that such a terrible thing had ever happened to her. She'd shoved the memory so deep that when she'd walked into this Albany police station to identify him, she'd nursed a growing fear that she'd distorted the memory so much that the monster she remembered no longer bore the faintest resemblance to the man he really was.

But that wasn't true.

He was the third one who swaggered in. The gray T-shirt he wore was a size too small, stretched across the pot of his belly. The ravages of alcohol had broken so many capillaries that his nose was beet red, malformed. He'd been in a few more bar fights since she'd last seen him, but he still had the chain-link neck tattoo, the split in his earlobe, the crescent scar gleaming white on his temple.

He looked brutish, stupid, and angry.

"Number three," she said.

"Look carefully." Jolie Sanderson, the assistant district attorney, spoke from the shadows. "Be absolutely sure."

"Number three."

The attorney stepped up and rapped on the glass. The guard on the other side led the men back out, shuffling single file. Tess watched the back of her rapist's balding head, probing her emotional temperature, trying to figure out what she felt—triumph or pity or fury or *something*. The prisoner now trudging out of the room was a stranger who'd done her terrible violence, but right now Tess just felt numb.

The district attorney flicked on the lights and turned toward the public defender with a slow smile. The public defender, sandwich in hand, shrugged and licked mustard off his fingers.

"Ms. Hendrick." Jolie pushed the door open and gestured for her to step into the hall. "Why don't you wait out here while I talk to the accused's attorney? I'll join you in a few minutes."

Tess wandered into the hall and stopped in the middle. Blue uniforms passed her by on either side and she resisted the urge to flinch. She'd always felt vulnerable since that terrible night. She'd spent so many years carrying a knife in her boot. She owned mace. She'd push a set of dresser drawers in front of her door whenever she rented a trailer at a man camp because she knew too well what could happen if she didn't. She felt dizzy because she'd braced herself to see the bastard who had made her like this—and now it was over.

She strained to hear Jolie's voice beyond the door, but all she heard was mumbling. Then she noticed Rodriguez leaning against the wall.

"You had the same look on your face," he said, "twenty-odd years ago, when I found weed in your pocket and threatened to charge you with possession."

"Scorn?"

"Shock."

Tess took the blow. Yes, she supposed she was in shock. So much had happened so fast, with Sadie … and now this.

"You were so skinny," Rodriguez said. "Hungry and young and scared and not street-hardened enough to hide it."

She turned her mind away from the image he'd projected of her, one she didn't like to think about. She waved toward the door where the attorneys were negotiating the future of her rapist. "I'm not used to putting control of my life in other people's hands."

"You're not telling me anything I don't know, Hendrick."

"And it's not just my life she's holding in there. It's Sadie's, too." Tess remembered the photo in his office. "Do you ever stop worrying about your kids?"

"Nope. And I've got one going to college in the fall."

Tess looked down at her feet, figuring if she concentrated on them long enough, she would finally feel like she was standing in place and not weaving like a drunk. She swallowed. "What if—"

"Jolie will drive a hard bargain," he said. "I called her in for this because she's handled more cases of sexual assault than any other assistant DA in the state. She knows this system inside and out."

"I want Sadie to be safe."

"I suspect what you want is for Sadie to have a life very different from yours."

She closed her hands into fists, tight enough to feel her fingernails dig into her skin.

"Hell, *I* didn't want you to have a life like yours, Tess." He squinted toward the light pouring through the windows down at the end of the hall. "Maybe if I'd had the sense to intervene when I brought you home to that mother of yours the first time, I could have saved you all of this."

Tess's eyes hurt. In her vision, Rodriguez washed out to a big, burly blue streak. Then Jolie saved her from weepy embarrassment by bustling out of the room while shoving a file into her overstuffed leather shoulder bag.

The attorney strode right up to Tess and put a hand on her shoulder. "It doesn't look good, Ms. Hendrick."

Tess's heart dropped.

"The public defender rejected the plea out of hand," the attorney said. "He said his client wouldn't accept it."

Rodriguez stepped in. "I warned you no felon would cop to a second felony."

"I wouldn't be doing my job if I didn't try." Jolie motioned for them to follow her as she strode with purpose down the hall. "Like I told you over the phone, if you positively identified the man who assaulted you, I would try a plea deal first and I would come in hard. But he didn't bite, which means we have to talk strategy."

Tess felt the first crack in the numb shell around her. The long, narrow hall echoed with murmurs, the swift rustling of hurried people, the clicking of high-heeled shoes, and the kind of muffled hum that she'd always associated with casinos and courtrooms—both places where the house always won.

"Explain this to me," she said, dropping back to match Rodriguez's stride.

"He's got one felony charge already." Rodriguez spoke too low for passersby to hear. "If he pleads to a second, he's looking at hard time. Since he's in jail now, he's got nothing to lose if he fights."

"This will do." Jolie pulled open a heavy door with a diamond-shaped window. Inside were a metal desk and three metal chairs.

Tess's stomach lurched. It looked like an interrogation room.

"We'll have some privacy in here to talk," Jolie said, slapping her bag on the desk and pulling out a pile of files. "My understanding, according to Officer Rodriguez, is that your first concern is for your daughter?"

"Yes." Tess sank into the chair, felt the metal steal the warmth from her thighs.

"I admit that concerns me as well." The DA spread out her files and chose one to open. "It took some convincing to get Officer Rodriguez to come clean to me that the child in question was a result of the assault."

Tess's throat tightened.

"I feel obliged to tell you, Ms. Hendrick, that in this state there are no provisions in the law that would prevent a rapist from demanding access, custody, even contact with any children born of rape."

That old fear, like ice water down her back. "It's the same in Ohio where she was born."

"Unfortunately that's a legislative issue. One that should be addressed in our lifetimes, but right now it's beyond our immediate abilities to change—"

"The bastard doesn't know about Sadie." Tess met Jolie's sharp gaze. "And I'm here today on the assumption that you'll guarantee he never will."

"He won't hear it from me, from my office, or from any of my officers," Jolie said, tapping the metal table with one painted fingernail. "I can assure you of that. But you should understand that whether he finds out depends largely on how hard he fights any charges we bring against him, as well as his resources—which I can only assume are slim since he has been assigned counsel by the court."

"You're telling me," Tess said, through an ever-narrowing throat, "that you can't give me any guarantees."

"Justice is often an unintended side effect of our criminal justice system, Ms. Hendrick. I can promise nothing but my very best effort."

Tess's blood went cold. She glanced over her shoulder and saw Rodriguez's face, the skin around his mouth pulled tight.

"First fill me in on some facts," the attorney said, drawing Tess's attention back to the matter at hand. "Your daughter is not in your legal custody, is she?"

"No."

"In fact, when you made your adoption plan, you surrendered all parental rights, am I correct?"

She nodded, the words like a slap.

"And because the biological father could not be found at the time of the child's birth," Jolie continued, "despite Officer Rodriguez's exceptional detective work"—she fanned the papers in the file—"the accused's parental rights were thus surrendered by default."

Tess said, "That can't be undone. Right?"

"Answer the question, Ms. Hendrick."

The attorney had an eye that skewered you right to the back wall. So Tess thought very carefully about those months after she'd discovered she was pregnant. The agency's legally worded questions about the birth father were easily satisfied when she'd admitted that she'd been raped by a stranger. They'd asked her about the father again, in those thirty-six hours after Sadie's birth, amid a blur of unexpected emotion and confusion and indecision, so nervous they'd been about whether the father would show up at some future date to challenge custody. He won't, she'd told them. So she'd given Sadie up and then disappeared into the world, just to make sure of it.

"Yes," she said. "That was my understanding."

"Good." Ms. Sanderson picked up a pencil on the desk and tapped it to get Rodriguez's attention. "Even if the accused found out—even if he could afford to fight to have the adoption plan made null and void fifteen years after, he'd be looking at years of battles ahead of him trying to convince a court the parental rights custody limitations should be overturned for a man convicted of sexual assault." The attorney turned her gaze on Tess again. "You protected your Sadie well."

Tess blinked at the disorienting sensation of having an authority figure in a tailored white shirt telling her she was right.

"I understand," the attorney asked, "that you've had some recent contact with your—with Sadie."

"She came looking for me."

"Any chance there'll be a change in the custody situation?"

Tess gripped the ends of the armrests. She told herself Sadie deserved what she'd had before—a nice house in a quiet suburb full of at-home mothers—someplace rural like the Ohio farm town she and her adoptive aunt lived in. "No," she said, "no, Sadie will be staying with her adoptive aunt." No reason to muddy the waters with the possibility of Riley's offer.

"Very well." The attorney slipped on her glasses to write something down. "And how old is Sadie now?"

"She'll be fifteen in a month." The date of her birth approached like a rising ache.

"Three more years and she'll no longer be a minor." The attorney nodded. "We can do this. We can protect her until she's eighteen."

"I don't want her to be protected just until she's eighteen. I want her to be protected for good."

Rodriguez said, "Kids grow up and go away from you, Tess, whether they're in your custody or not. At eighteen they become their own legal entities, with the right to do what they want."

"Ms. Hendrick," Ms. Sanderson added, "it's just a legal definition, and the limits of our—"

"I'm not interested in limits. I'm interested in keeping that bastard away from Sadie for as long as I possibly can."

"Then we'll have to keep him in jail, won't we?"

Tess sat back. The hard slats of the chair dug furrows along her spine.

"The way I see it," Jolie said, pushing herself close to the desk and the papers splayed over it, "we've got strong physical evidence. Both in the DNA sample Officer Rodriguez had tested from your rape kit—which, by the way," she said, glancing at him over the rim of her glasses, "will be contested, considering the age of the sample. But we also have the physical evidence from your hospital records, which will confirm injuries consistent with a violent sexual assault."

The attorney was holding up a piece of paper. Through

the translucency of the fibers, Tess could see the familiar medical form, the list of her injuries, the typed-up doctor's comment. Black spots were starting to swarm in front of her eyes so she roped her fingers together and pressed them against her diaphragm to force herself to take deep, slow breaths.

"It's unfortunate but not surprising," Ms. Sanderson said, "that there are no material witnesses—"

"No cooperative ones," Rodriguez interrupted.

"—but these two pieces of physical evidence, plus the testimony of Officer Rodriguez when he first interviewed you in the hospital, make up a strong case. This is the kind of sexual assault case that I don't need to be convinced to take to trial."

Tess heard a quick *rat-tat-tat* sound and realized that she'd skip-jumped her own chair against the floor. "A trial?"

"It's rare," Ms. Sanderson said. "Only about five percent of the sexual assault cases that pass my desk ever go to—"

"But I've got a juvenile record."

"Long expunged."

Tess turned to Rodriguez, saw him shrug, saw the strangest twitch at the corner of his lips. Her mind couldn't keep up with the implications so she turned back to what preoccupied her, to what was, even now, making a migraine throb behind her right eye.

"What if during a trial"—the word thick in her mouth— "his lawyer asks me if I had a child?"

"I'd object under relevance."

"But then he'll know."

"It may not come to that. Bear with me, Ms. Hendrick. When I say I don't have to be convinced to take this to trial, what I'm really saying is that it's a strong case. If we win, he'll get some real time."

Rodriguez interjected, "How much more time?"

"Depends on the judge. He'll get a minimum five, maximum twenty-five for a Class B felony rape. An extra ten years for being a violent second offender. But if I threaten him with first degree rape," Sanderson retorted, "plus the charge of predatory sexual assault, plus being a second violent offender, he's looking at a hard dozen years at least if he tries to fight it against this evidence. I can't guarantee the outcome of any trial, but if I were a betting woman, I'd say he'd lose it."

Tess calculated swiftly. "Only a dozen years?"

"Absolute minimum." The attorney tossed her pen on the desk. "There is one thing I need to know, though, before I proceed in any direction. Officer Rodriguez tells me that you are a determined woman, but rape cases are difficult. I don't think I have to tell you that the trial is often a devastating moment of exposure for the victim. You'll have to sit up in the witness stand and tell us everything that happened that night. What you were wearing, whether you were drinking, if you'd taken any drugs, how many boyfriends you had. I can't tell you how many times I've witnessed strong women drop charges long before trial, or back off at the last minute."

A rivulet of sweat slid down her spine. A weakness spread through her, and she pressed her thighs together against a sudden urge to pee. They were looking at her, waiting for a response, waiting for her to tell them with confidence that she'd testify. But she kept imagining sitting in that courtroom talking to a crowd of people—some of whom she knew, many who knew her—about how he'd tied her wrists to her bedposts and did whatever he wanted, all while the rapist himself sat at the defense table, listening to it all, maybe even grinning.

She felt pressure on her arm and looked down to see Rodriguez's hand. She glanced up and found herself staring at the spot on the back of his head where his dark hair whorled, because his head was in his other hand, because he was gripping his brow as if he understood the price she'd have to pay.

And it came to her then, like a veil peeled from her vision. All of Rodriguez's gruffness, his angry speeches, his constant harassment, and all the frustration he'd expressed, may have been more than mean-spirited persecution from a cop who despised her. Because right now his concern for her burrowed so deep she felt it warm her heart.

Rodriguez really had been watching over her.

Rodriguez was a good man.

"There is another option," Jolie said into the stretching silence. "If you want to avoid a trial, I could offer a lesser plea—"

"No."

She knew that she'd spoken the word aloud because Rodriguez looked up at her with that black gaze. Until a few moments ago, she'd been afraid that laying eyes upon her rapist would bring it all back—not just the violence, but the horrible way she'd felt afterward. That unshakable belief that nobody cared for her. That Tess Hendrick, abandoned by her father and betrayed by her mother—the girl who played with fire—got exactly what she deserved.

Now Tess looked straight into Rodriguez's face and hoped someday the veil would be ripped from Sadie's eyes, too. Maybe then Sadie would understand that, in the end, her birth mother chose to do not what was easiest, but what was right.

"No plea deal." Tess said. "I'll testify."

Chapter Twenty-Seven

When Riley posted the old high school photo on her social media account, she told herself she did it as a reminder to the Pine Lake girls that the time had come to make their reservations for the mini-reunion at Camp Kwenback. Riley adored this photo. It had been taken moments after she and her friends had thrown their mortarboards in the air. There were twelve of them, crushed together, laughing in the bright sun, and everyone sported pink hair—their senior year prank. The picture even included Tess, her mouth open comically wide as she photobombed the shot.

On impulse, Riley tagged Sadie in the photo as well.

A few days later, Riley posted a second picture, tagging Sadie again. It was a photo of Coley's Point, a vista spot just outside town where locals went to camp. In it she and her friends couldn't be more than thirteen. She was swaddled in a ridiculous puffy coat, her face unrecognizable under hat and hood and scarf, her arms thrown around a couple of other girls just as bundled. Tess was the skinny one wearing the mismatched hat, scarf, and gloves.

Riley's friends made all kinds of snarky remarks about that memorable evening, but Sadie didn't say a thing.

So Riley waited a week before posting the third picture. Sadie was probably getting ready for the school year, but Riley hoped to take advantage of these waning days of summer to capture the young woman's attention before Sadie lost herself in the whirl of homework and clubs and events at her new high school in Ohio.

It was another shot of Pine Lake, this time on the local baseball diamond. Riley sported a catcher's uniform. The padding on her chest and guards on her shins made her look meatier than usual. Her helmet was falling off her head, and her hair was all sweaty, and she was about six inches off the ground as she leaped into the arms of another player—Nicole, the pitcher, all glossy dark hair—as they both screamed to the skies. They'd just won the regionals, the first time Pine Lake's softball team had done that in three decades, and this picture had made the front page of the *Pine Lake Ledger*. Riley figured it would take Sadie a moment of searching to find the black shadow in the background of the shot, hunched against the chain-link fence, a lit cigarette dangling from Tess's unsmiling mouth.

Riley was sitting sat at her desk with a mountain of paperwork spread in front of her when an instant message finally blinked on the screen.

Why r u tagging me in all these pics?

Riley reached for the keyboard so fast she nearly

knocked her coffee all over the contract she was perusing.

I was thinking of you. I thought you'd want to see some Pine Lake history.

Bad hair and ugly snow boots?

You got me there.

I know what you're doing.

Posting pictures for the amusement of my friends?

Funny how the stegosaurus is in all three.

Can't pull a fast one over on Sadie, Riley thought. Maybe she should have mixed up the photos a little.

Another message popped up. *Is she feeding u these pictures? Telling u to show them to me?*

Tess is gone now. Riley hesitated, wondering how much to say, suspecting what Sadie wanted to hear. *She went back to North Dakota.*

Tess left Pine Lake the day after she identified the man who'd assaulted her all those years ago. She'd told Riley she wasn't running away. She just needed to make sense of a few things. Riley thought she looked tired but calm, like a marathon runner after stumbling over the finish line. Tess promised she would return in a few weeks to witness the post-indictment arraignment, the first in what would probably be a long, difficult road to trial. Riley had promised a room.

A new message blinked. *U still there?*

Yeah, I'm still here. Phone ringing off the hook. Riley rolled her own eyes the moment she typed that. The only person she expected today was her mother, and she'd cleared the decks for that visit.

Thinking of mothers, Riley found herself typing: *The stegosaurus isn't so bad you know, once you get to know her.*

You're pushing it.

Does that mean no more photos?

Riley flexed her fingers, watching the box for something to pop up. It was a full minute before Sadie posted again.

Whatever. g2g.

Got to go. Riley typed a chirpy good-bye and added a happy face. She supposed "Whatever" was a whole lot better than "Stop."

Riley closed the window when a jangle of chimes brought her attention to the front door. Her mother strode in, thumbing the cell phone in her hand.

"Sorry I'm late," her mother said, as she hit a button then slipped the phone into her purse. "Remind me never to choose flowers for the luncheon tables with Betsy Muldoon. The woman has the attention span of a flea."

Riley patted the mountain on her desk. "I took the time to catch up on paperwork."

"I hope some of that paperwork is about the air conditioner." Her mother tugged on the collar of her button-down shirt. "It's like an oven in here, and there's no hum coming from those vents."

The unit needed replacing, but Riley didn't mention that. "It's barely eighty degrees outside, Mom."

"You've always been a little lizard. But it's so hot in here you could seriously grow weed."

"How about some sun tea?"

"Yes. Let's take it out on the back porch, shall we? Maybe we'll catch a breeze off the lake."

Her mother's sandals clicked across the floorboards as she headed toward the sliding doors. Riley slipped into the kitchen and poured two glasses of tea, taking her time adding ice. She felt a little shaky. She wasn't so sure that the conviction she'd worked so hard to cultivate over the past week wouldn't wilt under her mother's scrutiny.

Once outside her mother gave her a look as she took a glass off the offered tray. "No guests this week?"

"Not yet."

"Ever the optimist."

"I'm booked for the Labor Day weekend. Claire, Nicole, and Jenna have already confirmed." Riley slid the tray onto the table and took a glass for herself. "Dr. Jin says it depends on her patients; she'll tell me closer to the day. Sydney's coming, too."

"Are these lovely Pine Lake girls paying?"

"Mother."

"It's an honest question."

"Friends and family rate." Riley sank into a chair.

"You really are your grandparent's granddaughter." Her mother curled her legs up on the cushion. "I assume you asked me over to talk about your recent visit to Ben's office?"

Riley had thought she'd kept the secret well, but the tom-toms of Pine Lake beat constantly. "Yes, Mother, that's exactly why I asked you here. I've made a decision about this place. I've put in a call to the Adirondack Land Trust."

Her mother's head swiveled, her expression full of surprise.

"Ah, the tom-toms didn't beat the whole tale, I see."

"The land trust?"

"Yup."

"The last time I spoke to you, you had plans to update the lodge—"

"Yes, I did." Alice-in-Wonderland dreams, until she finally climbed out of the rabbit hole. "I thought you'd be thrilled that I was throwing off the albatross."

"But the trust will try to swallow up the whole place, make it a part of the nature conservatory."

"That's the usual MO."

Her mother blinked. "But they'll pay you pennies on the dollar, Riley. Not half the worth of the land, commercially zoned—"

"Well, it is a charitable trust."

"I take it," her mother said, as her glass dripped condensation on her well-creased capris, "that you never called that developer."

"On the contrary, I did. I heard what he had to say."

"Is this about your birds?"

"Really, Mom!"

"I just don't want you giving up a chance at some financial security just to save some rare woodland owl or something."

"I've got more important things on my mind right now."

"Well, I'm dumbfounded. Last time we discussed this,

you were in your complete redheaded mode, determined to make this place work at all costs."

"Instead I've filed for bankruptcy."

The word lay in her mouth like ashes. Riley couldn't seem to swallow the taste away.

Her mother said, "Riley?"

"Ben is filing the appropriate papers," she explained. "Camp Kwenback will soon have temporary protection from its creditors while I work things out."

"With the land trust."

"With whoever will give me a chance to keep the place afloat a little longer, and yes, that just may be the land trust."

"They'll change the zoning so no one can ever develop it again. They'll swallow it whole." Her mother threw her arm out to the pine woods, stretching on either side of the lake. "Every acre of it will be annexed into *that*."

"Every acre but one, I hope."

Her mother slid her glass on the table. She planted her elbows on her own knees and then did what Riley dreaded the most. She released a long, weary sigh.

This time Riley chose to shoot first. "Mom, when was the last time you were in the attic?"

"For goodness sake, what on earth are you—"

"It's full of old boxes. Grandma was as much a pack rat as Grandpa, in her own orderly way." Riley flattened the arches of her feet against the edge of the glass table and pressed back so the chair tipped onto its back legs. "Figuring I was going to lose the place, I started the process of cleaning it out. So I went upstairs and opened some of those old boxes. I found ledgers dating back to the turn of the twentieth century."

Her mother ran her fingers across her brow, like she was smoothing out a headache.

Riley said, "Did you know a Vanderbilt slept here in the early twenties?"

"Yes."

Riley started. "And you didn't tell me?"

"He was a third cousin to the Commodore's grandchildren, far from the money tree."

"But he was a *Vanderbilt*. You don't think that would have been worth a nice plug on the website? 'Come stay where the Vanderbilts played.'"

"Forgive me, Riley, but I'm failing to see what this has to do with the land trust and... bankruptcy."

"I made more than one discovery up there."

Riley didn't know if her mother would appreciate the thrill she'd experienced paging through all those ledgers. Sitting up there with a patch of sun passing across the floorboards, she'd seen an older, different Camp Kwenback come to life in her mind. It made her realize that no place was immutable—and it was fruitless to fight against evolution.

"What I found," she continued, "concerned the boathouse." She squinted at it through the trees to focus on the bleached piles, the coiling twig work. "Apparently, it was built by William West Durant around the turn of the twentieth century. The story was written up in the *Pine Lake Ledger* in nineteen nineteen. That builder did a lot of work in the great camps—the ones everyone knows. Camp Uncas. Camp Pine Knot. Sagamore Camp."

"Riley, those camps are all National Historical Landmarks."

"Exactly."

Her mother lifted her head from her hands. "You want landmark designation for the boathouse."

"And the lodge, as well, as an associated building. I've already spoken to someone in the State Parks and Recreation Department about the survey and evaluation process, just to get the ball rolling."

"But—"

"I'd have to tear down the cabins." She couldn't look at them, stretching in steps down the east side of the compound, remembering the hanging laundry, the tumble of toys, the families sitting under the trees watching the sunset. "I'll have to tear down the Viking obstacle course, the rope climb, the tree house by the marsh. Probably the swing set and the dock around the bend"—every structure bringing another sunlit memory—"but with landmark status pending, the Trust should be willing to split the lot, let me retain the main lodge, the boathouse, maybe even the mini-golf. They'd still get nearly thirty acres at a bargain, and I'd still be the proprietor of a small—possibly viable—suddenly historic inn."

Riley shot up from her chair and strode to the rail to grip it in her hands. Her face was hot, and not from the warmth of the August afternoon. Speaking the idea aloud again—this time to her mother—made her realize how far afield she'd strayed from rationality. Old Ben Eason had been kind when she'd outlined her idea, lowering his gaze so she wouldn't see his skepticism, but she was used to that. She'd experienced that every time she'd handed a bank officer her business proposal.

But she didn't have that much history with Ben. Standing half in the sun, with her mother listening behind her, she felt the shadow of a hundred thousand other failures darken her mind.

Her mother murmured, in an oddly neutral voice, "Landmark status could take a long time to establish."

"It's going to be a lot of paperwork," Riley admitted. "And I'll have to make sure the proceeds from the land sale to the Trust can cover the cost of running the lodge, at least until I figure out a way to make the lodge viable, or at least until preservation loans become available."

"Landmark status," her mother mused, "could mean special tax treatment, too."

"Uh-huh. I could bypass Pine Lake Union Bank when I need to hire an artisan to replace rotting boards."

"You won't be able change anything, not a door, not a window, not a twig—"

"There'll be no mediation pagodas or golf carts on the hiking trails."

"Just the way you want it."

Riley realized she was holding the rail so tight that her knuckles had gone white. She had her back to her mother so she couldn't see her face. Riley could hear only the rattling of the ice in her glass, the rustle of her clothes as she shifted her position, the creaking of the wicker chair. Riley's heart was beating far faster than it should, faster than she'd wanted it to beat. She'd told herself that her mother's opinion didn't matter, but her gut clearly thought otherwise. Nobody wants to be a failure in anyone's eyes, especially in the eyes of those they love.

Her mother mused, "You know, I never liked this place."

Riley dared a half turn.

"Oh, it's lovely now," her mother said, as she absently toasted the backyard, "worn to a nub, yes, but it's quiet and we've got the whole place to ourselves. But I remember how it was in its so-called glory days. I remember racing between the lodge and the lake, right up and down these steps, right here. I was constantly delivering dry towels to shivering children and drinks to their parents, always forced to smile and be happy no matter that sweat was dripping down the middle of my back, mosquitos were biting, and so were some of those children, once they were out of their parent's sight. It's been nearly forty years since I worked fourteen-hour days here, but I still twitch every time I walk through the door." Her mother shook her head. "So what brought on this sudden decision of yours?"

"Utter financial desperation?"

"Riley, you've taken sudden right turns before, but there was always a trigger and it was never money."

Riley knew her mother was referring to when Riley left her job—and Declan. Riley looked down at her fingers, a tiny bead of blood oozing from where she'd taken on a splinter. She wasn't sure it was quite the right time to tell her mother the other decision she'd made about her husband.

"Don't mistake me, Riley," her mother said into the silence. "Finality can be a good thing. Making a decision, even a crazy one, can be a good thing. But, Riley, I know you right down to the high arches in your tapered little feet. You need a push to make any decision. I'm just wondering what pushed you over the line this time."

Riley chewed on her lip for a moment, wondering how to explain everything that had happened since she'd returned from Ohio. She hadn't said a word to her mother about Sadie or all the drama that had happened here over the summer. She wasn't sure she wanted to compound the crazy by telling her mother about the moment she found Sadie perched like a wet fledgling in the shed, to when Sadie had looked up at her with those green eyes and asked if she was her mother, to the hours she'd spent in the car with the broken young runaway, trying to gather together all the shattered shards of her heart.

Instead Riley said, "Did you see what Tess did to the mini-golf?"

"I did." Her mother stretched out the word like she was stretching out her patience. "It's like one of Bud's hoary old stories come to life."

"When I first saw those bears under the moon, I knew that preserving this place—or at least a small part of it—wasn't just for my own sake." Riley leaned back against the rail, testing it with her weight. "Tess showed me that. She also taught me that you can't run away from making a decision forever. Sometimes you just have to commit, no matter how difficult the choice."

"I wish you'd told me about Tess."

An uneasy prickle spidered up her back.

"If I'd known the whole terrible story," her mother said, "I would have been much kinder to that woman."

Riley froze.

"I'm afraid," her mother said, noticing her reaction, "that the whole town knows about the sexual assault now."

Riley tried to form the word *how* but she'd somehow lost the ability to speak.

Her mother said, "Tess's mother had a fit, some kind of breakdown, just last week. Not alcohol related, so I hear, but they're keeping her in the hospital under supervision. Since then she's been talking to anyone who'll listen. Nurses, orderlies, candy stripers. She's blaming herself for not protecting her own daughter from the man who assaulted her. I hear that she's asked to see Officer Rodriguez."

"Mom," Riley said, "this is Tess's private business." How Tess would hate to once again be the subject of discussion among the ladies over lunch, or during a round of golf, or while planning for the next charity event for the Daughters of Old Pine Lake.

"You know," her mother continued, "I knew something about Tess's home situation when she stayed here. But I had no idea it was so bad." Her mother rolled a charm up and down the chain around her neck. "Bud and Mary were right. Tess would have been better off if she'd taken up their offer."

"Offer?"

"They asked her to stay." Her mother looked up at her. "You two being so close back then, I thought you knew about that."

Riley shook her head. "Why didn't she stay?"

"We don't get to choose our mothers." Her mother gave her a wan smile. "And when you're that young, I guess you have to believe that you can fix the one you've got."

And suddenly Riley remembered her own mother on her knees in the grass squeezing the glitter glue around Riley's social studies poster. Riley thought of her mother marching into her sixth grade teacher's conference, her chin high, holding Riley's hand tight. Riley thought of the anger in her mother's eyes when she caught Riley's older brother teasing her over her homework. Riley thought of her mother jumping up and down in the stands at every softball game, cheering her on as Riley rounded the bases.

Riley heard herself saying, "There's one more thing I have to tell you, Mom."

Her mother groaned and reached for her glass. "I should have asked for something stronger than sun tea."

"I signed the divorce papers." Riley imagined she could still taste the gum of the envelope on her tongue. "I mailed them last week."

"Oh, dear."

"I held on to them for too long. I gave Declan false hope that I would return to a relationship that had serious problems from the very start." She spread her arms to encompass the land that would soon belong to someone else. "It turns out I have a bad habit of clinging to broken things."

Her mother listened in stillness. Condensation dripped on her mother's capris. Her mother made no attempt to wipe it off.

"I know," Riley ventured, "that you and Declan blame my behavior on the whole thing with my biological mother. You're right, but not in the way you think."

Those finely trimmed eyebrows raised a fraction.

"That woman's reaction to me was so much worse than I'd ever expected that, eventually, I realized the problem was all hers. I mean, really. No baby is that unlovable."

"Oh, Riley." Her mother's voice broke. "You're the most lovable soul I know."

"You have to say that," she teased. "You're my mother. My *real* mother."

Her mother's head bobbed a little. A faint flush rose to her cheeks. Her lips moved but no sound came out. The Cross women rarely spoke in such sentimental terms, but Riley figured that was one old habit she could break.

"Well," her mother said, "I wish you'd told me about signing the papers earlier." Her mother peered into her glass with more intensity than the drink seemed to warrant. "Moments like that should be enacted with some kind of solemnity. I'd have taken you out."

"To mourn?"

"To honor the passing. Though I would have tastefully celebrated with you, if that's what you really wanted."

Riley blinked back a sudden prickle of tears.

"So this idea of yours, for the camp," her mother said, in a brighter voice. "It's vintage Riley Cross, you know."

"I . . . guess."

"It hovers in that gray area between crazy and genius."

"Is that a vote of confidence?"

"Are you sure this is what you want?"

"Yes." The word came out, swift and unbidden, a reflex that just barely beat out the ripples of doubt.

Her mother said, "I think I might have waited thirty-odd years to hear you say that."

"Say yes?"

"To say it like you mean it." Her mother raised a glass in a toast. "In that case, bombs away, Riley. I'm glad you're moving forward in the direction you want, even if it's not in the direction I would have chosen for you."

As Riley absorbed those words, a great, swelling affection rose up in her, a wave of emotion that compelled her across the porch to perch her hip on the arm of her mother's chair.

"Riley, what are you, six years old?" Her mother chuckled as she got nudged. "There are plenty of chairs—"

"I know."

Then Riley pressed her nose in that fine blond coif, fiercely grateful for the opinionated, exasperating, magnificent woman who'd chosen to be her mom.

Chapter Twenty-Eight

During the long summer days in Ohio, Sadie did a lot of hard thinking.

She had no real complaints about living in her aunt's house. Her aunt couldn't cook to save her life, but there was always something on the table at 6:30 p.m. There was food in the fridge that Sadie didn't have to shop for and clean clothes in her drawers that she didn't have to wash. She didn't have to make everyone's bed—she didn't have to make *anyone's* bed if she didn't want to because Aunt Vi didn't care about things like that. She didn't have to pay any bills or clean the bathroom, even if Aunt Vi made her take in the garbage cans and occasionally watch the kids after day camp in the afternoon. And her cousins were like oversize puppies, rolling over one another, often making her laugh even if sometimes she wanted to crack them on the nose with a rolled-up newspaper.

The problems really began when Aunt Vi brought her to the high school to register for the new academic year.

She'd soaked it all in—the just disinfected smell, the gleaming black tables of the labs, the way the halls echoed every voice. But when she tried to cast her thoughts toward her future here, the images that tumbled in her mind looked a lot like Riley's stupid pictures.

She'd mentioned this to Izzy online—Izzy, whom she missed like a lost tooth, though there was nothing that she could do about that now that Aunt Vi was selling the house in Queens. Izzy had confessed that she sometimes had dreams about green, terraced hills she'd never seen before. They'd looked up the phenomenon online, found terms like "genetic memory" and "ancestral memory," and marveled at the possibility that they could have remembrances in their heads that were not their own. Sadie thought—*no way*. But that itchy, restless feeling just wouldn't disappear. Pine Lake was like a book she hadn't finished, one that promised adventure, mystery, or at least some kind of happy ending.

So one Saturday, despite Aunt Vi's reservations, Sadie took a bus to the local library, found a quiet cubby, opened her notebook, made two columns, and came up with a plan.

And now...here she was.

Sadie laid that same notebook on the weathered boards of the boathouse and then squinted up at the sunshine winking through the trees. When she'd arrived in Pine Lake last week, Riley had warned her that it got cold quick in the mountains and the chill could start even in September. Sadie had been skeptical at first, but now she could feel it. The sun was warm on her hair, the boards hot beneath her palms, the light bright on the paper of her notebook, but the late afternoon breeze raised goose bumps on her arms.

She loved it, all of it, the way the water gurgled against the piers, the way she could sit here in the quiet while still hearing Riley and her friends hooting in laughter on the back porch of the lodge, chattering in high-pitched excitement at seeing each other again. The laughter reminded her that she'd see Izzy again, eventually. Riley said Izzy could come next summer and stay with her in the attic room they'd built after tossing some of the old boxes. She and Izzy could make a little money working in the mini-golf if they wanted to. Riley also said Sadie could go back to Ohio any time she wanted—Christmas, Easter, February break, too. People should always have options, Riley said. Choice was good.

Some choices were harder than others, Sadie suspected. She was just beginning to understand that.

Sometime later Sadie heard footsteps *whoosh-whoosh*ing on the grass down the hill. She slid her book off her lap. Riley had told her that Tess would be in town to say hello to her old friends from school. With her stomach lurching, Sadie had told Riley that she wouldn't mind. She was cool with Tess being around.

Still, her heart did a little stop trip as she stood up.

Tess came into view, a blur in the boathouse shadows. Sadie patted her chest to grab the prescription glasses she'd hung on the collar of her T-shirt, the glasses she hadn't even been aware she needed until Aunt Vi took her to the optometrist. She still marveled how they put the distant world into sudden focus.

Sadie looked through the glasses at Tess pushing the sleeve of a fuzzy white sweater higher on her arm. The sweater looked so odd on Tess's black-clad figure that Sadie figured she had to have borrowed it from Riley. The sweater covered all the tats and reflected a strange light onto Tess's face.

That must be why Tess looked so pale.

"Riley tells me," Tess ventured, "that you've decided to stay here and go to Pine Lake High."

"Uh-huh."

"I almost lived at Camp Kwenback once, too." She stopped fussing with the sleeve and instead shoved her hands in her back pockets. "I wish I had, actually. This is a very good choice, Sadie. I'm happy for you."

Sadie nodded, looking at her feet, feeling a pressure growing in her throat, the pressure of so very many questions. About the troubled grandmother she'd met by accident in the grocery store, about the grandfather she didn't know at all, about the ancestors before them, where they'd come from, how they'd ended up in the mountains of upstate New York. She wanted to know the difficult things, too, how Tess managed living with an alcoholic for so long, whether Tess would be willing to come back to Pine Lake once in a while, you know, just to visit.

Instead Sadie blurted, "You can't be my mother."

Tess blinked and then dropped her gaze to her feet. The folds of her sweater caved around her abdomen.

"I mean," Sadie stuttered, "I know you're my birth mother. But I just can't *call* you 'Mother.'"

"Of course not. You already have a mother." Tess cleared the hoarseness from her throat. "I understand that."

"I'm just saying—"

"I remember her, you know. I remember when she came to the hospital to bring you home." Tess's brow furrowed. "She wore a blue skirt and sneakers. She had long black hair and a great laugh."

Sadie bobbed her head. Of course Tess knew her mother. Tess had chosen her mother. Tess had placed Sadie in her mother's arms.

"Sadie," Tess ventured, "I'd like to visit the camp now and again." Tess tugged on her fingertips, looking up at the twig work of the boathouse. "I know you're going to be living here now, but I hope you don't mind if I pop in occasionally. I'll make sure Riley lets you know when I'm coming so it won't be a big, ugly surprise." Tess wandered a step closer, stepping into the brightness of the bay, looking at her with odd, hopeful eyes. "We don't even have to talk when I'm here, if you don't want to."

Maybe it was the way the sunlight hit Tess's face, but Sadie noticed a certain pattern of freckles on her jaw. She saw the way her nose wrinkled right at the bridge when she squinted. She saw in those hesitant, questioning eyes the same tentative hope that she felt curling within her own heart.

Sadie didn't remember crossing the space between them. She just heard Tess make a strange, choking sound. She saw Tess's arms fly open.

Then, against her pressed ear, she heard the racing of her mother's heart.

A NOTE FROM THE AUTHOR

Dear Reader,

Some stories flow like cool, clear water and other stories flow like tears. I knew, as a mother of three wonderful daughters, that writing *Senseless Acts of Beauty* would be the latter. So I just want to say to those daughters—if any of you dare to pick up Mom's book—that there are no secret babies I gave up for adoption, and you were all born happily from a loving relationship. This book isn't about you.

And yet this book is all about them.

When Tess sees her daughter for the first time "it felt like a scrim had peeled off her eyes, and she could see the whole, wide world in all its goodness and badness, all its capricious randomness, complicated and full of senseless acts of beauty." That was the feeling that gripped my labor-addled mind when the doctor first put each daughter squalling into my arms. When Riley talks about the "full-body, twenty-four-hour, never-ending immersion" that is parenthood, the "crazy three-a.m. feedings, the emergency room visits, the moments when you thought you lost them," that was my anxiety hidden behind a smile from the days when I had to free them so they could learn how to dive, to drive, and to date.

But as I researched the many issues in this book—sexual assault, the reproductive choices a woman faces, the fate of children born of rape, and the intricacies of open and closed adoptions—I discovered a deep level of pain beyond the everyday highs and lows of parenthood. For some, the experience of becoming a mother is so fraught with confusion, complexity, and conflicting emotions that many women still can't talk about it.

To the mothers and children who so bravely shared your experiences, I thank you. I hope I did your stories justice. I hope I reveal to others the same wisdom you gifted me—that every child born is an act of beauty.

And to my readers, thank you for joining me on this journey. I hope my story will help you appreciate all the beauty in your life.

DISCUSSION QUESTIONS

Lisa Verge Higgins loves to meet readers. If your book club has chosen a book by Lisa and you're interested in arranging a phone or Skype chat, feel free to contact her at http://www.lisavergehiggins.com/contact.

1. *Senseless Acts of Beauty* circles around the idea that beauty and reason don't always coexist, that beauty is inexplicable, often random, always in the eye of the beholder, and that the most heartbreaking, amazing creations can arise out of whimsy as well as serious intent—or even from no intent at all. In your own life, can you pinpoint a moment when you've witnessed a senseless act of beauty?

2. Tess's discovery of her pregnancy months after the rape extends her emotional and psychological trauma, but also forces her off the streets. What if Tess had never become pregnant from the assault? How do you see her life evolving if Sadie never existed?

3. "Mothers cast long shadows," Tess tells Sadie as she explains why she felt compelled to make an adoption plan. Certainly Tess's mother, an unrepentant alcoholic, gave Tess no good

example of parenting. But other mothers in this novel cast long shadows, too. Who do you think wields the most influence over Riley during this story—her adoptive mother or her birth mother?

4. Sadie sets off to find her birth mother claiming she has no expectations. ("I'd be pretty mad if my birth mother was an alcoholic or a drug addict or something. It would totally suck to have come all this way just to find out she didn't care about anything but her next fix.") But considering her reaction to meeting Riley, the research Sadie tackles, and later her reaction to discovering Tess, what do you think Sadie was really hoping for in a birth mother?

5. Tess and Officer Rodriguez have a long, contentious, and complicated relationship. That relationship begins to change as Tess realizes how deeply he regretted not stepping in to remove her from a dysfunctional home. How do you see that relationship evolving? Will Rodriguez become a father figure? Will they become friends? Or is there a possibility for a deeper relationship, among equals?

6. Riley describes herself as "a mute brown wren tumbling helplessly in the gale-force winds of other people's advice," yet when we meet her at the start of the novel, she has already quit a good job in New York City and left her husband. What combination of factors instigated this first startling life change?

7. Sadie said a lot of terrible things about her aunt Violet not wanting her in her house, yet when Riley and Tess reach Ohio they discover a woman doing the best she can for the many young children under her care. Why do you think the

eight-year-old Sadie didn't like living in Aunt Violet's house in the first place?

8. Mother-daughter relationships, in all their fraught complications, inform many of the themes of *Senseless Acts of Beauty*. Considering all the examples in the book—the dysfunction of Tess and her mother, the fraught but loving relationship between Riley and her adoptive mother—how do you envision Tess's relationship with Sadie evolving as time goes on?

9. When Riley hesitated to sign the divorce papers, her husband, Declan, nurtured hopes for a reconciliation. He even coaxed Riley's own mother—who adores him—into arranging a meeting at the diner. What did Declan do wrong in this marriage? What did he do right? Was there any chance that they could have worked things out?

10. One of the major themes of *Senseless Acts of Beauty* is that no matter how smoothly and well thought out an adoption plan, it's all but impossible to avoid anxiety, lasting emotional trauma, and doubt on the birth mother's side and—later—a range of hard questions on the part of the adopted child, no matter how well loved by her adoptive family. Is open adoption the answer to these issues? Then what about situations like Sadie's, where the pregnancy was brought on by terrible violence? What are the mother's rights? What are the child's?

11. Riley is haunted by failure—her less than stellar academic youth, her failed marriage, her failed business proposals to the banks, and now her failing camp. And yet, for a long time, she's paralyzed by indecision. What keeps her from accepting one of the developer's plans that would put her

on better financial footing? Why is she so stubborn, at first, about not changing the nature of the camp? What, in the end, convinces her that bankruptcy—the ultimate failure—could actually mean a new beginning?

12. What do you think are Sadie's feelings about her birth father, now that she knows about the circumstances of her conception? Do you think Sadie will someday seek him out? Should Sadie seek out his family, too? Should Tess help Sadie in this search?

13. As mentioned in the novel, thirty-one states in the United States have no laws on the books preventing rapists from claiming parental rights to biological children from those assaults. What rights—if any—should such a man have with regard to the children of those assaults? What protections should the children have? The mothers? Why do you think this lapse in the law exists?

14. At one point in her life, Tess made a stab at domesticity with Callahan, going so far as to keep a garden and raise chickens in Kansas. What factors do you think contributed to the destruction of that relationship? What elements in Tess's background undermined the possibility of happiness? Do you think she set her farmhouse in Kansas on fire?

15. These three women—Riley, Sadie, and even Tess—yearn, consciously or unconsciously, for some sort of permanence in their unsettled lives. Riley has to lose what she most loves before she can build something new. Sadie discovers, at the end, that she has the privilege to choose. But the future of the most unsettled of them all—Tess—remains a mystery. What do you think Tess will choose to do going forward?

16. Riley's biological mother stated, in the most brutal way, that she wants nothing to do with Riley. Do you think Riley would ever try to contact her biological mother again? Should Riley try to find out who her biological father is? Would Riley even want to? Is it possible to come to terms with living with such a mystery?

ABOUT THE AUTHOR

While studying for her PhD in chemistry, Lisa Verge Higgins wrote and sold her first novel. Now an author of seventeen books, this opera-loving mother of three has been twice named in Barnes & Noble's General Fiction Forum for their top twenty novels of the year. Her stories about women's lives and women's friendships have been described by reviewers as "joyous, uplifting life lessons" that "inspire us to focus on what's really important in our lives." When not writing stories, Lisa works as a reviewer for *The New York Journal of Books*. She currently lives in New Jersey with her husband and their three teenage daughters, who never fail to make life interesting.

LisaVergeHiggins.com
http://facebook.com/lisavergehiggins